I0771639

GRAND THEFT AND A LITTLE DEATH

AN ELLIE GARCIA MYSTERY

KYLEE AWIECH

Sequential
House

Copyright © 2025 by Kylee Awiech

All rights reserved.

No part of this book may be reproduced in any form or by any electronic or mechanical means, including information storage and retrieval systems, without written permission from the author, except for the use of brief quotations in a book review.

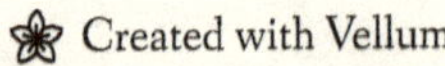 Created with Vellum

To Mom, Dad, and Tanner. Thanks for always listening.

To preschool teachers. You are the unsung heroes of society, and my sanity. I would never had been able to write without you.

CONTENT WARNING

This book discusses topics like mental health, violence, police brutality, intrusive thoughts, and suicidal ideation. They are not described in detail, but mentioned. There are multiple panic attacks that are described. Please take care of yourself and your mental health when choosing to read this book.

"The 988 Suicide & Crisis Lifeline offers 24/7 call, text and chat access to trained crisis counselors who can help people experiencing suicidal, substance use, and/or mental health crisis, or any other kind of emotional distress. People can also dial 988 if they are worried about a loved one who may need crisis support."

ONE

Thursday January 19th 6:50 AM

EVERY GIRL WANTS TO SPEND HER 18TH BIRTHDAY arguing with her parents about going to her brother's prison release. On a day that's supposed to be about me reaching adulthood, all they can talk about is *him*.

"I'm legally old enough to go to war, buy spray paint, and get married. You can't make me go," I repeat, grabbing my notebooks from my desk and stuffing them in my backpack.

My dad leans closer to the mirror above my dresser, redoing his tie for the third time. His forehead is covered in wrinkles, as if concentrating harder will smooth out the silk fabric around his neck.

"Ellie, please? Entering society after being in prison can be difficult for people. It would help your brother to know he has all of our support right now." The tie is beyond crooked now, so he unknots it and starts again.

I don't know why he's even wearing a tie. He's not the one that needs to make a good impression. My brother is.

"He should have planned his reemergence for a different day then."

Dad tilts his head and lets out an exasperated sigh. "You know the date was changed twice already and Evan has no control over it."

I do. Still. It's the principle of the thing. You only turn eighteen once, and I don't want to spend my whole day taking my brother out to buy new underwear.

I grab my backpack from my desk and head downstairs to the kitchen. Mom is leaning against the counter, finishing up a cup of yogurt. She licks the spoon, then chucks the container in the trash.

"Happy birthday," she says to me brightly.

I give her a quick hug, then glance at the table expectantly. We're not huge birthday people. I never had a special plate that I ate off of. I'm not expecting gifts, or a social media worthy balloon display. But, every birthday for as long as I can remember, there's been a raspberry jelly donut waiting for me from the bakery on Main Street.

She notices me looking and curses. "I'm sorry Ellie. I'll get it on our way home."

My throat tightens and I feel a slight burning in my eyes. I blink quickly, willing the impending tears away. I will not cry right now. I have cried too much the past few months; I'm not going to lose it over a donut.

I exhale, the burning subsiding slightly. "I'll get it myself. I have time since I'm going to school like *a responsible adult*," I add for Dad's benefit as he walks in the room. I sling my backpack over my shoulders and head for the garage.

"You thought begging her to come today was a good idea?" I hear Mom say as I'm closing the door.

The second I'm outside I yank up my hood. It's freezing out; the cold wind already starting to make my head buzz. The sidewalks are clear enough of snow I can ride my bike instead of trudging through drifts or begging Topher to pick me up. I pedal quickly, imagining the warmth of the donut shop. When I turn onto Main Street, red and blue lights reflect through all the shop windows. My chest tightens, and my eyes automatically flit toward the river. I can't see it from where I am, but it's there, frozen over for now. *Please let ice be the only thing in the water. Please.*

The lights aren't coming from the riverbank. There's a cruiser parked in front of a house caddy corner from the bar on Main Street. If the sky wasn't so gray, the lights wouldn't have been visible this far away. I stop pedaling and watch. There are two officers talking with an older white woman in a bathrobe. A younger man with black hair is holding her steady. They don't look distressed enough for it to be a murder. I watch for a few more seconds, then force myself to look away and keep riding.

Ten minutes later with a box of donuts in hand, I walk into Anika and Sophie waiting for me right inside the school doors.

"Happy birthday!" Sophie says, wrapping me into a hug. I hesitate for a moment. She's never hugged me before. I awkwardly hug her back while still holding the donut box.

Anika types something on her phone, and then mine buzzes in my pocket.

"Your newest birthday playlist for your listening plea-sure," she says. "Is that jelly on your face?"

I swipe at the corners of my mouth, then look down at the link on my phone. It's a playlist titled "Parental

Warning No Longer Necessary." The first song has most of the words in the title replaced with symbols. I laugh, then wrap Anika into a hug. With this weird morning, I'm glad that my annual birthday playlist tradition hasn't changed.

We start walking down the hallway to our spot where we usually wait for Topher. Sophie has been joining us more and more the past few months. Since coming back after winter break, she's been with us every morning. It's easy to see why Anika likes her. Sophie's passionate about community, knows about all the events happening in town, and super sweet. She's convinced Topher and I to join her in a fun run, and help at a community dinner. I'm glad to know her, even if it's still awkward figuring out how we all fit together. Once Anika and her become official, they'll be the first relationship in our friend group.

Anika and Sophie are talking to each other in hushed tones now. "It's your idea, you ask her," Anika murmurs.

"What's going on?" I ask slowly.

Sophie looks guilty, opening and closing her mouth like a fish. She looks at Anika, who raises her eyebrows at Sophie. Sophie stays silent.

"Sophie's house has had a lot of police activity lately. Every few nights, stolen cars end up parked out front. The police want to talk with her grandma each time, and it's wearing on her," Anika finally says.

"Do you live off of Main, across from the bar?" I ask.

Sophie's eyes widen. "Yes, do you know something?"

She sounds so hopeful; I wish I did. "No, I saw a patrol car there this morning. Was another stolen car parked there last night?"

Sophie's face instantly falls. "Yeah. The police keep promising to do extra patrols, but that hasn't stopped it from happening."

"Do they have any idea why your house?" I ask. Is there something shady going on with Sophie that Anika hasn't told me about? Or maybe on her street? Although, if you had something to hide, leaving stolen cars parked on your street would be plain foolish.

Sophie shrugs. "The police have no idea. They said there's been an increase in thefts, and they've been finding stolen cars all over town."

I nod, then glance at Anika. This is interesting, but I'm not sure why Sophie was so nervous to tell me this. There has to be something else going on here.

"We were just wondering if you had any ideas on what her family could do. They got security cameras, but it hasn't helped much. Everyone caught on camera is wearing coats or hoodies, so you can't identify them," Anika says.

I pick at the edge of my cuticle. "Maybe a floodlight?" I finally suggest. Google could have told her that, but it's all I can think of that she hadn't already mentioned.

"Yeah, maybe," Sophie says. She looks at the ground, then plasters a smile back on her face. "I've got to get to class. Happy birthday again." She gives Anika another hug, then walks away.

"What was that about?" I ask Anika once Sophie's out of earshot.

Anika is watching Sophie as she walks away. "Her grandma is struggling; she won't even get out of bed most days now. She's had some bad experiences with the police before, and now she has to talk to them every few nights about the cars. Her family needs it to stop."

"That's awful, but why did she think I would know something? I don't go to Pathfinders in this town anymore; I have no secret inside knowledge."

"I know that. She kept asking me to ask you since, well, you know." Anika trails off.

Sophie thinks I can do something because I caught the River Killer. Or killers, to be more accurate.

Stop. Don't think about that. I try to stop them, but the memories are too fast. A scalpel glinting in the sunlight. The tickle of grass on the backs of my hands as I picked up the warmed metal of the gun and turned to face Brooke. The ringing of the gunshot in my ears. The scream. The blood. I squeeze my eyes shut, trying to get the noise out.

When I open my eyes and see the look of pity on Anika's face, I try to play it off as getting an eyelash out of my eye.

"I said I'd ask to make her happy," Anika says. "Don't worry about it, okay?"

I nod, feeling a sliver of guilt creeping in. Anika—and Sophie—have been there for me the past few months. I want to be able to help with this. But I can't.

The warning bell for first period goes off. "Make sure your headphones are connected when listening to that playlist," Anika says before walking in the direction of her class.

Oh, I will. I toss the box of donuts in the trash, then press play. Profanities start screaming in my ears. I turn the volume up, hoping the music will shake the memories of the riverbank, the desperation in Sophie's voice, and my brother's prison release out of my mind.

TWO

Thursday January 19th 2:45 PM

My phone buzzes—again—in Bio. I glance down reflexively, and almost throw it across the room. It's not a "happy birthday" text. It's *another* update from my parents. They've been sending them all morning, letting me know they were outside the jail, inside the jail, getting Evan's things. And now? There's a picture of my parents with their heads pressed close to a stranger, standing outside our house. All three of them are smiling.

This is the first time I've seen Evan in five years. All of my memories of him are covered in a haze, his features always morphing. There aren't a lot of pictures of him from the year before he went to jail. He wasn't around much, and when he was, he was strung out. Not exactly the types of moments worth documenting.

The person standing next to my parents doesn't match my memories of Evan at all. They're standing next to a man with a full-on beard that desperately needs beard oil. There are a few shining grey hairs on his head. He looks... solid. Muscular. Nothing like the gaunt brother I remember. I keep staring, wondering if he'll look familiar the longer I look.

Maybe my parents should double check that they didn't bring the wrong Evan Garcia home.

The message under the picture says that they're grabbing a few things from home before taking Evan to his halfway house to get settled.

School ends in fifteen minutes. They'll still be there if I go straight home. I lean across the lab table closer to Topher, Anika, and Sandra. Sandra joined our lab group after her best friend Brooke was arrested. Creatures have to still be dissected, even when your best friend killed multiple people.

"What are you doing after school?" I ask the three of them.

"I was scheduled to volunteer..." Anika trails off.

"My sister has a basketball game and I have to wait for her there," Topher says. "Why?"

"Evan is at our house and I don't want to see him," I say.

"I'm sure he'll be gone once you're off work," Anika reassures me.

I shake my head. "My boss realized it was my birthday and gave me the day off."

Anika and Topher share a quick glance. It's so fast I would have missed it if I hadn't been paying enough attention. They've shared quite a few of those looks the past few months about me.

"I can see if someone else can cover my shift," Anika says.

"Maybe my dad could take my sister," Topher adds.

"I'm going to study at the library," Sandra offers.

Topher and Anika both look relieved at her offer. My gut twists. I don't want a pity hangout. Studying sounds awful, but not as bad as seeing Evan today.

"I'll come with," I say, trying to sound enthusiastic. Sandra beams at me, and I'm glad I said yes. We've never hung out. This could be good for both of us.

"Text me if it gets too boring," Anika teases.

"Or if you can't find an answer," Topher adds.

"Pretty sure my grade is higher than yours," Sandra says, rolling her eyes at Topher.

He glares at her. "By a point."

The bell rings and I gather my things up to walk with Sandra. Wheeling my bike next to me, I turn my face to the sun, soaking it in. You've got to love Colorado weather and its ability to squeeze multiple seasons into a day. The two of us are silent as we walk, turning onto Main Street. My eyes immediately drift a few blocks down to Sophie's house where the police were this morning.

"Have you heard anything about cars being stolen?" I ask Sandra.

She stops walking. "You're not interrogating me for another crime you think I committed, are you? Is your friend going to jump out of the bushes?" She looks around dramatically.

I groan. Our friendship got off to an odd start when I ambushed her last year because I suspected her of being involved in the deaths of our classmates. Which she *was*, just not in the way I thought. "How many times do I have to apologize for that?"

"One more wouldn't hurt," Sandra says.

"I'm sorry," I say, dragging the word out. "I promise to never do it again."

"Holding you to that," she says with a smirk.

We start walking again, and I note everything surrounding Sophie's street. The houses in this area are older, and many are rented out to college students. It's easy to spot which homes are filled with students: the lawns littered with discarded ping pong rackets, rubber ducky shower curtains in the front windows, and a lone lawn chair on a roof.

Sophie's house is well maintained. The skeletons of rosebushes line the walk up the driveway. There's a hedge that lines up perfectly with the front window. The flickering light of a TV is barely visible through gauzy curtains.

Since Sophie's house is on the corner, the sidewalk is wider to accommodate the crosswalk and stoplight. Crossing on Sophie's corner leads directly to the back of the Drunken Lizard bar. I slow my pace, taking in all angles of the bar. There's a mural of lizards drinking on a beach wrapped around the building. It's seen better days; the paint sun-bleached and peeling. I step off the sidewalk, glancing to the front. The neon OPEN sign is off, and there are only five diagonal parking spaces.

I'm pretty sure more than five people go there every night, and Main Street gets extremely busy on the weekends. Maybe people are parking in front of Sophie's and walking over? But why in stolen cars?

I stumble on the edge of my bike tire when I step back onto the sidewalk.

Sandra is staring at me. "You good?"

"Mhmm," I murmur, rejoining her.

She shrugs, then keeps going. I keep my head forward, the bar and Sophie's house in my peripherals. The police know about the stolen cars. There's nothing more I could do about it.

Sandra and I finally reach the library, and she leads me

up the stairs to one of the study rooms. She was serious about this. She pulls out her textbooks, notebooks, pens, and two protein bars. She slides one across the table to me. I start chewing on it while staring out the study room window. As fate would have it, I can see the front of the Drunken Lizard from here. I start scrolling through my phone, trying to ignore the bar.

No one has posted anything exciting on Instagram. However, a blue sedan just parked in front of the bar. I watch as two women get out. They walk farther down Main Street, entering the gem and mineral shop two buildings down. I stare at the sedan. Nothing about it screams stolen. If only I had access to the police database so I could run the license plates like I've practiced at Pathfinders.

"Are you trying to sneak into that bar?" Sandra asks.

I startle. "What? No."

"Then why won't you stop staring at it?"

"I'm not." I go back to scrolling on my phone. After a few minutes my eyes are drawn back to the bar. There are two bicycles chained to the bike rack that weren't there before, and a white sedan is parked out front too.

"Money laundering?" Sandra asks. She's still looking at her textbook, highlighting something.

I turn to her. "Excuse me?"

"What do you think is happening at that bar?" she asks.

"Nothing," I say defensively. "Can't a girl just admire a beautiful day?"

Sandra raises an eyebrow. "I think you doth protest too much."

"Shut up," I grumble, crossing my arms.

Sandra snorts, writing something in her notebook. Suddenly her head whips back to me, her eyes lit up. "Do you think they're stealing cars from there?" She angles her chair so she has a better view out the window. Together we watch cars drive up and down Main Street.

"That would be weird, considering the police keep finding them in front of Sophie's house," I say, pointing across the street.

"Is this your new investigation?" Sandra asks.

"No," I snap.

Her forehead wrinkles as she raises both her eyebrows. She doesn't believe me.

"I don't do investigations. That was a one-time thing."

"Then why can't you stop staring out the window?" she asks.

I ignore her question, glancing at my phone. It's 4:02. That's over an hour since my parents said they were grabbing a few things from home for Evan. By the time I bike back, they should be long gone.

"I should get going," I say, grabbing my backpack from the floor.

Sandra looks panicked. "No, stay. I won't say anything else about it."

I swing my bag onto my back, adjusting the straps.

"We have a test in a few weeks, we could start studying," she offers.

I snort. I stopped studying for things a while ago. "I'm good."

She stands up from the table, her eyes pleading. "It's your birthday, I don't want you to be alone."

I stare at her. "You know how everyone treated you differently after what happened to you?"

She cringes.

"I know I've been, not quite myself, but I'm better now. I don't need you—or anyone— to baby me."

Sandra looks torn. Expressions flit across her face, and

she looks down at her own phone. Finally, she nods. "You're right. That's the last thing you need." She sinks back into her chair. "Have a good night."

"You too," I smile, then speed walk all the way out of there.

***

There's movement inside my house. I hesitate before pressing the final number in the garage code, staring at the front window. We don't have any pets. There's no reason the front curtains should be moving. I keep watching, and I swear they move again.

I should call the police. But what if it's something simple, like air from the vents moving them? I picture an officer walking through the house and there being nothing. It would be humiliating, and I'm sure word would get back to Officer Ken on his latest trip, and then to my parents.

I grab my bike lock from my backpack. It's pure metal, and I could do some serious damage with it. I creep around the side of our house, looking for any signs of an intruder. There are no broken windows. The back patio door is still closed with the curtains drawn. I watch them for signs of movement, but there aren't any.

Did I imagine it? I press the palms of my hands into my eyes. Have the lost sleep and panic attacks finally caught up with me? I rub my chest absently as the all-too-familiar ache twinges. I've almost made it two weeks without a panic attack. I don't have time for this.

I go back to the front yard and punch in the garage code. On the off chance there is someone inside right now, and they're your typical robbers, they'll try to get out once they hear the noise. To my surprise, both of my parents' cars are parked inside. Are they already back from dropping off Evan? Or are they still inside with him? Their cars being here would explain the movement inside. It wouldn't explain why all the lights are off.

Lock firmly in hand, I cross the garage to the door. I hesitate, then press my ear to the wood. There are voices inside. Way more than three. Horrible scenarios flash through my mind. A robbery gone wrong. A hostage scenario.

A voice comes scarily close to the door.

With all my strength, I fling the door open. If the owner of the voice is as close as they sound, they'll be trapped behind it momentarily, and that extra second will give me an advantage. The door presses against something large, and someone moans. I hold the bike lock up, ready to strike as I pull the door away from them. The metal is inches from a man's face when I realize that it's my dad, holding his stomach where the door handle flew into it.

There's a cacophony of noise. The dishwasher running, music playing, laughter. I look in every direction, trying to locate it. People come flooding into the kitchen, and I'm still holding the lock in the air, ready to strike.

"Surprise!" they yell.

Someone blows on a horn, and confetti flies into the air. I stand there, my arm heavy.

Anika puts down her phone and runs over to me, grabbing the lock from my hand. Dad comes out from behind the door, a grimace on his face. I look around wildly, not sure where to focus. Mom, Topher, and Sophie stand there. I was inches from seriously hurting my dad, and all of my friends are here, staring at me.

Anika sets the lock down, then wraps an arm around my shoulders. "Ellie needs to freshen up," she says to everyone staring. She drags me to the bathroom upstairs, and locks the door.

"Splash some water on your face," she commands.

"That never actually works," I protest.

"Maybe this is the time it will," she says. When I don't move, she turns on the sink herself and flicks a few droplets of water at me.

"Stop it," I whine. I sit down on the closed toilet lid and put my head in my hands. "I could have killed my dad."

"Killing is a bit dramatic. A head contusion seems more likely." When I don't laugh at her horrible joke, she sighs. "I knew a surprise party was a terrible idea. Your parents wanted us to pull it off when they found out about Evan's new release date."

This party was my parents' idea? "Everyone's going to think that I'm psychotic."

"No they're not. Only your friends are here, and they all understand."

Understand? That's what my friends do now. They understand that at first, I was fine in the aftermath of shooting Brooke. But then, that facade slowly started cracking until it all broke during the regional Pathfinders competition. Now it's been bad for so long, that the idea of me hurting my own dad at my surprise party is completely understandable.

Anika flicks water at my face again, but my hands get most of it. "I'm going to keep spraying you until you look at me."

Water hits me, again. "What?" I snap.

"It all happened so fast, I bet your dad didn't even realize what was going on."

I finally remove my hands, looking up. "You think so?"

She nods emphatically. "Come on. It's your birthday and we're here to celebrate you. Don't make my fight with Topher about streamers be for nothing."

"Fine," I say, standing up. I examine my face in the mirror. It's paler than normal, and my eyes look wide, but otherwise I look the same. I splash a little more water on my face for good luck, then follow Anika out of the bathroom.

Voices climb up the stairs. Lots of voices. Who did they invite? Could *he* be here? My heart skips a beat, but this time for a good reason.

Downstairs music playing. There's a curtain of streamers hanging in the hallway from the living room to the kitchen. A card table is filled with bowls of snacks and a cooler of drinks. People are mingling in different corners of the living room. I spot Sophie talking with Sandra on the couch. Sandra smiles when she sees me.

"I tried to stop her, but it didn't work," she tells Anika.

"Can any of us stop a determined Ellie?" Anika grins.

Oh. So Sandra wasn't babying me. She was trying to stop me from crashing my own party. And Topher and Anika weren't worried about me in Bio. Everyone's strange behavior is making sense.

Topher is talking with DJ, and our team leader from our new Pathfinders group, Layla. I'm touched she'd come here for my party on a Thursday. We've never hung out outside of practice.

The curtain of streamers starts moving as someone walks through them. My heart begins to race again. All of my friends are already here except him...

A tiny blonde head walks through. It's Ben. The annoying twelve-year-old from my old Pathfinders team. I have never been more disappointed to see him. He doesn't even look up at me when he walks through with a plate of nachos.

I go over to the curtain of streamers and peek through it, checking to see if anyone else is here. The kitchen is empty.

"Did we forget to invite someone?" Anika asks.

"No," I say, a little too quickly.

Her eyes narrow for a second, then she smiles. "Come on, we're all here for you."

"Did you see that Ben is wearing gel?" DJ calls from across the living room, wrapping an arm around Ben's shoulders. Then he tries to rub his fist through Ben's spiked hair, which turns into play fighting. They almost crash into the snack table.

"Knock it off," Topher yells, pushing them away from the food.

"It's nice to know you two haven't changed at all," Anika says.

"Or you," Ben replies, rolling his eyes.

"Why did you invite him?" I whisper to Topher.

"I forgot how obnoxious he was," he whispers back.

Me too. I'm glad that he chose to join another Pathfinders team so I don't have to see him on a weekly basis anymore.

The streamers move and Mom bursts through them, Dad behind her. I search him for any signs that I seriously hurt him, but he looks completely normal. Except for the fact he has his phone out and is recording me. Does he really need another video of me blowing out my candles?

"We know that it hasn't been an ideal birthday, especially for such a special one. Hopefully this last surprise will help make up for it," Mom says. "This is from us and all your grandparents." She grabs my hand and leads me to the front door.

Dad stands next to the doorframe, the camera still on me. Are my grandparents waiting out there? If so, Mom completely ruined the surprise. Maybe she did so I don't end up accidentally punching my grandparents in the face.

I don't think they would be able to survive that, especially if they've been standing outside in the cold waiting.

The front door swings open, and I stare at the empty porch. I peek around the corners, wondering if my grandparents are in the bushes. There's nothing except for the yellow glow of the streetlights and tiny flakes of snow falling through the air. Great. I'm going to have to bike in that tomorrow.

I look behind me. Everyone is staring at me expectantly. There's nothing out here. I search the street again, my eyes landing on an unfamiliar car parked on the curb. It's an older Toyota. There's no one waiting inside it. Maybe it's Layla's. Then I see the tiny gift bow on the hood. It's miniscule in comparison with the car, nothing like the commercials.

"Is that, for..." I trail off, hoping that someone will fill in the blank. I've always been told that if I wanted a car, I had to pay for it. I've been saving up from work, but I'm nowhere near having enough.

"My coworker was selling their car and we thought it'd be a perfect first one for you. It's a beater, but you won't have to ride your bike everywhere," Dad says.

"No way," I breathe. Excitement flutters through me. My first car. I can go so many places. My ears won't ache every morning.

I turn to my parents and wrap both of them into a hug. Mis abuelos call on Facetime, and I thank them. Then I chat with the rest of my extended family members who call in between dancing with my friends. I eat all my favorite snacks. And at 8:30 everyone leaves so we can all finish up homework for school tomorrow.

When I get into bed, I scroll through my phone and post a few of the pictures from tonight. My face smashed close together with everyone. A video of us dancing to "Anti-Hero." Even one where I'm posed ridiculously with a birthday crown and sash. It was definitely the weirdest birthday I've ever had. But also, one of the best. I close my eyes, trying to erase the image of my dad when the door hit him in the stomach from my mind.

I'm drifting off to sleep, when my phone buzzes.

QUINN

Are you free tomorrow? We need to talk
—ASAP

THREE

Friday January 20th 3:04PM

I re-read my texts with Quinn again. He wouldn't tell me what he wanted to talk about, only that we needed to meet up. The last time we texted before last night, was back in November. I sent a skull emoji in reply to a TikTok he sent me. What is so important that he'll only say it in person after two months of silence?

I stand in the pickup lane with my bike by my side. I forgot that driving means scraping windows and didn't have enough time to clean them this morning, so I ended up biking in the snow instead of taking my new car. Which means Quinn is picking me up and stashing my bike in the back, just like old times.

"Don't get yourself killed," Topher says as he walks to his truck with Anika and Sophie. I stick my tongue out at them, then keep watching the line of cars coming through the parking lot. I'm careful not to look toward a spot five-hundred feet to my left, near the basketball hoops. That's where Quinn pulled up in his Jeep three months ago, and was forced back inside at gunpoint. I close my eyes and take a deep breath, trying to picture the beach scene that's my safe place.

A car gives a quick honk, and I open my eyes to see Quinn in his Jeep right in front of me. He looks different. His hair is so long the ends of it curl from under his beanie. His tan has faded, and he seems... older. I run around the side of the Jeep, about to open the passenger door. Then I stop. Someone is already sitting there.

It's Kacey, Quinn's roommate. She's typing furiously on her phone and doesn't look up at me. She's been nice the few times I've met her, but I didn't expect her to be here. That eliminates 75% of the scenarios I thought this might be about. I load my bike into the back, then climb in behind Kacey, grateful for the heat blowing on me.

"Thanks for meeting with us so fast. How much time do you have?" Quinn asks, turning to give me a quick smile.

Looks like we're getting right to it, whatever this is. "My shift starts at four," I say, reminding him of my job. So he knows that I have one. Like the adult I now am.

"Where are you working?" he asks as he pulls out of the school parking lot.

"The frozen yogurt place near campus."

"They're still in business?" Kacey asks.

I glare at her through the seat. I feel protective of the shop, especially since the sister store in Loveland recently closed. I'm supposed to meet the lone employee my boss is keeping today. "Yes, and they're doing great. Everyone hates on froyo until they're craving it."

Kacey doesn't reply, going back to typing on her phone.

"What have you been up to? Not tackling anyone else I hope," Quinn asks.

I remember the first time we met, the smell of mud from the riverbank. The flashing red and blue lights everywhere. The fear when he reached behind his back and I thought it was a weapon. The weight of him beneath me as I tackled him, and then zip-tied his hands. I couldn't stand him when I met him. Now? Now I'm wondering if that day could technically be a meet-cute.

"Does almost wounding my dad because he was throwing me a surprise party count?" I ask.

He bursts out laughing. "Same old Ellie. When was your birthday?"

"Yesterday."

"Happy belated," he says.

So this doesn't have anything to do with my new adult status. Which is technically good. It's creepy to have men waiting until the day you turn eighteen to ask you out. But whatever this is, why couldn't he just text it?

We're at the end of Main Street, and Quinn keeps driving until we're in the overflow parking lot two blocks away. During the summer it's impossible to get a spot here, but now the lot is mostly deserted.

Kacey gives a dramatic sigh, then puts her phone on her lap. "My car was stolen two days ago, and my family is flipping out." She starts rubbing tiny circles on her temples.

My stomach sinks. This is the second person in twenty-four hours to mention stolen cars. "What happened?" I ask.

"A lot of cars have been getting stolen from our apartment complex, so I double check every night that it's locked. It was there around ten, but it was gone in the morning."

I'm instantly in analysis mode. "Why are so many cars getting stolen from your lot? Are there floodlights? Any cameras?"

"There are. It hasn't stopped the thefts at all," Quinn says.

"The police aren't even bothering to check the footage anymore," Kacey adds.

I adjust myself, sitting up straighter. "Why would they stop checking it?"

"The building manager said they stopped a while ago. For me they made a report, told me to be patient, and that's it. They won't return any of my calls now," Kacey says.

"So we figured we'd talk to you," Quinn says, fully turning around in the driver's seat, giving me the perfect view of his hopeful face. "Do you know anything the police might not be telling us?"

Disappointment floods through me. This is all he wanted. They're hoping that I have some secret power in the police department, just like Sophie did. I've spent all day hoping that maybe Quinn missed me, or even returned some of the feelings I feel toward him, and that's why he wanted to meet up. Instead, it's because of who I once was. The girl from last year, who regularly went on ride-alongs and knew all sorts of secret happenings in town because of Pathfinders. Whose body didn't spike with adrenaline at every loud noise. Who felt like she could do anything.

"No, I'm not in Pathfinders for this city, and I haven't heard anything in Loveland."

"Do you know a different officer we could talk to?" Kacey asks.

I shake my head. Officer Ken retired and is traveling the world. He sent me an actual postcard from Greece a few weeks ago. A postcard. There's Detective Zhao, but she works homicides and probably wouldn't know much about the cars.

"Have you asked your aunt?" I ask, picturing Patty, the

coroner. "She could get information out of them. Or reach out to the DA's office."

Quinn scoffs. "No, you know how she is."

That she's passionate and extremely intimidating? That I wanted to be like her one day? How she used to like me, but now I pray I don't die while she's still in office? Yeah, I can see why he hasn't involved her, especially since she's mad Quinn and I did our own investigation last year.

"I'm sorry. I wish I could help more," I say.

The little bit of hope that was in Kacey's eyes fades. She nods, turning around to face the front of the car and sinks back into her seat.

This is the second person I've disappointed in as many days. Sophie looked the same way.

Sophie. The person who *keeps having stolen cars show up in front of her house.*

I pause before speaking. If I tell them this, I'm opening a door I swore would stay closed. The last time I tried to do an investigation, people almost died. Two of us are in this car.

This is different, though. It's potentially finding a stolen car; not a serial killer classmate. Stealing a car is a misdemeanor. If we simply drive down the street, I won't be risking anyone's lives.

"Actually, I might have a lead on where your car could be."

Kacey whips around, her eyes wide, and Quinn puts his hand on her shoulder. "I told you Ellie would know something," he says, smiling at me.

My stomach tightens. That's quite the hype to live up to. The car better be there.

With the license plate of Kacey's green Subaru Outback written on my phone, we drive back down Main Street. The radio is turned off, and the three of us are scanning for any sign of Kacey's car. I spot three on our first pass, none with the correct plate.

"Turn here," I say, as we pass the Drunken Lizard. Quinn waits as a group of people use the crosswalk, then finally turns onto Sophie's road.

"Look," Kacey gasps. There's a green Subaru parked on the street, three houses from the corner. Did I pull this off? It was almost too easy. We get closer and the first three letters of the license plate even match. I clutch the headrest of Kacey's seat. Then she lets out an, "oh." The last two numbers of the plate don't match.

"Did they make a different plate?" I ask.

Quinn pulls up right next to the Subaru. We stare inside. There's a graduation tassel on the rearview mirror, and boxes in the back.

"It's not mine," Kacey says quietly.

"It's probably some other transplant who got their plates the same time you did," Quinn says.

All of the hope has disappeared from the car.

"Let's keep driving around. Maybe it's on a nearby street," I say.

The Jeep starts moving again, but Kacey turns her head away from the window. I catch a glimpse of her face in the side mirror. There are tears in her eyes. After ten more minutes of slowly cruising the side streets of the neighborhood she says quietly, "It's time to get Ellie to work."

The clock on the radio says 3:50. She's right. Quinn turns out of the neighborhood, driving back toward Main Street.

"Keep trying this neighborhood. Stolen cars keep showing up on that first corner we checked. Maybe it'll be there tonight."

"Maybe," Quinn says, hope in his voice. Kacey doesn't respond.

The Jeep pulls into an open spot in front of the yogurt shop. Quinn gets out of the car as I do. He opens the back of the Jeep and we both reach for my bike at the same time. Our arms brush each other and that familiar electricity shoots through me. I pull back, and Quinn unloads my bike for me.

"Thanks for trying. I'm sure it'll turn up soon. It's the waiting that's getting to her," Quinn says, shoving his hands into his pockets.

A gust of wind bites my skin and I shiver. "I wish I knew more."

"Don't sweat it. It was good to see you," he smiles.

"You too." This can't be over already. I want more time with him, but can't think of a way to prolong this moment. "Keep me updated."

"For sure. Take care of yourself." Quinn lifts up his arm, and pulls me into a quick side hug. I savor every second. It's over as soon as it started, and he gets back into the Jeep. I watch the two of them drive off.

"What are you doing here?" a familiar voice asks. I look up and freeze.

No.

FOUR

January 20th 4:00PM

"IN CASE YOU FORGOT, THIS IS *MY* CITY," I SNAP.

My nemesis is standing mere feet away from me, outside *my* work, and he has the nerve to ask me what I'm doing here? I look Jamie over. There are flecks of snow in his jet-black hair, making it spike up in sections. His brown eyes are narrowed as he frowns at me. He's only wearing a hoodie and jeans, so he must have driven here, otherwise he'd be freezing. This is the first time I've seen him in casual clothes, instead of our navy-blue Pathfinder uniforms. It feels so, wrong.

Jamie and I are co-assistant team leads at the Loveland chapter of Pathfinders. He's been suspicious of me since I started here, thinking that I want to start a coup and take over the group. That's the farthest thing from the truth. After the disaster that was our last competition... he downright loathes me. The holiday break from Pathfinders has been a welcome relief from seeing his arrogant face. So why is he standing here, outside my job?

I look Jamie over again, my eyes landing on the tiny logo stitched onto his hoodie. Fro Yo Information. The exact same logo on the t-shirt under my coat.

No. No. No!

I push the door open to the shop, not checking to see if Jamie is behind me. My boss Angie smiles when I walk in.

"You're both here! Perfect," she says, walking out from behind the counter and pulling her red hair out of her ponytail. "Ellie, this is Jamie. He was working at my Loveland shop, and he's such a great employee he agreed to transfer here."

Maybe there's another boy named Jamie behind me, wearing a hoodie with the company logo. I keep my eyes forward, giving the evil Jamie a chance to disappear and a new one to arrive in his place. Angie frowns at me. Completely ignoring someone isn't a good example of my customer service skills. Only because she's watching, I turn to Jamie and give him my fakest smile. "Nice to meet you."

Jamie is barely able to stop himself from snorting. "You as well."

"He knows most of the ropes, you'll just have to show him where we keep things here. I've got a meeting with the moving crew at the other shop, so I'll leave you two to it," Angie says, clapping her hands.

I drop my backpack and coat off in the back, as does Jamie. We keep our fake smiles on our faces until the bell on the front door rings, signaling Angie is gone.

I whip around to run to the cash register. It's the best spot. You don't have to keep gloves on, and you can leave your phone or a textbook on the counter while you work.

Jamie has the same idea and he sprints to the doorway. We reach it at the same time, unable to both fit.

"I'm supposed to be showing you around, let me out," I grunt as I slam my shoulder into his.

"I can figure it out myself," Jamie says, shoving against me. We both keep pushing back and forth, until I hook my leg around Jamie's in an attempt to trip him. He braces the doorway with both of his arms and stays upright, shoving me down instead. I duck under his legs as he tries to swing out of the doorway. Crawling on the floor, I get ahead of him and upright, running into the front room of the yogurt shop. A young mom is standing there with two toddlers, trying to stop them from pulling the yogurt handles them-selves. She glances at me and I smile, saying, "welcome."

In the millisecond it takes me to greet her like a decent employee, Jamie slides behind me and runs to the register. He holds his hands out wide, like he's blocking someone in basketball, to keep me away. I could take him down, but the mom and kids are at the topping counter now. I'm not going to stoop to his level of unprofessionalism; at least not in front of customers. Instead, I stand uncomfortably close behind him. When he messes up, I'll let him know.

Jamie starts punching keys into the register to log in. The little box at the top says ERROR and makes a beeping noise. He tries again, but the same thing happens. Over and over he types, and it keeps beeping at him.

"You must not be in this system yet," I say, pulling on his shoulder to move him out of the way. He glares at me as I log into the register, purposefully typing as fast as I can to show off. He huffs, then walks over to the cleaning supplies, going to wipe down a table with a few leftover sprinkles on it. When the mom and kids finally make it to check out, I give them stickers and even let them pick which color spoons they want. Suck on that customer service, Jamie.

When there's no sign of anyone else coming, I grab a rag to wipe down the dispenser handles. I can feel Jamie's judgement as I walk throughout the room. I have to show him that I'm the best frozen yogurt employee there ever was. Am I potentially compensating for what happened during the Pathfinders competition? Maybe.

The mom and boys finish eating their yogurt and stand up to leave. Jamie and I are both eyeing their table from separate corners of the room. As soon as the door closes behind them, we're both dashing to the table. We reach it at the same time, furiously wiping the top of it with our towels. Our hands keep bumping into each other, until I move on to wipe the chairs. They're practically clean, but I can't leave a surface untouched.

When every surface is gleaming, my phone buzzes in my pocket, and I reflexively look at it.

QUINN

Thanks for trying.

Keep me updated. I'll let you know if I hear anything.

"Are you texting Angie to quit?" Jamie asks, nodding at my phone.

"What? Of course not."

"That's good. It's nice to see you're loyal in some areas of your life."

I look up at the ceiling and groan. The second I saw him, I knew he'd say something like that. He's been finding every opportunity to remind me of the fiasco at the competition for months.

"That was quite the stretch," I say.

"It's still a better job than you did in the SWAT scenario."

I glare at him, trying to think of anything else but that dark room. The muffled sounds of gunshots in the distance. The way my lungs closed off and my vision swam, and how...

"At least I can log into the cash register." I saunter back behind the counter, claiming my territory.

"I'm going to tell Layla that I think it's best you're relieved from your duties as co-assistant at our meeting on Monday," Jamie says. "Especially since you've missed so many practices."

I freeze. Would Layla actually listen to him? She wouldn't, right? Yes, I missed a few practices, but I made it to the last one of the year, and I'm doing much better now.

"I'm going to tell Angie how horrible of an employee you are," I say.

He rolls his eyes. "Go ahead and try. She likes me so much, she brought me here."

"Probably because she felt sorry that nowhere else in your own city would hire you."

"I think you're describing yourself," he says, then starts sweeping the already clean floor.

I'm about to tell him to go back to his own city because this one's mine, but my phone buzzes again.

ANIKA

Another one? Want to come to my house
while you wait?

Sorry, that was for Sophie

I frown at the screen. They could be talking about anything.

Another what? Stolen car?

ANIKA

Yeah.

Don't worry about it, okay?

I lean over the counter, looking out the window down Main Street. I can't see Sophie's house from here. There hadn't been any cars in front of her house when we'd driven by; the Subaru we'd spotted had been two houses down. How did someone have the chance to ditch a stolen vehicle in broad daylight *and* the police to find it in less than an hour?

"Texting your boyfriend?" Jamie asks, standing in front of the register.

"Just because I have friends doesn't mean you won't make some one day," I say sweetly to him. I tune out his response as I look back at my phone. Leaving a stolen car out in the middle of the day seems like an escalation. One that's affecting multiple of my friends.

Sophie's worried face as she asked me for help yesterday flashes alongside Kacey's hopeless one today. I might be failing at Pathfinders. Barely getting by in school. My nemesis works here now. But these stolen cars? My mind is spinning with ideas.

Tell Sophie we're going to stop this.

33

FIVE

Friday January 20th 10:30 PM

Aɴɪᴋᴀ ʙᴜᴍᴘs Sᴏᴘʜɪᴇ ᴡɪᴛʜ ʜᴇʀ sʜᴏᴜʟᴅᴇʀ, ᴀɴᴅ Sophie giggles before pushing her back. The force of it bumps me into Topher who is perched on the bench next to me. I keep my eyes forward, not wanting to stare at the two of them, even if their method of flirting is annoying. Things with Anika still feel fragile after our big fight last year. That tends to happen when you suspect your best friend of being a serial killer. Then the darkness that was November ... Things are still settling into their new normal, and I'm not messing with it.

"If you're going to flirt, can you do it somewhere less crowded?" Topher asks, shoving me back into Anika as he gets up from the piano bench we're all squished on. We're set up in Sophie's front window, the four of us taking turns watching every car that goes down the street. It's a tight fit, and the cold air seeps through the thin pane of glass in front of us.

Sophie's face turns bright red. "I'll get more popcorn," she says, leaving the room. Anika and I are alone.

"Thanks again for doing this," she says, bumping my shoulder now.

"Of course," I say, keeping my eyes out the window. Snow is falling steadily, but people are still out and about, heading toward Main Street. So far, no strange cars have parked on this street though.

"Are you okay?" Anika asks tentatively.

I keep my gaze out the window, not wanting to miss anything. "Of course."

"Are you sure? I don't want to set you back—"

"I'm good," I snap, instantly regretting it. It's not her fault. It's perfectly reasonable for her to ask that after the past few months. She was there for my overreaction at my party yesterday.

Will there be a time when those around me aren't afraid of me breaking? When *I* won't be afraid of that?

"You don't hate Sophie, right?" she asks, her voice cracking on the last word.

I finally turn away from the road to look at her. "Of course not. Why would you say that?"

She pushes a strand of hair behind her ear. "I don't know. This year has been weird."

"Sophie is great. Really. And if she makes you happy, that makes me happy." I grab her hand and squeeze it, trying to convey the truth. Change is hard to get used to, but this is a good change.

Anika's cheeks flush, and she smiles. She doesn't get a chance to respond because Sophie and Topher walk back into the room. Topher grabs a few popcorn kernels from the bowl Sophie is holding.

"What'd I miss?" he asks.

"Nothing," I say, turning back to the road.

"Can we watch a movie?" Anika asks. She gets up from the bench, stretching dramatically. Then she runs to the blue suede couch in the corner of the room, diving into the cushions for something. She sits up, the remote for the TV in her hand.

Topher and Anika fight over what to watch, while Sophie comes back and stares at the road with me. She places the bowl of popcorn in the middle of us.

They finally settle on The Mummy. And then promptly fall asleep thirty minutes into the movie.

"Have you seen this before?" Sophie asks.

"My parents showed me it once I think," I say. Parts of it look familiar, but I have no idea what's going to happen next.

Sophie turns back to the screen to watch for a moment. "My grandma is obsessed with Brenden Fraser. She rewatches George of the Jungle all the time for the scene where he's in a towel."

I choke on the sip of water I just took and start coughing. I hold a thumb up to Sophie when she looks concerned. Imagining the older woman with thick, red framed glasses, and thinning white hair cut in a bob openly ogling Brenden Fraser is hilarious.

"She wasn't surprised I'm gay because I never joined her in all her rewatches," Sophie grins.

I laugh. "She seems nice."

"She stepped up for me after my parents were arrested. That's why I want to make this stop," she says, gesturing out the window. "Every time the cops show up, it brings back bad memories."

"I get it. Has Anika told you about my brother?" I ask.

"Vaguely," Sophie says. "You don't have to share though, it's okay."

"Gossiping about crushes at sleepovers is so 2000. Now it's all about trauma bonding."

Sophie's the one who snorts while drinking now, water spraying from her nose and mouth. We both start laughing so hard, I'm surprised Topher and Anika don't wake up.

The faintest light hits the fence across the street from us. The circles of white get brighter as a car approaches. It turns onto Sophie's street, followed by the sound of wheels crushing snow. It's a white sedan, not Kacey's Subaru.

"Do you recognize that car?" I ask Sophie.

"No," she breathes.

There's nowhere to park on that side of the street, so the sedan slowly flips around. It backs up, then pulls forward so it's perfectly lined up with the edge of Sophie's driveway, not blocking it. Are thieves usually so considerate? The interior light turns on and two people rummage around inside. Sophie is breathing so hard it's fogging up the window. It squeaks as she furiously wipes it away.

"Maybe they're lost, or stuck," she says.

Car doors open and two people get out.

I jump from the piano bench, fling Sophie's front door open and run outside. I've been wearing my coat and boots this entire stakeout in case this moment came. The snow that's been falling has piled up more than I expected, and I start slipping down the driveway.

"Stop," I call out.

The two people who got out of the car turn around and look at me. One has long blonde hair peeking out of her coat. The other is wearing a beanie. They see me running and take off to the corner.

I chase after them, my boots crunching in the snow with each step. I'm gaining on them. They run across Main Street, a car horn blaring as it barely misses them. The car slides through the intersection, tires groaning as they struggle to gain traction. More horns honk in warning, and relief floods me as the car regains control. I bounce up and down on the street corner, waiting for the intersection to clear. I track my targets as they run to the front of the bar. They're both wearing black coats. I didn't have enough time to identify anything unique about them. The light finally turns red and I sprint across the road.

When I get to the front of the Drunken Lizard, I push through the crowd of people taking quick huffs off their vape pens in front of the bar. I run to the window and peek inside. It's crammed with people, black coats flung onto chairs everywhere. I'm holding onto the door handle, when I hear my name screamed into the night.

I sprint back to the intersection, and run across the road. Sophie is standing in her driveway, waving her arms wildly. An SUV is idling in the middle of the street, next to the white sedan. I run to Sophie and the cars. If these are car thieves, they won't like that she's out here watching them.

The SUV hits the gas, spraying snow in every direction. It jerks forward, and hits a patch of ice, fishtailing toward me on the sidewalk. I jump into Sophie's snowbank of a yard, barely getting out of the way. Tires screech as the SUV tries to reverse. I get back to my feet, so close I can see inside the front window of the car.

Hooded faces look at me, wearing ski masks. The driver side window starts to roll down, and something cylindrical points at me.

I stand there, staring back at it. My brain is refusing to

compute what that is. What's happening. I've trained and practiced so that I wouldn't need to think, I'd know what to do. But right now I'm absolutely frozen.

There's a gun. Pointed at me.

Finally I duck, curling into a ball in the snow, my hands behind my neck like in a tornado drill. I can't hear anything over the sound of my heartbeat racing and my ragged breaths. I wait for the pop-pop, the explosion of pain. There's nothing. Am I already dead? Did it happen so quickly that I didn't even hear it?

My heart is beating. I'm still alive.

Hands touch me and I kick forward, trying to get whoever owns them away from me.

"It's me," Topher says, hands up in the air. Sophie is standing next to him with Anika. I stare back and forth between the three of them. Anika and Sophie reach down to pull me out of the snow, and I let them. I look up and down the street for the SUV. The road is empty both directions, except for the white sedan.

"What happened?" Anika asks. "I heard the front door slam and you both were gone."

Sophie describes what we saw, and how I took off. "Then the SUV pulled up, and someone got out, walking toward the white car, but they saw me. I got a picture of it though," she says.

"No way?" I breathe.

She nods.

"You're amazing." I tell her.

Anika and Sophie both grin. Topher rolls his eyes.

"Why do I always miss out on the fun?" he asks.

"You can call the police if you want," I say as we all head back inside.

Everyone stops walking. "Why?" Sophie asks nervously. We'd discussed earlier that we wouldn't call unless we really had something, to save her grandma the stress.

Topher pulls his phone out of his pocket, looking at me for confirmation.

"Because they pointed a gun at me."

SIX

Saturday January 21st 12:30 AM

HE SUCKS HIS TEETH AGAIN. IT SENDS A WAVE OF irritation through me.

"Let me get this straight. You were nice and warm inside, and then you willingly chased after the passengers of a *potentially* stolen car."

The way he says it isn't a question, but I say yes anyway.

"Then another car pulled up, you chased after it, and they pointed a gun at you," Officer Erving says. He's an older guy with a suspiciously black mustache that doesn't match his eyebrows. He definitely dyes it. I've never worked with him before, and honestly, I'm glad for it.

"Yes," I say. I don't even try to keep the irritation out of my voice.

Sophie and Anika are upstairs, trying to calm down her grandma while Officer Erving talks with me. Since I'm legally an adult now, I can talk to him by myself.

"Do you think they might have felt threatened that you were chasing after them, and that's why they pulled out the weapon?" Officer Erving asks, tilting his head dramatically.

"No, I think that they're running a stolen car operation and they were threatening me because we're onto them."

Officer Erving raises his brows and gives a low whistle. "Well maybe I should give you my badge and let you do the investigating," he says.

"Maybe you should," Topher mumbles.

The officer turns his complete attention to Topher. "What'd you say?" His voice has completely changed.

Adrenaline starts pumping through me. Officer Erving is being a jerk, but Topher is a black man. Others have been killed for much less.

"This is Ellie Garcia, the girl who caught the River Killer. Maybe you should listen to her," Topher says in a soft, measured tone.

Officer Erving stares at Topher a beat longer. I will him to look away, to let it go. Two breathes later, he turns back to me, examining me from head to toe.

"Now it makes sense why you ran after it. You think you're some kind of detective?" Officer Erving asks, raising his brows.

I hold my hands up. "I'm just trying to help my friend. They keep having stolen cars show up here and it feels like no one is listening."

Officer Erving sucks his teeth again. "Do you know how many cars have been stolen this week alone in the county? Forty-four. That's forty-four families calling every day to check in on where their vehicles are. That's just the cars from this week. Last week there were sixty-two, and we still haven't located all of them.

"Do you know how we find these stolen cars? By

running license plates. They're everywhere. The airport, Main Street, by the grocery store, parked in neighborhoods. That's a lot of license plates we have to run, meanwhile we have officers quitting left and right. Then there's the increase in gang activity, overdoses, and gun violence that we're dealing with. So I'm sorry if we don't have the manpower to sit outside this house 24/7 in case someone drops off a stolen car."

He was trying to make me feel inferior, but Officer Erving just gave me a lot of valuable information. First off, I have more ideas of places for Kacey to look for her car.

"I'm assuming the gangs are the ones stealing the cars?" I ask.

Officer Erving gives a bark of a laugh. "Are you trying to get information from me for your little investigation? Listen, you might have gotten lucky with the River Killer, but those were high school girls. You stay the hell away from the gangs," Officer Erving says, pointing his finger at me aggressively.

When I don't say anything, he steps closer to me, leaning down so his face is level with mine. I stand up straight, refusing to appear weak to him. "Do. You. Understand? This isn't playtime. If you mess with the wrong people, they won't hesitate to kill you."

The image of the gun barrel sticking out the car window floods into my mind again. I nod.

"Good. Now let us do our jobs, and you stay safe. Inside."

Officer Erving's radio beeps, and he takes that as his excuse to leave. He heads to the front door and lets himself out.

Topher walks out of the room, to the back of the house. He slides the patio door open, then closes it behind him before letting out a yell. He's kicking at the piles of snow in the backyard, saying something. I slump onto the couch, thoughts whirring. The gun. Officer Erving focusing in on Topher. Increased gang activity.

Evan. If there's increased gang activity in town, does that mean increased drug access as well? The last thing my brother needs right now is more temptation to slip up. I'm glad he's over an hour away in Denver.

Sophie and Anika come down the stairs, trying to walk quietly, but stepping onto even more creaks.

"Is your grandma okay?" I ask. I tried to catch the car thieves so she could feel safe in her home and stop having the police show up. Instead, the situation seems even worse, and all we have is a blurry picture for our efforts.

"She'll be fine," Sophie says tightly.

"What'd you learn?" Anika asks.

Topher comes back in from the snow, slowly closing the door and kicking off his boots in the kitchen. The three of them join me on the couch.

"I need to get out of this town," he says tightly.

"Only a few more months," Anika says, patting his shoulder.

"I don't know if I'll make it," he murmurs.

I stare at him. I had no idea he was so eager to get out of here. I know he applied to CU Boulder, but haven't heard if he got in yet. This declaration sounds like it's about more than Officer Erving.

"What happened?" Sophie asks.

I give them a summary. Everyone is silent for a long moment once I finish.

"So now what?" Anika asks.

"What do you mean?" I ask.

"Are we going to figure this out, show them how incompetent they are?" Anika asks.

Sophie slaps Anika's thigh. "No, we're not. Someone pointed a gun at Ellie tonight. This is way over our heads."

"We've been through worse," Anika mutters.

Topher doesn't say anything, his eyes flashing with emotions after his encounter with Officer Erving.

"I think you can do this," Anika says, turning to me.

It was in a different house where I begged them to help me figure out who was killing our classmates and dumping them in the river. When I'd feared that I'd somehow get in trouble because of my connection to one of the dead boys. Anika and Topher both shot me down that day, absolutely refusing. Anika had been angry I'd even considered it. Is that why she's pushing so hard right now? To make up for that day? Or does she actually believe that we can do something?

"Let's go to bed. It's late," Sophie says. She busies herself with pulling out blankets and pillows, and converting the couches into a pull-out bed.

I lie on my side of the couch bed I'm sharing with Topher, tensing as soon as the lights are turned off. Now that it's quiet, that I'm still, fear rips through me. I am a panic attack bomb, always one wrong thought away from going off. At school. In the grocery store. In the middle of a Pathfinders competition. Night after night alone in my room. Someone pointed a gun at me. What is my body going to do now?

I listen to the slow breathing of my friends around me. When it sounds like they're all asleep, I crawl back to the front room, to the bench we were sitting on. I look outside to where a tow truck driver is hooking up the white sedan. It *was* stolen. Officer Erving must have checked the plate when he was done talking with us. I stare at the car with smug satisfaction.

My eyes trail to the bar again, trying to fit the pieces together. Why would those people steal a car, and then leave it out here just to go to the bar? How are they getting home later? An uber? Another stolen car? Is there some sort of shady operation running out of the Drunken Lizard? Maybe I should peek inside one night, see what I can find out. Am I even allowed to walk in there? Would Quinn know something?

I keep sorting through ideas, watching the snow fall, anticipating the panic attack. Is it waiting for the moment I let my guard down? Will it wake me up once I finally drift to sleep? There has to be one coming. I had an *actual* gun pointed at me. That has to be more panic-attack-worthy than some of the other things that started one.

I stare at the snow until my eyelids are burning and it's a fight to keep them open. Is it really not coming? I tiptoe back to the couches, and gently lower myself onto the bed, not wanting to jostle Topher awake. I lie on my side, the sound of my friends' slow deep breaths soothing. I'll be safe tonight with all of them surrounding me.

Maybe figuring out what's happening with these stolen cars is good for me. There's a piece of me that feels alive in a way it hasn't in months.

No. I need to think about this when I'm not half asleep. When I make decisions too hastily, people get hurt. And I'm not risking anyone else again.

SEVEN

Monday January 23rd 5:15 PM

"How were your holidays?" Layla asks as she twists her hair into a perfect bun. There are no bumps or flyaways. And she did it without a mirror. Why is everything better here in Loveland? Perfect buns, a sizeable Pathfinders team, and a driving track. They don't even have to take down the tables and chairs at the end of every meeting because this room is *only* for Pathfinders. It's always set up, ready to go for practice.

Or, for leadership meetings.

"Fine," Jamie and I say at the exact same time from opposite sides of the table. We're mirror images of each other, arms crossed on our chests and leaning back in our chairs while glaring.

Layla looks back and forth between the two of us. Then she gives a dramatic sigh. "I was hoping with the winter break, we could all move on and start fresh. You two leave me no choice. It's time for an intervention."

"Is this really the best use of our time?" Jamie asks.

I glance at the clock. There's only forty-five minutes left until the rest of the team gets here. It's the first meeting in a month, and we need to strategize how to make a comeback. Thanks to me.

"Yes, it is. We need to up our game if we're going to make it to Regionals this year, and I can't have you two at each other's throats the whole time."

"We're not always at each other's throats—" I start.

Layla tilts her head. "Good. Prove it. I want you both to tell each other one thing you like about them."

I glare at Jamie. He looks at me for a moment, then rolls his eyes.

"If you two can't name one single thing that you both like about each other, I'm going to assign you to be partners on every single activity until you figure it out."

"I feel like that's a disservice to everyone else. I could really help mentor the other kids," I say.

"I would be a better mentor to them because I wouldn't be trying to secretly overthrow you as team leader," Jamie says to Layla.

"How many times do I have to tell you that I don't want anything to do with being the leader!" I yell, smacking the table in emphasis.

"That's not what it looked like during the SWAT scenario," Jamie retorts.

"That's not what happened," I say, glancing at Layla. I've never talked about that day in the dark of the warehouse building with her. Or how I missed four meetings after that. Jamie's made his interpretation of my actions more than clear. What does she think about it?

She only shakes her head. "You two are worse than I thought." She drums her fingers on the table, staring out into space. "Do either of you have ideas for a team building activity we could do?"

She's moving on that easily? Is that good, or bad?

"How about paintball?" I suggest.

Layla looks to Jamie. He looks down, then mumbles, "that could work."

I try my best not to smirk. See? I have good ideas that even he can't argue with.

Layla smiles. "Great, we'll do that. Now for the schedule."

She goes over a list of trainings to do. I completely forgot that tonight's activity is hostage negotiations. That familiar tightness in my chest starts to creep in, but I try to ignore it. Tonight's training has nothing to do with what happened at the riverbank. I mean, *technically* Quinn could have been viewed as a hostage. And, I was trying to convince Brooke to let him go. But that's not going to be the scenario we're practicing tonight. So, no reason to think about the riverbank and have a panic attack.

I didn't have one when someone pointed an actual gun at me Friday night. If that's not proof that I'm getting better, I don't know what is. I've got this.

Maybe.

We go through the rest of the schedule, Layla and Jamie having an in-depth discussion about whether we should use the real cruisers when learning traffic stops in a few weeks. By the time we wrap it up, people are arriving for practice. I stop myself from running over to Topher and DJ when they walk in. Jamie is always accusing me of not integrating with this team, so I need to prove him wrong. I sidle up to one of the younger members, a girl with brown hair, named either Desirae or Deidre. I've messed her name up multiple times now, and I can't ask her what it is again.

If I talk to her long enough, maybe it will come up naturally.

She gives me a quick smile, then turns to her actual friends. They all start laughing. I wait for them to finish so I can join the conversation, but one of the girls snorts, sending them all into a fresh fit of giggles. I slowly start backing away. They don't want me here, and that's fine. The old me who was a team leader wouldn't have had to hang around awkwardly to try and remember someone's name. I would have known Desirae/Deidre's entire back-story, along with her favorite drink for her birthday.

Another reminder of how far I've fallen.

Lieutenant Sanders walks in then, looking us all over. I hurry to Topher's side as Layla calls us to attention for the weekly uniform inspection. Since coming here, I've realized how lax we were with the program. It makes sense why the Loveland team often makes it to the national competitions, and we didn't. The money for extra things like their own practice track probably helps too.

Layla comes over and stands in front of me, yelling in my face. "What are the three different shooting stances?"

My mind goes to that quiet place, and I focus solely on her. "Isosceles, weaver, and fighting."

"Demonstrate them," she barks.

I hold up my plastic weapon, and go between the three stances, moving my shoulder blades and feet for each.

Layla nods and moves on to yell at Topher. DJ ends up on the floor doing push-ups since he answered his question wrong. The extra hair of his mullet flops around each time he goes down to the ground.

Once Layla and Lieutenant Sanders have finished questioning everyone, they both go to the front of the room.

"Today we're prepping for hostage negotiations, since it

will be in the final competition," Lieutenant Sanders announces.

I half listen while she goes over the steps of de-escalation, and techniques to try. I tune back in when Layla says my name.

"Ellie, Jamie, you'll practice together," she says. She smiles, walking over to hand me a script. I'm about to beg her to let me work with anyone else, but there's a fire in her eyes that shuts me up.

"Switch with me," I hiss at Topher.

"Absolutely not," he says before walking over to his partner. It's Desirae/Deidre. Of course it is.

Jamie appears next to me, and he looks like he's in physical pain.

"Think of a compliment for me, and we can be done with this," I tell him.

"You think of one," Jamie retorts.

I stare at him, trying to think of something. My mind goes completely blank. The two of us wordlessly walk to an empty corner, standing opposite from each other.

I glance down at my script. I'm the person in distress, holding my family hostage after a domestic dispute. Jamie will be the officer. Perfect. I can handle that. I grab the fake plastic gun from my belt and point it at Jamie.

"Get out, or I'll shoot."

Jamie arrogantly throws his script behind him, and holds both his hands up. "I'm Jamie, and I'm not here to hurt you. I'm here to help."

I skim the next few lines of the script, then drop it to the ground. I got the gist of it; I'll just wing it from here. "You can't help me."

"What's your name?" he asks.

"You don't need it," I say.

"I'm here with you and I thought it'd be good to know."

"So you can manipulate me?" I shout, taking a step closer to him, slipping into the role.

He blows out a long breath. "Your family is scared. Why don't we just calm down a little?"

"Don't tell me to calm down!" I wave the gun around wildly.

Jamie still has his hands up. "I'm going to take a step back right now. Is there anything you need?"

He's on the give physical space step. I shake my head wildly. "No, get out of here."

"I'm not leaving you until I know everyone is safe. We're going to figure out something that works for everyone."

I pace back and forth with the plastic gun, pretending that I'm thinking.

"You don't care about us. You're just a cop."

"I get why you'd think that."

Now he's trying to be empathetic. He sucks at it. He probably tells people that he's sorry if they chose to be offended by what he said when he apologizes. "Of course I think that!"

Jamie's eyebrows pull together and he's chewing on his lip. He still hasn't gotten me to give my name like his script told him to.

"What's the difference between ice cream and frozen yogurt?" he finally asks.

"Yogurt is full of probiotics," I start saying automatically. "Hey. That's cheating." He stole that from the poster on the wall at work. I re-read it over and over whenever I'm bored.

He throws his hands up in frustration. "You're not following the script, what am I supposed to do?"

"De-escalate. They're not going to have a script for you to check against at the competition," I say.

"No, but they're at least going to be a little fair."

"Life isn't fair. Be better." I cringe internally as I say it. Hello inner-tough-love-parent from a movie.

He rolls his eyes. "If you're so good at it, you do it."

Layla appears then and hands him a different script with a new scenario on it. She offers me one, but I don't take it. I don't need it. I shake out my hands and close my eyes as Jamie looks over the pages. I hear Anika's voice in my head, telling me the steps of de-escalation over the phone. I'll never forget them, even if I wanted to.

"Get out of here," Jamie yells.

I open my eyes. It's time.

I hold my arms out at my sides, palms facing Jamie. This feels less threatening to me than having my hands by my head.

"Sorry, I didn't mean to startle you. I'm Ellie. What's your name?" I ask, my voice slow and soft.

"I said go away," Jamie yells.

"You want me to get away, I understand that," I repeat, making sure he knows I hear what he wants, even if I'm not doing it.

"Get out, or I'll shoot them," Jamie says, pointing the plastic weapon behind him.

"No one needs to get hurt. Let's talk, you and me."

"I don't want to talk to you," he spits.

Isn't that the truth. "Lots of people say that about me. Can you help me understand what's going on?"

"Stop talking to me like a child," Jamie says.

All right, I'm stuck. I stand there quietly, my mind spinning. One of the steps of de-escalation is actually silence though. I stand there with my palms still facing outwards, a neutral expression on my face. I keep waiting, and see Jamie glance down at his script.

"Someone called me an abuser. That's a lie," he finally says.

Yes. The silence made him crack, slightly. "Do you feel like no one will believe you?" I ask.

He nods.

"I'm here to listen. Tell me why they said that."

Jamie stares at me, then looks down at his script. I press my lips together so I don't smirk.

"Our neighbors heard screaming. The kids were just messing around."

That's probably not the truth, especially if his character is willing to create a hostage situation over this. But I have to stay with his truth until everyone is safe.

"Kids scream sometimes, especially when they're playing."

"My neighbor hates us, they're out to get me," Jamie says.

"I'm not listening to your neighbor. I'm here with you right now."

Jamie looks down at his paper again. I realize the rest of the room has gone completely quiet. They're all invested in our standoff, watching carefully. Lieutenant Sanders is watching from her spot at the front of the room.

Jamie realizes it too, because he raises his plastic gun in the air, straight at me. "Get out or I'm going to shoot!"

I don't know if it's because he's so close and I can see the anger in his eyes, or because this is the second time someone's done this in a week. But staring at the barrel of his bright blue plastic gun pointed straight at me brings me right back to the riverbank. I can hear the slow gurgle of the water, feel the autumn sun on my arms. My heart starts racing and adrenaline courses through me, preparing me to fight. I take a step backward on shaking legs, keeping my eyes focused on that blue barrel. Thoughts swirl in my head. *Do I tackle him? Do I run? How can I keep everyone safe?*

"Stand down Jamie," Lieutenant Sanders says. She's standing next to me and places a firm hand on my shoulder. The weight of her hand brings me back into the room. I'm in the police station. That gun is plastic. Everyone else is here. No one is in danger.

My body won't turn off though. My head is swimming and I feel unstable. Am I going to pass out? Or have another panic attack? I can't have a panic attack right here. Everyone is staring straight at me. I'm going to crawl out of my skin if they don't stop looking at me.

"Whoops," Topher yells from the opposite corner of the room as an entire stack of chairs clatters to the floor. Everyone turns around to look at him. I step out from under Lieutenant Sanders hand. Then I bolt to the door out of the room, taking off down the hall to the bathroom.

I need to take deep breaths, but I don't think I can. I'm going to hyperventilate and they're going to find me passed out here from lack of carbon dioxide. I can't do this. I'm never going to be a cop if this keeps happening to me. I can't even look at a plastic gun without losing it. That day by the river, it broke me.

A sob rises in my throat and I try to stop it. If it escapes, there's no stopping the flood of them. I turn on the cold water in the sink, splashing it on my face. Maybe it will actually do something this time. When it doesn't, I hold my wrist under the tap, hoping the cold there will shock my system. I stare at my face. My eyes are wide, pupils dilated even in the light. My skin is so pale, I could pass for fully white. Which makes the zit forming under my nose stick out. I lean closer to the mirror to look at it, accidentally brushing against the wet edge of the counter.

Great. There's a huge spot on my uniform. I move to the dryer, spinning it so it's aimed at my shirt. Thankfully it's navy blue and the stain doesn't show too much. I tuck my shirt back in, then go back to the mirror to get a better look at the zit forming under my nose. As I poke at it, wincing in pain, I realize my heart isn't pounding in my ears anymore. I'm breathing.

My chest is still tight, and I feel weak. But I'm breathing. I'm not sobbing. I wait a few seconds, seeing if the panic is about to come roaring back to life. It doesn't.

I walk back to the practice room. The chairs are all picked up from the floor, but everyone is still staring at Topher who is standing facing Desirae/Deidre.

"I love that Topher kept talking in a soft voice so that Desirae naturally lowered her volume. That takes skill because we naturally want to match volume with someone who is already yelling at us. Nice job," Lieutenant Sanders says to the room. She claps him on the shoulder.

Instead of looking thrilled about the public praise, he's frowning slightly.

What's that about? I'm glad he got a chance to shine. Topher knows his stuff and the younger team-members can learn a lot from his example.

"That's enough for tonight, I'll see you next week," Lieutenant Sanders says. She looks around the room and her eyes land on me. She starts walking over.

"Topher, I'll meet you in the parking lot," I yell at him, holding my keys in the air. I don't check to see if he heard me, then go right back out the door.

I don't want to talk to Lieutenant Sanders right now.

She'll probably hint that I should take a longer break from Pathfinders like she told me to last year. Then tell me she's always here to talk. I can't take any more time off. Jamie would never let me hear the end of it. And as nice as she is, I can't tell her about what's happening. What if she writes it in a file, and it stops me from becoming an officer one day?

It was a baby panic attack. Nothing to freak out about. If Jamie hadn't been so aggressive, it wouldn't have happened.

The real world doesn't have a script, and it's going to have even more pointed weapons. What will you do then?

Shush, brain. This is Jamie's fault. Speaking of the devil, he's standing in the hallway.

"Where'd you go?" Jamie frowns.

"Period emergency," I say. It's a lie, but if I have to suffer through them every month, I'm going to milk them for all they're worth.

He opens and closes his mouth like a fish, miraculously staying quiet as I pass him to get to the parking lot.

EIGHT

Tuesday January 24th 2:40PM

Ms. Lions hands back our quizzes. Topher is laughing with Sandra until the paper slides across his desk. He picks it up and stares at it. A C stares back.

"What?" he asks no one in particular. He keeps staring at the paper. I get my own back and it's a B-. That's the highest grade I've gotten in a while.

Topher glances at my paper. "You got higher than me?" he says in disbelief.

"I'll try not to let that hurt," I say.

"You were having your meltdown last semester," he says.

I look up at the ceiling exasperatedly. "Can everyone stop bringing that up?"

He's not listening. He snatches Anika, Sandra, and my quizzes and compares his answers with ours.

"I don't think college is going to care about this little pop quiz," I say.

"I care," Topher says. His stool screeches across the floor as he walks up to Ms. Lions' desk.

Anika, Sandra, and I exchange a look. What is going on? He's never cared this much about grades before, especially a little pop quiz.

My pocket buzzes. It's a number I don't recognize.

KACEY

THEY FOUND MY CAR!

Can you come over?

This is Kacey btw. I stole your number from Quinn.

"They found Kacey's car," I tell the table.

"Ooh, where?" Anika asks. She pulls out her phone, presumably to text Sophie about it.

"I'm glad they found it before you had to interrogate anyone," Sandra says, her lips in a smirk.

"You need a new joke," I reply.

Sandra laughs.

Sure. What do you need me for?

KACEY

I need your expertise on something.

I'm going to ask her about what, but Topher is coming back to the table, looking dazed.

"They found Kacey's car. She wants me to come over and check something out. Do you want to come?" I ask him.

He shakes his head, as if clearing it. "What?"

"I'm going over to Quinn and Kacey's. They found her car. Do you want to come?" I repeat.

He frowns. "Why would she need you now?"

I shrug. "Not sure. It would be nice to get some closure on the whole thing though."

"That's code for she wants to see her boyfriend," Anika says in a sing-song voice.

"Is not. I'm going there to see *Kacey*," I emphasize. If Quinn happens to be there, well, that's not the worst thing in the world.

"Are you really going to put yourself in harm's way for a boy again?" Topher asks.

"I'm going over to their apartment, in broad daylight, to see her returned car. Come with and supervise me if you're so worried," I say.

"I can't," Topher says. He pulls out his textbook and starts flipping through it.

"Fine, just don't complain that I never involve you in things. Anika, do you want to come?"

"I've got volunteering with Sophie, otherwise I would. Don't do anything dangerous without me."

"Sandra?" I ask.

She shakes her head. "No thanks."

Well fine then. I bite my nails in anticipation. What could Kacey need my expertise on?

When a girl with blue hair opens Kacey's door, I'm confused. I step back and look at the apartment number. 212. This is the right door.

"Hi," she says slowly.

"I'm looking for Kacey?" I ask.

Kacey comes running to the door, standing behind the girl with blue hair. "She's here to see me, Ronnie."

Ronnie. Probably short for Veronica. Ronnie shrugs and walks back into the apartment. Straight to the couch where she sits next to Quinn, laying her legs across his lap. I pause in the entryway, staring at them. Quinn's typing on his laptop with headphones in and hasn't seen me yet. Ronnie picks up a physics textbook from the coffee table and starts writing. He didn't even look up when she came back to the couch, like this is something they do all the time.

"Let's go to my room," Kacey says, pulling on my arm.

How long have I been staring? "Sure, sounds great."

Quinn's head snaps up and he pulls his ear pods out. "Ellie, what are you doing here?"

"I invited her over," Kacey says.

"Why didn't you tell me?" Quinn asks.

"Because I don't have to," Kacey says simply.

"What's going on?" Ronnie asks, looking at me with curiosity.

Quinn's head whips back and forth between the three of us. "Ellie was helping Kacey with her missing car. But she got it back this morning. Was it stolen again?"

"Wouldn't you like to know," Kacey says. She pulls on my hand, leading me down the hallway. "They're so obnoxious," she says once she closes the door of her room.

"Oh really, why?" Do I sound too interested when I ask that?

"Ronnie is smart as hell, but she's super outdoorsy. She's always inviting us to go hiking and climb fourteeners, and Quinn pretends that he's in shape enough to do it, but then he just comes home and moans all night soaking his feet."

"Oh," is all I can come up with. He must really like her if he's willing to do that.

"They have tickets to go snowshoeing in a few weeks. They were expensive. Can you imagine paying hundreds of dollars to get permission to walk around with tennis rackets on your feet?"

I try and picture it, then shudder. Snowshoeing sounds awful. I don't hate the snow, but I wouldn't willingly spend hours and hours out in it. They'll probably walk together hand in hand, then snuggle up afterward to get warm...

"What did you want to show me?" I ask.

Kacey goes to her desk. There's a stack of papers sitting on top next to a tiny pink Christmas tree. "When they turned my car back over to me, I decided it was time to clean it out. I brought up all of these papers, and I found some things that don't belong to me."

"Did you call the police?" I ask.

"I did, and they don't care. Surprise, surprise." She rolls her eyes. "Which is why I wanted to show them to you."

It's painful to hear how they've been treating Kacey. Is it because they have so much going on right now? Or is it something else? I don't know the officers that she worked with personally, but I was in the Pathfinders program. I'm sure I received a level of respect that the general public might not because of that.

She hands me the papers with a few folded receipts on top. I'm immediately overcome with the scent of burnt vanilla. It reminds me of my mom's favorite lotion when I was a kid, until they changed the formula and it smelled awful. I look around Kacey's room for a bottle of lotion, or maybe a diffuser. I don't see anything that would explain the smell, except for the papers right in front of me. I bring them up to my nose and sniff them.

"What the hell? Do you think you're a bloodhound or something?" Kacey asks.

"Do these smell to you?" I ask her.

She stares at me. Then shakes her head no.

"Sniff them," I urge her, putting the papers near her nose.

She stares at me, probably to see if I'm joking. Then she takes the papers and gives them a quick sniff. And then another. And a third.

"How did you smell that?" she asks.

"It's my mom's old lotion. I hate it. Whoever's these are must use it too, or maybe had it in their backpack."

I look through the papers one by one. They're all school papers. One of them is a test, but in the spot where a name should go, there's a bunch of numbers. "What's this?" I ask Kacey.

"A student ID number. Some professors have you put them instead of your name so that they're not biased while grading."

"Can you find out whose this is?" I ask excitedly. If we find out whose number it is, then we'll know who was in the car.

"No, I tried digging, but I couldn't get anywhere unless I had a last name."

We keep going through the rest of the papers. I sit down on her floor and organize them into piles. There are three quizzes with the same student number on them. A Starbucks receipt. A folded-up flyer for a campus movie night that already happened. Kacey goes through the trash-bag of stuff she collected in her car and we double check there isn't anything we missed.

"So, we have someone who is taking a math class, visited a Starbucks, and maybe went to a movie night," Kacey says.

I stare at the quizzes. They're all math, but look nothing like anything I've learned yet in school. There are a bunch of shapes with circles drawn on the corners, and squiggly lines.

"Do you know what kind of math this is?" I ask Kacey.

She shakes her head. "I'm a good-old-fashioned calculus kind of girl myself."

I stare at the paper for a moment longer, then hop up from the floor, heading to the living room. My stomach immediately sinks as Ronnie kiss Quinn's neck. She says something to him, and he laughs. I go backward and then reenter the room noisily. Ronnie is sitting up now and Quinn's cheeks are red.

"Hey," I force a small smile at Ronnie. She's done nothing wrong, it's not fair for me to be angry with her. Quinn told me months ago that there was a girl he was sort of seeing. This is probably her. She's been around longer than I have.

Jealousy still slithers through me as I see all the places their bodies are casually touching. I try to shove it down. People who take physics also take math.

"Do you know what kind of math this is?" I hand her the paper, and she stares at it for a few seconds.

"Discrete math. Probably from Professor Kingston, he always makes his students use their student numbers," she adds with a smile.

Kacey wasn't lying about her being smart. "Thank you," I smile back.

Quinn grabs the paper from Ronnie. "Where'd you get this?"

"Wouldn't you like to know," I say, snatching it from his fingers before speeding back to Kacey's room.

"Is there a way you can look up what classes a Professor Kingston teaches?" I ask as soon as I'm back inside.

"Definitely." She pulls out her laptop and sits on her

bed, typing. I sit next to her, watching her navigate through some kind of portal. She puts in discrete math, and a few time offerings pop up. She opens each one up where more information shows the professor's name. It turns out Professor Kingston only teaches discrete math once a week on Thursday nights from 3:30-6pm. I take a picture of the screen.

"What are you up to?" Quinn asks from the doorway.

I search for any signs of Ronnie behind him. "Nothing."

"I'm going to avoid discrete math at all costs," Kacey says.

"It's not that bad once you get the hang of it," Ronnie calls from the living room.

Quinn raises an eyebrow. "Where'd you get some random quiz of it?" he asks. His eyebrows pull together. Then they rise up. "Was that left in your car? By whoever stole it? You're trying to figure out who it was, aren't you?"

"Of course not. Why would I do that? It's not like the police would help me even if I did," Kacey says.

"Exactly. You have your car back and we added extra security measures, so let's all just let it go." His eyes are on me.

"Why are you looking at me?" I ask.

"Because you're the one with a history of struggling with that."

An image of Brooke running the scalpel over his neck pops into my mind. I close my eyes for a second, begging it to go away. When I open them, I can clearly see the scar on his neck, peeking out just above the top of his hoodie. My head starts to spin.

"I've got to go," I say, grabbing my half-zipped backpack and clutching it to my chest. I cannot have a panic attack in front of them, and one might be coming.

Quinn frowns. "Do you need a ride home? It's starting to snow out."

"I actually have a car now, so I'm good."

"When'd you get a car?" he asks.

"When did you care so much?" I snap.

"It was just a question," Quinn says, tilting his head.

I push past him and practically run through their living room to the front door. Kacey puts a hand on my shoulder as I turn the knob.

"You okay?" she asks.

"Yep, I'll text you."

"It was nice meeting you Ellie," Ronnie calls out as I make my way out the door.

My chest burns with each of my shallow breaths. "You too," I barely manage to say. I slam the door behind me before they can see me fall apart. I run down the stairs, sinking to the ground on the last step. My vision is blurry and I'm scared I'm going to pass out. I put my head between my knees, willing myself to stay conscious. Behind my closed eyes, I see the image of blood running down Quinn's neck, over and over. The hate in Brooke's eyes. The sound of the gun as I fired it at her, that instant where I didn't know which one of them was screaming.

No. No. No.

My butt is soaking wet. The snow on the bottom step has slowly been seeping through my jeans. I leap up from the step, then slip on a patch of ice. I fumble for the railing, slamming into it. My right thigh immediately starts throbbing. That's definitely going to bruise.

By the time I'm standing safely on the sidewalk away from the stairs and ice, my vision has cleared. My chest still hurts when I breathe, but it's less intense. I slowly walk back to my car and slump into the driver's seat.

Quinn is okay. He's alive and cuddling another girl on his couch. An instant wave of jealousy burns through me, thinking of the two of them.

I'm feeling jealous. I laugh. I can handle jealousy. Feeling jealous means I'm not about to have a full-blown panic attack, or pass out on the bottom of those stairs. It means I'm okay.

More than okay, actually. I have something new to focus on. I open my photos, rechecking what time Professor Kingston's discrete math class meets. It's time to catch a thief.

NINE

Thursday January 26th 5:40PM

"DOES THAT LOOK LIKE A SCIENCE BUILDING?" I ASK Topher.

He squints at it. "With that kind of tiling and columns? Definitely not. It says more history to me," he says.

"Seriously?"

"No, who do you think I am?" he snorts. "Definitely not an architecture student."

I laugh, glad that Topher's weird mood from the other day is gone. I pull on my backpack straps, turning in a circle, then glance down at the map on my phone again. It only gives the official names of the buildings, which are all named after rich donors. How am I supposed to know which donor was chosen for the science building?

"Hey," a voice calls. We turn around and see an out-of-breath Kacey bounding over to us. "I've been calling your names forever. The science building is over there." She points to a different brick building. There are no decorative columns in front of it.

"You were onto something with the columns," I say to Topher, then we follow after Kacey.

"You can think of this as your unofficial college tour. Except, I know where all the best things are, and I'm not going to shove statistics down your throat," she says.

"Can you talk about how the price of tuition went up drastically after you built your new stadium, even though you already had one? And how the new field doesn't make you any better at football?" Topher asks.

Kacey stops in her tracks. "Are you a CU kid?"

He shrugs. "Potentially. I know I'm not going here. I'd like to be smart about where I acquire my debt, and it's not going to be for a stadium."

Kacey rolls her eyes. "Why is he here again?"

"To make sure Ellie doesn't get shot," he says.

I glare at him, silently begging him to shut up.

"What do you mean?" Kacey asks.

"There was the whole incident at the riverbank, and then the guy who pulled a gun on her last week during the stakeout trying to find your car."

Kacey stops walking.

"It's not as bad as he's making it sound," I say quickly.

"Why didn't you tell me? I didn't know these people were armed," Kacey hisses.

"That was probably a one off. Do armed people really take discrete math and go to Starbucks?" I ask.

"Maybe, you can't stereotype people like that," Kacey starts. "There are soccer moms whose entire personality is being armed."

"Nice science building," Topher interrupts.

We're finally in front of the brick building. While it

doesn't have decorative columns, I can picture myself with textbooks in my backpack, feeling excited to rush off to class and finish up my homework. Okay, that's unrealistic. I'll be there with my backpack, excited to run off and meet up with friends.

I feel a sudden pang. I'll be losing my friends soon. Topher is going off to Boulder most likely, and Anika is leaning toward Denver. As for me? I don't want to think about it.

Topher walks to the door of the science building and opens it. "Can we hurry this up? I've got homework."

Kacey spins her keys on her wrist, looking back and forth between Topher and me. She gives a dramatic sigh, then walks through the doors. We follow after her through the long hallways of the building. There are people on laptops tucked into nooks and crannies everywhere. On the floor with backs against the wall, in little groups of tables at the ends of the hallways. We pass tiny café with metal shutters over the door, surrounded by more tables and chairs.

Finally Kacey stops in front of a classroom. "I got the number off the registration portal," she says.

I glance at my phone. 5:55. Here with only minutes to spare. I bounce up and down on my heels. We're actually doing this.

There's no bell, but the door of the classroom next to ours opens. It's 5:57. My teachers would die if they saw this —students leaving early—especially the ones who demand they dismiss us, not the bell. We get it; you like power. Just let us go.

At 5:59, the classroom door in front of us opens. I start looking at the students, trying to figure out who might be a Starbucks fan, invited to a pizza party, and steal a car. I want to think that a car thief would be dressed in all black with a beanie, but I know that's ridiculous.

I look through people's hands, seeing if any of them are carrying Starbucks. There are a few, but most are carrying hydro-flasks. One is holding a half-eaten ice cream cake. College students bring ice cream cakes to class? What is this place?

No one is wearing a black beanie with a shirt that says, "I like to steal cars," though.

"Maybe we could ask the TA who the paper belongs to?" Kacey asks, pointing to someone still inside the classroom.

I try to peek in, but a final group comes out of the door, and I move out of their way. That's when I smell it. Burnt vanilla. The same scent I caught on the papers. I follow after the last group, trying to sniff the air surreptitiously. I pull out my phone and stare at the screen, pretending to be oblivious as I move to the side of their group. I can still smell the vanilla, along with the scent of weed. There are four possible people it could be, three girls and a guy.

There's a fork in the hallway and the group splits into two. I have to choose which to follow. Is it the two girls who went left, or the other girl and guy who went straight? I hesitate, taking in big breaths of air. I'm getting lightheaded from all the sniffing. This is absolutely ridiculous.

The girl and guy who went straight are at the front doors of the building, walking out into the cold night. Unless I want to track them down in the dark, the only way left to go is left. A few steps down the hallway, I'm rewarded with the burnt vanilla smell again.

The two girls are about to turn into another hallway, so I jog to catch up with them. This is it. I swing my backpack to my chest, pulling out a piece of paper. Topher and Kacey are right behind me, but there's no time to fill them in.

"Excuse me" I say to the girls. At first, they ignore me, but I repeat it. They both turn around and stare at me.

"Are you talking to us?" the blonde, white girl asks me.

"Yeah, I think you dropped this in my friend's car," I say, handing the test forward. The blonde girl stares at me in confusion, but the white girl with red highlights lights up with recognition.

"Oh thanks. Sorry about that." She takes the paper from me and opens up her backpack to drop it in. I'm hit with the scent of burnt vanilla as soon as the zippers open. There's definitely a spilled bottle in there. She smiles at me and is about to walk away.

I'm confused. Why did she admit to the paper being hers so easily? Does she often ride in stolen cars and leave her stuff there?

"Are these yours too?" I ask, pulling out the receipt and flyers.

Red highlights nods, taking them from me. "I must have dropped them when I was looking for some gum. I wasn't feeling the best," she says.

She freely admitted to it again. Not only was she in Kacey's car, but she felt comfortable enough there to leave a mess. Do car thieves do that?

"Were you feeling sick because you're a car thief?" Kacey asks, standing next to me.

The blonde girl's mouth opens up, and red highlights takes the tiniest step backward. They look at each other, then back at us.

That's the type of reaction I was expecting.

"What do you mean?" the blonde girl asks.

"My car was stolen last week, and I found your test

inside. Care to explain?" Kacey asks, her arms folded across her chest.

Red highlights holds up her hands, the Starbucks receipt and flyer still in them. "Whoa, I didn't steal your car. We were just leaving a party and got an Uber."

"It wasn't Uber, it was that new one. Unter? Under? My roommate gave me the code for it," the blonde girl says.

Wait, what?

"Can you show us the app?" I ask.

The two girls look between each other.

"Your stuff was found inside a stolen car. You should show us the app," Topher says. "How about at those tables over there?"

We're near the closed café. All the tables in front of it are empty. We all take seats at one of them. The girls both look worried.

"We didn't know it was a stolen car, promise. We were just trying to get home safely," the blonde girl says.

"We wouldn't have ridden in your car if we knew it was stolen," red highlights agrees.

Kacey nods. She has that faraway look in her eyes again.

I pull up the App store on my phone, and type in Unter. An app shows up, but when I go to open it, it asks for an invite code.

"Can I have the invite code?" I ask.

Both girls shake their heads. "You only get one invite, and we already used ours. Each code is different," red highlights says.

"You can look at it on my phone," the blonde girl says, handing it to me.

I stare at the homepage. This thing is interesting. I've only used Uber once, but this looks nothing like it. There's a choice to request a ride, or find an available car. I click on request a ride, and it says there aren't any available right now, but to check back later.

I go back and click on available cars. It takes me to a map of the city. There are blue dots all over it, the majority of them around campus and then Main Street. I click on one near me, and it lists the price of $10 per one ride, or $25 for the whole day. I choose one ride. It asks for credit card info, which is already filled in from a previous ride. I hit confirm to see what happens. Once I pay, it shows me a picture of the car, and says to keep the app open to unlock it when I get there. The screen says to leave the app open until I'm finished, when I can hit a big red FINISH RIDE button.

I take screenshots of everything, then text it to myself. "How can you run the car with no keys?" I ask.

"Usually there's a USB in the glove box. Most of them are push starts," Red Highlights says.

"It's a little glitchy, but totally worth the savings," the blonde girl says.

Of course it is. All of the cars are stolen so whoever is running this app can charge as little as they want. I hand the blonde girl her phone back. "I can Venmo you for the ride I just bought."

"Don't worry about it. Is there anything else you need?" she asks, her eyes flitting down the halls.

I look at Topher and Kacey who both shake their heads.

"Do you have any idea who made this app?" I ask.

"None. I heard about it from my roommate. I swear, we didn't know the car we rode in was stolen. Do you think all of them are?" Red Highlights asks.

"Probably."

"Should we call the police?" Red Highlights asks.

The blonde girl gives her an anxious look.

"Yes, you definitely should. And tell all your friends to stop using the app," Kacey says.

They nod solemnly. After a moment of silence, the blonde girls slowly stands up from the table. Red Highlights follows her lead. They look down at us, waiting for an objection.

"Thank for your help," I say. "If I have more questions, I'll be in touch." I have the blonde girl's number from the screenshots I sent myself.

They nod, then practically run away from us.

"That's it?" Topher asks once they're out of sight.

"What do you mean that's it?" I ask.

He shrugs. "I thought it'd be more thrilling. That you'd bang on the table or something."

"Sorry that figuring out who stole my car isn't enough entertainment for you," Kacey says deadpan.

"Anika got to have more fun," Topher grumbles.

I ignore him, looking at Kacey. "You okay?"

"Not really. I thought I'd feel better after confronting them, but I'm just annoyed. Even if the police find that app, what are they going to do about it?"

"They could work on getting it shut down," I offer.

Kacey shrugs. "Maybe." Her eyes go vacant and she disappears back into her thoughts.

"What are you doing here?" Topher calls out to someone behind me.

I turn around to see who he's talking to. Of course. It's Quinn.

Quinn comes over and joins us at the table. "Topher, it's been too long." He claps Topher on the shoulder, then sits down in the chair next to Kacey, across the table from me.

"What brings you all here on this lovely night?" Quinn asks.

"Nothing—" I start.

"We found the girls who took Kacey's car," Topher says.

Quinn's eyes widen. "Here? The two who were practically running away?" He points over his shoulder with his thumb.

"Technically they didn't steal it, they thought they were using a car share app," I say.

"Hold on, how did you figure any of this out?" Quinn asks.

"How *did* you know it was them?" Kacey asks, tilting her head.

I look down at the ground. "They smelled like vanilla," I mumble.

Kacey bursts out laughing. Topher and Quinn keep exchanging looks.

"Ellie smelled the papers like a dog and matched the scents," Kacey explains.

Topher snorts and Quinn keeps staring at me, his forehead wrinkling from the intensity.

I glare at Kacey. "It's a very particular scent."

Kacey smirks back at me. I'm glad my distaste for vanilla lotion can at least make her smile.

"Start at the beginning," Quinn says.

I look at Topher. "We've really got to get going back," I say, standing up. "Topher has homework."

"It can wait for this," Topher says, leaning in his chair and wrapping his arms around the back, his eyes gleaming.

Why is he the way that he is? I sit back down and glare at him while Kacey explains the papers in her car.

"So what's next?" Quinn asks when she finishes.

"Nothing," Kacey says with finality. "Because whoever is running this pulled a gun on Ellie and—"

Quinn's head flips so fast to look at me. "What? Why didn't you tell me?"

"Because it wasn't a big deal," I say.

He looks around the table in shock, running a hand through his hair. Then he leans forward on the table so that he's only inches from my face. "It wasn't a big deal? Ellie, you could have gotten hurt."

I lean even closer. "But I didn't. I can take care of myself."

"I know you can. That's not the point. You shouldn't have to be in that situation in the first place."

The way he's looking at me, it's like we're the only two people here. I can't help staring at his eyes for a moment too long, taking in the color. They're so many different shades of brown, with a few gray streaks and hazel mixed in.

"This isn't only affecting you. It's hurting my friend's family, and everyone else who is losing their cars. The police haven't been able to shut this down. Maybe we can help," I say.

Quinn shakes his head back and forth. "No. When I reached out about Kacey's stolen car, I figured that you'd have an in with a police officer who knew what was going on. I didn't mean you need to solve this for the city. You need to stop, now. Before someone else gets hurt."

Irritation flashes through me. "No one's getting hurt."

"You don't know that," Quinn says. His fingers go to the scar on his neck, whether intentionally or not. I get an even better look at it now from here. It's already a silvery color. If you didn't know to look for it, you might just miss it.

If Brooke had pushed a little harder...

I stand up quickly from the table, my chair sliding backwards loudly. "I have to go."

Everyone looks startled, but I don't give them a chance

to reply before taking off down the hallway with my bag. I'm outside, the cold air biting my face, when Topher catches up with me.

"You good?" he asks.

I hesitate, searching for any signs of an oncoming panic attack. Why not have three in a week? I must have left in time because I feel fine. Just annoyed. "All good."

"You sure? Because that's your second dramatic exit from a building this week. I'm not always going to be around to follow after you."

He doesn't even know about the one I made at Kacey's apartment on Tuesday. I look at him. "I'm sorry. I'm being ridiculous."

He shrugs. "Whatever. At Pathfinders you were having a panic attack. But Quinn's a good guy making some valid points."

"I know," I sigh.

"It was fun having a little stakeout sleepover, and I can't believe you and Kacey figured out who was in her car from some smelly papers. But." He stops speaking.

"But what?" I ask.

He shoves his hands in his coat pockets, looking up at the sky above us. "It's been hard seeing you fall apart the past few months. I've missed you, and I feel like we're just getting you back. I don't want you to go back to that dark place over some stolen vehicles. Kacey has her car back. Isn't that enough?"

"What about Sophie? Or that app?" I ask. I'm already anticipating all the research I'm going to do tonight.

"Those aren't your problem. You're still having panic attacks when you have plastic guns pointed at you. Let the actual police do their job."

His words prickle against me. "I didn't have one when

the real gun was aimed at me. Maybe I only have them at Pathfinders because Jamie's such a jerk."

He rolls his eyes. "That's not it. Please. Leave it alone."

I cross my arms. "Anika thinks I can do it."

"Because it benefits her girlfriend," Topher huffs. "Whatever. Can we go?"

He thinks that I'm still broken. That I'm going to break even more if I keep doing this. Is he right?

"Let's get you back to your homework," I finally say. Arguing about this more right now isn't going to get anywhere productive. I need to think.

Topher smiles, wrapping an arm around my shoulders as we walk in the dark.

TEN

Thursday January 26th 10:30 PM

ELLIE, PLEASE. LEAVE IT. TOPHER'S WORDS ECHO IN MY mind as I stare at the cursor blinking at me in the search bar. I only have to type five letters. Five. I throw my phone across my bed, getting it as far away from me as possible.

I can leave it alone. Totally. It's not like those five letters are going to rattle around in my mind, constantly reminding me I'm only a few taps away from getting answers.

If I do search the word Unter, it's not going to notify anyone. I won't be under an oath to find out who's running the app, involve all of my friends, and get someone hurt. Topher isn't an FBI agent monitoring my search history. He'll never know. And I'll be able to go to sleep because my brain will be able to shut off and stop wondering.

I fish my phone out of the crevice between my mattress and the wall where it fell. I go to google, and finally type those five letters. The first result is that unter means under, among, or below in German. It's also the opposite of uber. The listing for the app store doesn't appear anywhere in the search results. Interesting.

I try a new search. *Uber like app Colorado.* I scroll past the sponsored results and don't find much. *Rideshare. Carshare.* I comb through the pages of search results, each of them getting less relevant. Three pages in, I find a link to an article that mentions my high school. I tap on it.

THREE RIVER'S EDGE HIGH SCHOOL TEENS DEVELOP CARSHARING APP FOR STUDENTS
April 22, 2022

Three students from River's Edge High School spent all year developing their own app for a business competition. While they were only required to come up with a proposal, seniors Devon Burton, Mason Wilkins, and junior Jake Peters decided to go the extra mile and coded their own app to see if any of your acquaintances are available to give you a ride.

"Ubers are expensive, and after the pandemic a lot of people don't feel comfortable using them. Sometimes you need a ride and your best friends aren't available, but maybe someone else you know from math class Is. This is going to help with that," said senior Mason Wilkins.

"We wanted to see if we could actually code the app. Turns out we're a better team than we thought," said junior Jake Peters.

"We hope to get it fully operational in the next year or so," senior Devon Burton added.

The article was written last year. So if Mason and Devon were seniors, they'd be college students right now. What if they finished up this app and found that trying to find a ride from someone in math class didn't actually work, but running their own carsharing service with stolen cars did? By using stolen cars and not worrying about things like insurance, or having employees, they can keep all of the profits and undercut all the competition.

I screenshot the article and email it to myself. I know better than to assume it will still exist later when I need it. My mind is the spinning rainbow wheel on a computer, thinking of all the new directions to look into, unsure of where to go next.

Ellie, please. Leave it. Topher's voice replays in my head again. I was only going to find out what came up when I googled Unter so I could go to sleep. That's it. If I keep looking into this, what if I can't stop? I press the lock button, then lay my phone face down on my nightstand.

Friday January 27th 1:00AM

I can't sleep. I can't stop thinking about it.

Devon Burton has a public Facebook profile. He's wearing a blue suit with a nametag, holding up a blue book. There are palm trees in the background, and some kind of ornate church building behind him. It says he currently lives in Chile. Five months ago, he started writing his posts in Spanish, and when I auto translated them, they were all religious. Unless he's psychotic and went through the effort to fake all of this, it looks like he's been out of the country on a religious mission. It'd be difficult to run a car theft ring outside of the country, especially with all the maintenance the app would require.

So, talking with Devon wouldn't even be an option. If I wanted to chat. Purely from a research perspective.

I set my phone back on the nightstand and roll over again, trying to turn my brain off.

Friday January 27th 1:45AM

Mason Wilkins only has Instagram. The account goes back ten years, with embarrassing photos of him and other preteen boys doing cannonballs in a pool, wearing camo while throwing up peace signs, and driving four wheelers. Then there are the memes he posted before Instagram stories existed. The more recent photos are of computer parts. I have no idea what any of them are, but the people who commented under each post are impressed.

There's a single photo of a man with his arm wrapped around an older woman. The caption for that post is a GoFundMe link that no longer works. There's also a picture of him holding up a hoodie for the campus ten minutes away. The caption says, "college bound."

Devon Burton might not be in town, but it appears Mason Wilkins is.

Not that it matters. Since I'm not investigating this.

I slide the phone back onto the nightstand and flip my pillows over, hoping the cool side will help me finally fall asleep.

Friday January 27th 2:15AM

I can't find Jake Peters. His name is too common, and I have no idea what he looks like to sort through all the profiles. I go through my friend's accounts, seeing if any of them have him as a friend. They don't. I think of the popular kids at school, the ones who know everyone. I find Leah Gallegos, the student body president. I gawk at the thousands of followers she has, then search for Jake Peters. No one pops up.

Friday January 27th 5:57AM

I've taken a crash course on coding your own app, and it's finally a reasonable-ish time to text. I've had the group message open for hours, crafting and recrafting my message. I double check to make sure Topher isn't in the group, then hit send.

All the Single Ladies

> Do any of you have a class with or know a Jake Peters?

ANIKA

> Why are you up already?

SOPHIE

> I had gym with him last year.

SANDRA

> He's in my first hour. Why?

I leap from bed, grabbing random clothes from my dresser. I need to get to school, now.

ELEVEN

Friday January 27th 7:10AM

"THAT'S HIM," SANDRA SAYS, POINTING TO A GUY IN
the crowd. He's blonde with blue eyes, and I never would
have found him on my own. He blends in. There are a few
details that stick out: his pristine Jordans that scream expensive, the glittering diamond earrings in both ears, and the
smartwatch on his wrist.

"Does he always dress like that?" I ask Sandra.

"No, he definitely changed the past few months. Like
he came into a load of cash or something," she adds,
wiggling her eyebrows.

"For not wanting to get involved, you seem to be
enjoying this," I tell her.

"Good luck doing an interrogation before the bell
rings." She bumps me with her elbow before walking into
her classroom. I don't get the chance to tell her this isn't an
interrogation. I simply have a few questions for the coding
genius who happens to go to my school.

"Jake, wait up," I say.

He's smiling as he searches the hall for who called his name. When he sees it's me, he frowns. "Ellie," he says, his voice shaking slightly. He looks up and down the hallway.

He's nervous, and he has no idea what I'm going to ask him about yet. It seems my reputation proceeds me. Does that fill me with a tiny thrill? Of course.

"Hey Jake," I say. "I was hoping we could talk."

"About what," he says slowly. "My name wasn't on any of those lists, I swear."

"I know you weren't. It's not about that," I say reassuringly. Brooke would have been happy to know that her lists and letters still fill people with fear here. I shove the thought of her down, down, down. I can't think about her right now. I need information from Jake.

"I was researching last night and I saw this article about you." I hold up my phone, showing him the screen. There's a picture of a younger version of him holding up a trophy with two other boys.

"Oh yeah, that was a good time," he says, putting his hands in his pockets.

"It's pretty impressive. My brother tried to make an app once, and it was more involved than he originally thought," I say.

Evan has never tried to make an app. But I figured that story sounds less threatening than the fact I did hours of research this morning so I could talk to him.

He nods. "Yeah, people don't think about the upkeep. Every time a phone system updates, you have to make minor tweaks to your app as well, for multiple processing systems."

I raise my eyebrows dramatically. "Wow, that's a lot.

Then there are probably legal things you have to look into that are different for every state."

Jake runs a hand through his hair. "I'm not sure. We didn't get that far. We worked mostly on the mainframe of the code."

"Did you three keep on working on it?" I ask.

He shakes his head. "No. Devon left the country on a mission trip, and Mason went to college. They got busy, and the idea kind of fizzled out."

"That's too bad, especially after everything you put into it," I say.

Jake shrugs. "I guess." He looks at the doorway of his class, shifting his weight. He's about to leave.

This is it. There's an invisible line, waiting to see which side I choose to stand on. I can stop here, walk away, and believe his story.

Or I can push and find out the truth.

"So is that why you revamped the app all by yourself?"

He freezes, his eyes widening. "What? What are you talking about?"

"This," I say, holding up the screenshots I have of the Unter app. "It's funny, my friend's car got stolen, and it turns out it was being used for this app. Which looks eerily similar to the one that you created with your friends."

"That, I don't, you can't, I've got to go," Jake says, looking up and down the hall. No one is paying attention to us.

I step in front of him, stopping him from getting away. "No, you don't. You're going to tell me what's going on."

"Someone else must have stolen it," he says. "It's up there in that article, anyone could have seen the idea and changed it."

"You didn't post the code online for someone to copy,

and you're the one with the expensive accessories," I say, kicking at Jake's shoes.

He flinches. "These were a gift."

I snort. "I'm sure they were. From yourself."

His eyes are wild, and he takes his hands out of his pockets. He clenches and unclenches his fists. I place my feet hip-width apart, ready to fight back if he tries to attack me. He's only a few inches taller than me, I can take him.

The bell rings.

He glares down at me, rage in his eyes. Then he shoves past me into the classroom, the door slowly closing behind him. I take off down the halls to my own class, sliding into my seat. My teacher doesn't even glare.

My phone buzzes.

BIO CREW

ANIKA

Soooo... how'd it go?

TOPHER

How'd what go?

No. Anika used the wrong group message; Topher's in this one. I start typing in the other one, telling them to switch over, when the next text comes in.

SANDRA

Jake looks like he's going to be sick.

ANIKA

WHAT HAPPENED

TOPHER

???

All plans of doing a tiny bit of research without Topher getting involved are gone. I type furiously.

Jake Peters. I found out he and some friends created a rideshare app last year. He screams guilty. He practically started shaking when I talked to him.

Anika

You do have a reputation. Maybe he thought you were going to beat him up.

Shut up.

Along with acting guilty AF, he has Jordans, diamond earrings, and an expensive watch.

TOPHER

Could have been Christmas gifts

SANDRA

He got them before that. And he can't stop running his hands through his hair right now.

ANIKA

The drip doesn't make you guilty.

You should have seen him. I have a feeling.

TOPHER

Didn't you have a feeling about Anika too?

Did he *seriously* just say that?

ANIKA

💀

Thank goodness. She took it as a joke.

SANDRA

He's texting more than we are right now.

Does he usually do that?

SANDRA

Yeah...

ANIKA

Maybe because he's busy running a car theft ring.

TOPHER

Switching sides?

Anika sends a TikTok with the "switching sides" audio.

The texts stop coming in after that, all of us settling into our classes. I reread the messages. Is Topher mad? Does he know that I purposefully left him out of a group message this morning? My stomach knots. I'll see how he's acting at lunch.

I try to listen in class. But Jake's expression when I brought up the app is the only thing I can think about. He wasn't confused, or outraged. If I'd worked as hard as he had on something, and found out someone else stole it and was making money off it, I'd be furious. Instead he looked scared. I'm onto something here, I can feel it.

Leah Gallegos kicks my foot. I glare back at her, but she tips her head at my leg. I've been bouncing it mindlessly, shaking the floor.

"Sorry," I mouth, tucking my leg under me.

She's already turned away. It's too bad she probably thinks I'm annoying. As student body president, she has to be a trove of inside information about what's going on in this school. Searching through her Instagram followers is one thing, but I'm not going to bother her in real life for, whatever it is I'm doing right now.

What *am* I doing?

Research. Only research. I've never had to sign a waiver or watch a safety video about the risk of death for doing research. Yet we have to do those every semester for gym class. I'm simply asking questions and googling things. That won't put anyone else at risk.

I've opened the door with Jake. One of his partners is out of the country. But the other one is still in town. I'm not stopping here.

Hey Kacey, do you know a Mason Wilkins?

TWELVE

Wednesday February 1st 4:30PM

In the end, Kacey found Mason Wilkins. She even found out when his math class was. The only problem is how.

"So," Quinn says, breaking the silence.

"So," I say back, fidgeting with my backpack straps as I walk next to him on campus. I almost run into him again as I avoid a patch of ice on the sidewalk.

The fresh snow crunches beneath our boots. "What's wrong?" he finally asks.

"Nothing," I say too quickly.

"You've been acting weird since this whole thing started."

"I have not."

He side-eyes me. "Ellie, come on. There are no doors for you to run out of here. Talk to me."

I stop walking and look at him. "You don't know me well enough to know if I'm acting weird."

He snorts. "We stopped a serial killer together."

"Yeah, and?"

"We're friends. I can tell."

"Are we?" I ask.

For the first time he looks unsure. "I thought so," he says slowly.

"Friends talk to each other outside of investigations."

His eyebrows pull together. "Do you want me to send you more TikTok's?"

I roll my eyes and start walking again, even though I have no idea where I'm going. He was the *one* person I asked Kacey not to involve when looking for Mason Wilkins. Quinn made his opinions on me looking into this pretty clear the last time I saw him. While Topher hasn't been outright hostile about my research, he's grumbled under his breath more than once when Anika and Sandra ask for updates in his presence.

Kacey kept me updated on her search for Mason. I'd tried messaging him on social media but he never saw it. We both tried his school email, but there was no response. As a last resort, Kacey had asked her roommate Seb if he knew him, only to have Quinn walk out of his room and announce that he knew Mason. They had a math class together.

Yes, I'm a strong independent woman. Topher being obnoxious and Quinn thinking this is a bad idea shouldn't mean anything. But I still feel wobbly after climbing out of that dark place, and I'm scared of what could send me back.

Quinn touches my arm. "I thought you didn't want to hear from me."

"What?" I whip toward him.

He runs a hand through his hair, his messy waves rearranging themselves. "Your texts got shorter and shorter. I figured you had better things to do, or were annoyed, or I don't know what. Then it was the holidays and finals, so life got busy."

My hand grazes my back pocket, about to pull my phone out and pull up my texts with Quinn. I want to read them line by line and dissect where this all went wrong. I can't do that in front of him, so I move my hand back to my backpack straps.

"What were you busy with?" I ask.

He stares at my face for a moment, his eyebrows pulling together again. Then his expression smooths. "I went back home to Arizona for break, and I've been doing overtime at work. Have you heard about that mortician in the news who just got arrested?"

"The one selling body parts for a profit?" I ask. The story is horrifying. A mortician in town has been selling body parts, and sometimes full corpses, to labs without the families' permission. Then she was mixing dirt and other ash in with cremated remains to try and cover it up.

He nods. "That's the one. I may or may not have been able to help with that investigation."

I open my mouth to ask a question, but he holds up a finger.

"I can't give you specifics. Let's just say that it's been a lot of sorting through ash."

I picture him in a white suit, wearing a mask and purple gloves, moving tiny pieces of ash around with tweezers.

"What about Ronnie?" I ask. That's something a friend would ask, right?

He smiles. "Yeah, that's new too."

I stumble on a small piece of ice, my arms going out to rebalance. Quinn's hand brushes my elbow, but when I don't fall it disappears.

"What've you been up to?" he asks.

"School, work." I leave out the other parts.

"You're still doing Pathfinders, right?" he asks.

A sigh escapes me. "Yep."

"What's that about?" He taps on my arm lightly when I keep walking forward while he turns down a sidewalk. I cross over the tiny bit of grass to rejoin him.

"It's different, that's all. How's Patty doing?" I ask, quickly changing the subject. Pathfinders is the last thing I want to talk about.

"She's cooled down quite a bit since the last time you saw her," he smirks.

That was at the police station when she told me to stay away from Quinn because I'm a bad influence.

"Give her my best," I say.

He snorts. "I'm definitely not going to do that."

"What would she do if she knew where you were right now?"

"She's never going to find out," he says with finality. We're outside of another brick building that looks the same as the rest. He stops to the right of the entrance and faces me, standing mere inches away. "Why are you doing this?"

"For research purposes."

He raises a single brow and waits. A burst of wind whips my hair, making me shiver. He's not going to show me where the classroom is until I answer.

"I've already learned more in a few days than the police have. I'll ask some questions, compile everything I find, then take it to Detective Zhao." My plan has solidified in the days it's taken to find Mason.

"She's a homicide detective."

I roll my eyes. "Then she can give it to whoever will stop it."

"Won't you digging into things ruin their chances of prosecuting since the information wasn't obtained legally?"

I sigh. "I'm asking a few questions, not doing a sting."

He looks at me, searching for something. "I don't think you should do this, especially since someone already pointed a gun at you."

"Stop. Just stop!" I shout. I cover my mouth with my hand, surprised how loud that came out.

His pupils flare, but he crosses his arms and waits.

"All anyone tells me lately is what I can and can't handle. Sometimes, they're right. I'm not the same Ellie from before the riverbank. The last three months have been..." What am I doing? I don't want to tell him any of this.

"Looking into this app has been the first time I've felt like myself in a while. I learned from my mistakes, and I'm not putting anyone else in harm's way. This is purely research," I say quietly.

His face is a flash of emotions I can't read. Then he glances at his smartwatch.

He swears. "This conversation isn't over, but we've got to go."

He holds the door of the brick building open for me. It's not as nice as the science building from last week. There's no café, or designated sitting areas. It's purely hallways and classrooms. Quin heads down the hall, ducking in between students. He stops abruptly in front of a classroom, then peeks his head inside the doorway.

"Follow me."

It's an auditorium with curved rows, just like in the movies. The back rows are already filled with people scrolling on their phones. Another group is scattered in the middle, and a few lone people sit in the first four rows.

Quinn leads me to the third row, squeezing past three people typing on laptops. I scan each face, but none of them look like the few pictures I was able to find of Mason. Quinn stops in the middle of the room, directly behind a man with shoulder-length hair pulled back with a headband in the second row. Mason. He has a beard and is typing briskly on his laptop.

"Let's sit next to him," I whisper to Quinn.

"No. Too risky," he says. He settles down in the tiny folding chair beneath him, and I sit next to him. I shimmy, trying to make more room for my hips. Do they expect actual adults to sit in these?

"Hey Mason," Quinn says.

Mason turns around to look at Quinn. His forehead is scrunched, seemingly confused. "Hey."

"We were in a group last week. I'm Quinn. This is my friend Ellie."

I give a tiny wave and a reassuring smile. More people are filing into the room, picking random seats all over the auditorium.

"Okay," Mason says slowly.

"It turns out Ellie went to the same high school as you, and she was telling me about this competition you and your friends won last year," Quinn says.

Mason's face brightens a bit. "The statewide business competition. We shocked them when we showed up with a functional app, not just a plan on paper."

"I can't imagine how much time the three of you must have spent together to pull that off. Are you still close?" I ask.

"I wish. Devon left the country and I haven't talked to Jake much since graduation."

I hesitate, deciding what to ask next. If this was like our

last investigation, Quinn and I would have gone over the list of questions beforehand and he'd jump in.

"Are you going to launch the app?" I finally ask. "You went through all that work."

Mason sighs. "No. Devon and Jake were chatting about it before Devon left, but by that point I decided it wasn't worth my time. We would have needed substantial funding to get it running. If this was the kind of idea that I thought would go viral, maybe it would have been worth securing that. You can just as easily ask the kid in your math class for a ride, without having to get an app involved."

I share a look with Quinn, trying to communicate silently. Is now when I reveal that the app exists? My telepathic message goes through because Quinn gives the tiniest nod. I reach into my pocket and pull out my phone, opening up the app store.

"That's weird, because—"

"Let's talk causality," a voice booms through the room.

During our conversation with Mason, the professor entered the room, connected her laptop, attached a microphone to her shirt, and loaded up her PowerPoint.

"What do I do?" I hiss to Quinn. He's pulled out a notebook and pen and is scribbling frantically.

"You could leave," he says. "Sorry."

I think of the Office episode when Pam gets up to leave a lecture and is immediately told to sit down again. I'm in the third row from the front. It'll be painfully obvious if I get up. Plus, I wouldn't get the chance to show Mason the app and see his reaction. It looks like I'm about to sit through my first college lecture.

"How long is this class?" I whisper to Quinn.

"An hour fifteen."

Great. I was counting on being home before then, and

that's not even factoring in time to talk with Mason after class. My parents are going to worry.

My telepathic messages have quite the range because my phone buzzes on the tiny desk then, flashing my mom's name.

MOM

What are you doing on campus?

Taking a college tour

Pics or it didn't happen.

Really, mom? She needs to get off Facebook. She sees old TikTok's months after they came out on there and thinks she's so cool. I sneakily pull up my phone and try to take a selfie while the professor is changing slides.

"You're not taking a picture of me, are you?" the professor asks.

She's looking straight at me. I look behind me reflexively, making sure there isn't someone else who is also taking a picture right now. There isn't. Everyone in the auditorium is looking straight at me. I turn back toward the professor.

"I wasn't," I say shakily.

"Then you thought right now would be the best time for a selfie? Or one of those Be Real things?"

I shake my head again.

"What were you taking a picture of then?" she asks. She isn't going to let this go.

"My mom wanted picture-proof I was in class."

The professor stares at me. Then she takes her glasses off her face, and swipes her hands down the sides. "Helicopter parents," she mutters, but since she's wearing the microphone, everyone hears her.

I slide down in my seat, trying to appear as tiny as possible. I can never go to this school after this. What if I have to take a class with this professor and she remembers this day?

"Is your mom really freaking out?" Quinn whispers.

I give the tiniest of nods, then text the picture. I paid for this dearly, she better print this off and have it framed.

MOM

Why didn't you invite us to go on the tour
with you?

I heard about it last minute.

If you go on another one, let me know.

If I do go on any campus tours, I'm purposefully *not* going to take her after making me go through this. It's been a bit since I've gone anywhere besides work, school, and Pathfinders. I forgot that my parents have two tracking apps to see where I am at all times, just in case one of them fails. Why was seeing that I'm at the college campus alarming enough that my mom texted and wanted proof of what I was doing?

I glance to the side at Quinn, still taking rapid notes. Is *he* why? She's worried I'm with him? I try to pay attention to the lecture, pushing that thought away.

"Would anyone like to explain what I mean by correlation does not equal causation?" the professor asks.

Mason raises his hand. "It's the fact that even though two things seem to be statistically related, it does not mean that one caused the other. For example, violent crimes and ice cream sales tend to go up at the same time, but it's not the ice cream that caused the rise in crimes, it's the heat."

"Thank you," the professor beams. She then pulls up graphs and starts explaining them.

I should make my own graph. Maybe it'd help me sort things out. The first one would be the increase of stolen cars in town, and the appearance of the Unter app. The police have chalked it up to an increase in gang activity. It looks like they're the ones who're missing the correlation and causation.

My second graph would be Jake versus supposed involvement. He has a lot of new expensive accessories, which can't be chalked up to the holidays. He helped create the earlier version of this app, and according to Mason, wanted to keep working on it. Plus, he seemed pretty rattled after talking to me.

You do have a reputation Anika's voice echoes in my head. Which is true. He could have thought I was there to talk about the river murders and the lists of boys who'd done horrible things.

I tune in and out of the lecture, but start getting restless around the fifty-minute mark. There's still twenty-five more minutes to go. I shift in the tiny chair over and over, trying to find a more comfortable way to sit. It squeaks with each movement, and Mason turns around to look at me. I feel like I'm going to scream. I need to get out of here.

Quinn nudges me with his elbow. I look at him, and he motions to his notebook that he's pushed right next to me on the tiny folding table. There's a tic tac toe board drawn on it.

"Really?" I whisper.

He shrugs, drawing an x in the middle spot. I stare at the paper, then glance at the professor. The last thing I want is for her to call me out for playing games in her class. She's facing the board, drawing some sort of graph on it. I pull a pen out of my own backpack, then draw an O in the bottom left corner.

The game ends in a draw, so Quinn moves on to hangman. The first word is thrapple.

"That is not a word," I whisper.

"Google it," Quinn whispers back.

It is in fact a word. I do the word anthropometry next, which Quinn guesses.

"No anatomy terms this time," I tell him for the next round.

He plays poikilothermic.

I google it. "I said no anatomy terms."

"You didn't say anything about physiology," he says, facing the front of the room.

I kick his leg under the desk. "You're such a nerd."

He points to me, then himself. "Kettle. Pot."

I roll my eyes, fighting a smile. I'm trying to think of a word to play next when class finally ends. Quinn stuffs the notebook in his backpack, and I grab my own bag from the floor. No more games, it's time to get back into detective mode.

Mason turns to look at Quinn and I, still packing up his things. "Did you need something else?"

"I heard about a few kids on campus using an app like yours," Quinn says. "When I mentioned it to Ellie, she remembered your competition last year."

I hand my phone over to Mason, showing him the screenshots of the app. His forehead crinkles. He sits back down in the tiny desk chair. The plastic groans, much to my satisfaction.

"Wait a second." He flips through the screenshots I took. "This is almost identical to the app we made." He hands me my phone back, and pulls out his laptop. Since we're behind him, I have a clear view of what he's doing. He pulls up the website for the app, but it asks for a password.

"Do you know the code?" he asks.

"No, apparently you can only share it once, and the people we talked with already gave theirs out."

Mason makes a noise, then opens up a black window in the corner of the screen. He starts typing gibberish into it. Two minutes later, he's into the website. He's flipping through screens so fast I can't keep up. He finally lands on the page with the map, showing where the available cars are. Right now there are three around campus, and one off of Main Street near Sophie's house. Not nearly as many as the other night.

"Why all the secrecy? The security can barely be called that, and the time and energy for the invite codes is useless. If you're making profit off of this, wouldn't you want as many people as possible to be able to use it?" Mason asks.

"Not if the cars are stolen," Quinn says.

Mason flips around, his eyes wide. "What did you say?"

"We know at least one of the cars was stolen, if not all of them," I reply.

Mason runs his hands over his face. "He didn't."

Now we're getting somewhere. "Didn't what?" I ask.

"When we were originally making the app, car thefts were increasing after Covid. The news was playing in the background one day while we were working, and the reporter said people were mostly going for joy rides in the stolen cars, not even selling them for parts. Jake joked that we could run our business with stolen cars."

Quinn and I lock eyes.

"It was a joke. At least, I thought it was," Mason reiterates. "You don't think they're going to tie this to me, do you? If you already tracked me down, what are the police going to think? I had nothing to do with this." His voice is rising in panic.

"Take a breath," Quinn says, clapping him on the shoulder. "Tell them exactly what you told us."

Mason is shaking his head. "I can't believe Jake would do this. He was a pain in the ass, and now he's running an illegal enterprise with our app?"

"How do you think he's stealing the cars?" I ask Mason.

He chews on his thumbnail for a moment. "He could be cloning the key fobs. But how does he have time to do that? You have to be close enough to someone long enough to clone it, and then drive off with the car. Some models are easier than others. I'm assuming the police are finding the cars every few days, so he'd constantly have to be doing that to keep the app running. He has to be working with someone, if not a large group of people." Mason looks up. "It's not me. I haven't talked to him except for a few messages at the beginning of the summer. I've been taking care of my grandma. She's pretty sick," Mason says solemnly.

"I'm sorry to hear that," I say.

"Thanks." He looks around. "If you figure out how he's pulling it off, let me know. I can't believe my work is being used for this."

"Sure," I say, adding his number to my contacts. If we can verify what he's told us, the police should have an easy case to arrest Jake. As I hit save, my phone starts ringing. It's my dad. He rarely calls, preferring to text. My heart starts to pound and my legs feel a little weak. I turn away from Quinn and Mason, answering it.

"Hey kid, where are you?" he asks.

"Doing a college tour. I sat in on a math lecture," I say.

"Interesting. Are you going to be home soon?"

"Yeah, is everything okay?"

"Yep, just wondering where you were. Are you busy on Friday night?"

"I don't think so," I say. What is this about?

"We're having dinner with Evan in Denver. You should join..."

"No," I cut him off.

"Let me finish. It's low stakes in a neutral location, you don't have to say anything, and there's a full tank of gas in it for you."

"A full tank?" I say slowly.

"I'll pay the summer rate. Wasn't it almost $5 a gallon then?"

I try to calculate how much that is. Around $60. That's almost four hours of work. Four hours of not being with Jamie. Tempting.

"I'll think about it."

"Great! Drive safe, it's icy out." His voice is filled with excitement.

I glare at my phone after he hangs up. That could have been a text, and I wouldn't have gotten scared something bad happened to Evan. And if he'd talked with my mom, he would have known where I was.

Mason packed up while I was talking, and is walking out the door. Quinn waits until it's closed behind him before turning to me.

"What do you think?"

It takes a second to remember what we were talking about. "I'd like to believe him. But I need to verify everything he said."

"Agreed. Let's get you back to your car though. You need to get home young lady," Quinn says, shaking a finger at me.

I frown. "Don't call me that."

He shudders. "Yeah, that felt gross as I said it. Come on. I'll fill Kacey in on everything, and we can go from there."

We start walking. "You don't have to do that. I know you didn't want to get involved in this."

He raises a brow. "Do you really think she'll leave me alone once I get home?"

I laugh, picturing Kacey harassing Quinn. "That's true. But then you're done. This is a solo research project."

"What if I want to help?"

I shake my head. "Nope." My eyes go to his neck, to the scar.

He catches my glance. "About earlier. Are you okay?"

I look away. "I don't want to talk about it."

"I couldn't shave below my chin for a while afterwards. I had this nasty neck beard going, and then it was no shave November so it was socially acceptable. By December 1st it was so itchy, getting rid of it outweighed the fear."

He's probably trying to make me feel better, let me know that he was affected too. Instead it's a reminder that I'm the one who begged him to help me with my investigation in the first place, setting up the series of events that ended with that scar.

"I'd pay money to see pictures of your neck beard," I say, forcing a small smile.

He grins. "I was saving those for if I ever needed to

bribe you for information. Tell me how you're doing, and I'll show you one.

"I'm *fine*."

He clicks his tongue. "Yeah, that's not enough to earn a picture."

I try to elbow him in the arm, but he sidesteps me. "You're obnoxious. Especially when it comes to hangman."

We exit the building and the cold slams into me. He leads me across campus, the only light from the streetlamps.

"You said no anatomy, but you didn't say anything about physiology."

I roll my eyes. "They go together. It's anatomy *and* physiology."

He smiles. "Next time you'll have to be more specific."

It's quiet between us the rest of the walk to the car. I start replaying what Mason said. He seemed genuinely shocked that Jake was still running the app. Plus the fact that Jake allegedly mentioned using stolen cars years ago? It's too much of a coincidence.

Who is continuously stealing the cars for Jake? That's what I need to find out next.

By myself.

I made mistakes last time. But I can't stop looking into this. I realized the truth as I said it to Quinn. Investigating this *is* the first time I've felt like myself. I'm not letting that go. I'm going to figure out what's going on and bring the information to the police.

I glance at Quinn's face. He's clean shaven. He's been able to move past his fear of razors on his neck. I don't want to cause anyone else that kind of pain.

I can still do this. I'll just do it alone. Then I won't risk anyone else.

We've reached my car. Quinn leans against it.

"What's next?" he asks.

"Nothing."

He snorts. "Liar."

"It sounds like Jake is involved. I'll leave an anonymous tip, or talk with Detective Zhao." I fumble with my keys, struggling to make my cold fingers cooperate. I finally get the right key, and stand next to Quinn to unlock the door.

"How're you going to figure out how he's getting the stolen cars?"

"I'm not," I lie.

He stares at me, his breath forming clouds between us. "I know I said I thought this was a bad idea, but that was fun."

The door clicks and I swing it open. "Thanks for helping me talk to Mason." He doesn't say anything, so I throw my backpack inside, then slide into the driver's seat. I turn on the engine, cold air blasting out of the vents.

Quinn leans down, holding onto the edge of the door. His face is only inches from mine. "You don't have to shut me out. I'm here if you want to talk, or need help tracking someone down."

"Good to know," I say, knowing I won't. Tonight was more fun than I've had in a while. But I just figured out a way that I can keep doing this, while not repeating my past mistakes.

He stares at me a moment longer. "Drive safe." He closes my door, then jogs across the parking lot to his Jeep.

THIRTEEN

Thursday February 2nd 7:00PM

THE DOOR CHIMES AND I GRIN. ANIKA'S STANDING there, her face flushed and eyes practically sparking. She glances around the empty shop.

"Welcome," Jamie says to her from the cash register.

"Thanks." She goes and gets a tiny amount of yogurt and comes over to where I'm reloading the toppings.

"Ellie," she says, grinning.

"What happened?" I ask.

"Sophie kissed me," she squeals.

"No way? Finally!"

"It. Was. Perfect," Anika says, looking starstruck.

"I'm so happy for you," I say, reaching for her hands over the sneeze guard. It's like I can absorb the happiness radiating off of her.

"So are you two official now?" I ask. This is the first time either of us has been here. We've both had our crushes over the years, and Anika even went to sophomore homecoming with Brandon Waters, but we made a game of hiding from him once she realized all he wanted to do was grind. Neither of us have been in an actual relationship, so this is new territory.

Anika nods. "I may have said I loved her." She covers her mouth with her hand. "Was that ridiculous? I don't want to be that stereotypical queer girl who moves fast."

"Did you mean it?" I ask her, pretending I have some sort of expertise on the matter.

"I think so. This is the first time I've felt this way about someone."

"Then say it. You two have been flirting for almost six months, it's not like you met yesterday. What'd she say?"

Anika grins. "She started kissing me harder. And then her grandma called, so she had to go home." Her face falls. "She didn't say it back though."

I point at her. "Hey, no panicking. That doesn't mean anything."

"Excuse me, are you going to stay there all night?" Jamie asks, leaning toward us from his spot at the register.

Anika and I both glare at him. She puts her hand above her eyes, turning her head back and forth dramatically as she looks around the empty shop. "There's no one else here."

"True, but if they come in and see you standing there, they might think we're too busy and go elsewhere."

Anika scrunches her face up in confusion. "What planet are you from? When have you ever seen that happen?"

"I'd hate for today to be the day it does."

Anika stomps over to the checkout. She opens her wallet, and pays completely in loose change. Jamie painstakingly recounts each penny and dime as she hands them to him. I cover my mouth with my hand. I love Anika, especially when she's sassy to my nemesis.

"I'd like my receipt," she says when none comes out of the printer. Jamie struggles on the tablet, trying to figure out how to reprint one. The back of his neck flushes the longer it takes. He finally prints her receipt and hands it to her silently.

Anika takes the receipt and immediately tosses it in the trashcan. Jamie blows a long breath out of his nose as Anika walks to the farthest table in the corner, sitting down dramatically.

"Is this better?" she yells at Jamie.

He huffs. "Why can't you talk on your own time?"

She leans back in her chair. "This is my own time. I'm going to talk freely to the air, and if Ellie happens to hear what I'm saying and has a response, then that happens."

"What if I respond?" Jamie asks.

"I'd love to have a conversation with you, Jamie. Isn't it funny that I know your name but you're not wearing a name tag?" Anika asks.

He rolls his eyes. "I'm sure Ellie told you about me."

Anika smirks. "She sure did, and she described you perfectly."

He folds his arms. "How did she describe me?"

"How do you think she described you?" Anika asks. "Does it make you nervous?"

He frowns.

Anika cackles. "You should be more worried about Topher's description. Ellie just told me your height and weight."

"I did not," I interject.

"No, but you somehow perfectly captured his annoying intensity."

Jamie looks at me. "Intense?" he asks.

My face is burning, and I glare at Anika.

"Can you hang out Saturday?" she asks me.

I shake my head as Jamie says, "she has team building."

"Ooh what does that involve?" Anika asks, waggling her eyebrows up and down.

I snap off my plastic gloves, wad them into a ball, and throw them at her head. They bounce off her curls and she laughs.

"Paintball," Jamie says answering her question.

Anika's eyes light up. "Can I come?"

"You're not a part of the team," Jamie says.

"Fine. Jamie, you might want to invest in some butt pads because Ellie is going to kick your ass. Or shoot it."

"We'll see about that," Jamie mutters.

The door opens again and Kacey enters with a woman in a wheelchair I've never seen before. She has brown curls and tortoiseshell glasses. I give them a wave, and Kacey comes right to the toppings counter.

"Can we talk?" Kacey asks, hands in her pockets. She has purple circles under her eyes and doesn't look well.

"Are you serious?" Jamie interjects.

"I'm taking my federally protected break," I say to Jamie, opening the half door at the end of the counter to get out.

"It's actually not protected unless you work over—"

Anika is cackling from the corner again. "Is this guy for real?" she says in-between laughs.

I lead Kacey and her friend over to the table where Anika is sitting, as far away from Jamie as we can get.

"This is my other best friend, Anika," I say to Kacey. "Is it okay if she's here, or should we go outside? I only have fifteen minutes." I've never had one person visit me at work, much less three.

"Are you as annoying as Topher?" Kacey asks in a deadpan.

"Depends on your definition, but I can turn it off," Anika says.

Kacey grins. "Stay. This is Isa," she says, introducing her friend.

Isa extends her hand to me. "It's great to finally meet you. I've heard lots of good things."

"Thanks," I say, stretching out the word. I have no idea who Isa is or what she's specifically heard about me. No wonder Jamie was so rattled wondering what I told Anika about him.

"Isa is the editor in chief of the college paper. She's also had pieces published in bigger publications. I'm not sure if you keep up with college sports, but she was the one who broke the news about the basketball coach who got a DUI on the way to the game, and the police let him go to coach it."

"No way, that was you?" I ask. I don't follow sports, but even I heard about that.

"You're amazing," Anika says. "I've read quite a few of your articles."

"Thank you, that means a lot," Isa smiles.

It's great to meet Isa, but why is she here?

Kacey turns around to check where Jamie is. To my surprise, he went into the back, giving us some privacy.

"Quinn told me about your meeting with Mason," Kacey starts. "There was one thing he said, and I couldn't sleep last night thinking about it."

"What was it?" I ask, sifting through all the things we

learned, trying to figure out what would be the most troubling to Kacey.

"He said you were gathering all this information to take to the police."

Oh.

"We started this whole investigation because of my stolen car," Kacey says. "*My* car. A black woman. I'm lucky that my interactions with the police were able to be mostly phone calls. What if I'd needed their help because someone had attacked me? Would I still be alive? There's a chance I might not be."

I sit with her words. I want to protest, to say there's no way that would happen here. But the truth is I don't know that. I can't say that.

"If you're looking into this to bring everything to the police, I'm not helping. Did you see that story of the baby who was kidnapped in Indiana? How two black women found him, and the police got all the credit? This is my story, and I'm going to share it with Isa. Someone who is dedicated to finding out the truth, whatever that is, and bringing it to the light," Kacey says.

Isa is looking at me intently. I've never read her work. I did, however, read the articles about me last year when I refused to talk to the press. They would take the most random details, and make up an entire story about them. If I was walking with my head down because the wind was blowing in my face? I'm downtrodden with the guilt of convicting my best friend. I'm laughing at a joke Topher told me? I'm glad that those boys died and secretly conspired with Brooke and Shelby.

How can people be so manipulative and lie, and call themselves reporters?

"I know that you were burned by reporters last year,"

Isa starts. "That's not who I am, and I don't consider that good journalism. I want to expose this theft ring and the inaction of the police department, along with the laws that were changed that made this possible during Covid. I want to highlight all of the work that you've done that they didn't even bother to."

I shake my head. "No. I don't want to be in the news again. They're just starting to leave me alone from, you know." It wouldn't only be the articles. It'd be the TikTok's and Threadlit conspiracies. Constantly feeling like people are watching me, recording me, and not knowing if that's my anxiety acting up or actually happening. I had to change my phone number, the routes I took, and watch what I said.

Isa tilts her head. "I don't have to name you. Kacey wants to go on the record, but you don't have to. I can name you as an anonymous source."

"Couldn't you be making this all up if it's an anonymous source?" I ask.

Isa shrugs. "I guess technically. But I never would. I have a record for telling the truth, and only that. I wouldn't want to ruin that name. I'll also be corroborating everything you tell me, so that there's more than one source."

More than one source? How will she find those? The image of the guy in the car with the gun pops into my mind. "Whoever is stealing these cars, they have guns. They're dangerous. I don't want either of you getting hurt."

Kacey reaches her hand across the table and gives mine a squeeze. "We're going to be fine. Isa knows what she's doing. This article will help the public and make the police act."

"How?" I don't see how words will change things.

"For one, the police department will be so embarrassed that they're going to do something quickly for PR," Isa says.

"The app would most likely get shut down immediately. It would help people know what's going on in their neighborhood, and try to protect themselves by taking action to prevent their key fobs from being cloned."

Never mind. All of that would make a huge difference.

"I've already told Isa my story. Quinn is willing to tell her about what he heard yesterday. But this is all held together by you. You're the one who's been driving this and has all the information," Kacey says.

I pick at a hangnail, ripping a tiny strip of skin. Immediately a droplet of blood wells up. I press down on it, trying to stop the bleeding. I've spent the past few months actively avoiding reporters. Now, there's a journalist sitting across from me on my break, asking me to open up again and stop these car thefts.

Isa seems different from the ones who chased me. Kacey knows her, which is a positive. Anika has heard of her. I know that good journalists can change the world. I also know the pain a bad one can cause.

"Why don't you read a few of my pieces, sleep on it, then get back to me," Isa says. "I'm going to publish this on Monday, so there's plenty of time to think about it."

Someone clears their throat obnoxiously. Jamie is back, and he's looking at the clock pointedly. My break is over. Isa slips a business card to me from across the table.

"Thanks for your time. I'd love to hear from you, but understand if you don't want to talk." She rolls away from the table, then heads over to the yogurt cups. Kacey, Anika, and I stand.

"Please think about it," Kacey says.

"I will," I say. That's all I can promise for now.

She squeezes my shoulder, then joins Isa at the yogurt levers.

"Isa's really good," Anika says in a hushed tone. "If it was me, I'd talk to her in a heartbeat."

"I know, but the guy with the gun," I say. Yesterday I finally figured out a way to make this investigation work. I have to do it by myself. So no one else can get hurt. Writing an article and putting their names out there is the complete opposite of that.

"If whoever that was wanted to come after Kacey and Isa, they could do that even if you talked to the police first. The police can't even patrol Sophie's driveway and catch the stolen cars being dropped off. It's not like they have time to provide security to anyone these car thieves want to go after."

I shiver as her words hit me. "We need to stop them from writing the article."

Anika snorts. "What makes you think you can stop them? That article is getting written with or without your help. Which is why you should help."

"I don't want them to be in danger," I start.

Anika's eyebrows rise dramatically. "I didn't want you to be in danger last year. Did that stop you? No. And I'm glad it didn't. What you did saved lives, and now you and Isa can help stop these car thefts. We need more solutions in society that don't involve brute force."

"Have you been binge reading your sociology textbook again," I tease. That class has changed her outlook on so many things.

She rolls her eyes. "As if. That book is so out of date. I can send you this article I read though about alternatives to traditional policing..."

"Hey Ellie," Jamie calls from the register.

"She has one minute left," Anika snaps, holding up her phone.

"Not according to that clock," Jamie answers, pointing to the wall.

"Which one are you going to believe, the digital clock that is constantly being given the correct time from the cell network, or the wall clock with a battery that can run however it likes?"

Jamie crosses his arms on his chest. The time on Anika's phone changes right then.

"Make sure to come talk to the air more often on my shifts," I say to Anika, wrapping her into a hug.

"It would be my pleasure. At least think about helping," Anika says, squeezing my hand. She glares at Jamie as she walks to the door. I hop behind the counter, Isa's business card a heavy weight in my pocket.

FOURTEEN

Friday February 3rd 5:30PM

A FULL TANK OF GAS. THAT'S WHAT I HAVE TO KEEP reminding myself of. Four hours that I don't have to spend at the yogurt shop with Jamie. I would be ridiculous to turn that down. I can sit still and eat good food for an hour.

Maybe. My twisted stomach isn't so sure.

"Looks like he's already inside," Mom says, staring at her phone as we walk up to the restaurant. It's a beautiful brick building on the corner of a street in downtown Denver. Through the windows I see color everywhere. I focus on the little details, trying the mindfulness exercises my therapist gave me.

Five things I see

1. A giant chalkboard hanging above the bar with a quote from Zora Neale Hurston. *I do not weep for the world. I am too busy sharpening my oyster knife.*

2. Silver streamers hung up in the middle of the room.

3. A mural of Denver

4. The wooden bar covered completely in overlapping stickers.

5. My parents walking across the room to an unfamiliar man sitting at a table. He hugs Dad, then Mom. The two of them sway back and forth for a moment before Mom finally lets go. The man looks different from the selfie they sent me two weeks ago. Instead of a long scraggly beard, it's now short and neatly trimmed one. The thick black glasses have been replaced with fashionable clear framed ones. He's wearing a blue sweater that hints at how fit he is. The most shocking thing is the light in his eyes.

There's no way that man is my brother. My brother was sickly thin and drowning in holey t-shirts. His eyes were sunken with blue circles underneath. How could he look better after being in jail for five years?

Finally finished hugging, my mom turns and waves me over. I cross the restaurant, navigating around full tables of people. When I reach our spot, I stand slightly behind my mom, like a shy toddler.

Evan finally makes eye contact with me. "Ellie," he says warmly.

"Evan," I say flatly.

He holds his arms up tentatively, inviting me in for a hug. I keep my own arms down and stay put. He runs a hand through his hair, as if that's what he was originally intending the whole time. *Smooth, bro.* I'm surprised to catch a whiff of whatever soap he's using. He smells, clean. My last memories of him, he smelled like greasy hair and sweat. I'm glad I won't have to hold my breath for the whole meal.

We settle in our seats, and I grab the menu as a protective shield. I stare at it, as if I didn't already google it. I'm glad I did because it's confusing. There are asterisks and stars next to each item, listing other ways it can be prepared or customized, depending on if you want it vegetarian or vegan.

"I've heard the waffles are the specialty," Mom says, breaking the silence.

"That's what my roommate said too. Thanks for meeting me here."

His roommate? At the halfway house? Or maybe an old cellmate? Would it be rude to ask?

"How'd your interviews go?" Dad asks instead.

Evan's face falls slightly. "I haven't gotten any calls back yet. But I'm not giving up," he adds brightly.

"I'm sure your parole officer has some suggestions of felon friendly workplaces," Mom says.

"Yep, I'm making my way down the list," Evan says with a tight smile.

Hopefully someone calls back soon. I learned in Pathfinders that many people end up back in prison after reentering society because there are so many roadblocks, and not enough support. I don't know if my parents will make it if he goes back again.

"Are you coming over for the Super Bowl?" Dad asks.

"Umm, if that's still okay?" Evan says it as a question, glancing at me.

"Since when are you into watching the Super Bowl?" I ask Dad, hoping it sounds like a joke. We haven't even turned it on since Covid.

"It's an excuse to eat appetizers and have a party in the middle of winter. Who cares?" Mom replies.

"Can we have jalapeño poppers?" I ask.

"Of course. So you're in?" Dad asks Evan again.

"Sounds good to me. This might be a good time to mention that I've decided to become vegan," he says.

"Oh," Mom says, sounding surprised.

How surprised can she be when we're *literally* in a vegan restaurant?

"After being locked up, and researching animal cruelty, I don't want to participate in another creature ever being treated like that," Evan explains.

"That makes sense," Dad says.

"We'll have a gluten free, vegan, Super Bowl party," Mom says.

"So, where do we stand on jalapeño poppers?" I ask slowly. "If it's gluten free, that means no breading. But if it's vegan that means no cheese or bacon."

"There's substitutes you can use," Evan says. "And you don't have to make everything vegan for me, I'll gladly bring my own food."

"We'll make it work," Dad says, a little forcefully. His eyes shoot to me.

The waiter walks up then, clicking his pen multiple times as he smiles brightly at us. I could kiss him for showing up right now. How big of a tip would it take to get his number so I could text him to keep coming back anytime things get weird? When he goes to put our orders in, I almost beg him to stay. Especially when Evan looks right at me.

"How's senior year going?" he asks.

I shrug. "Oh, you know." Maybe he'll catch a hint and drop it.

"What are your plans for after school gets out?"

Looks like that's a no. "No idea. Everything kind of changed back in October."

Evan gives me a small smile. "That's alright. When plans change, you have to keep pivoting."

"I like that idea," Dad says.

Of course he does. He's always been obsessed with Evan, and with me having a good relationship with him.

Mom turns to me. "Have you finished up your applications?"

I look down into my drink, stirring the ice around. "I'm almost done."

"Ellie," she says, and I can hear the disappointment in her voice. "Your friends have already heard back. We're submitting them tonight."

"Okay," I say, so softly they probably don't hear me. I keep my eyes on my drink, dreading the thought of opening up those application portals and slogging through question after question.

"You can't let what happened in October halt the rest of your life," Dad says.

"I'm not," I snap.

"I know it's hard, but these are a critical few months, and you don't get a redo on them," he adds like he didn't hear me.

"I'd like to think that's not true," Evan says.

We all look up at him. He's sitting in his chair calmly, his hands clasped together. He could have just mentioned the weather. Not hinted at how he'd royally messed up the same time in his life, and what it had cost him.

"We didn't mean anything about—" Mom starts. Her face is flushed.

"It's fine. I know I made a huge mistake. I'm also aware how lucky I am to have gotten out when I did, and get a chance at another life. Give Ellie some slack. You don't have to have everything figured out right now."

The waiter pops up again with refilled glasses for us. I try to catch his eye, blinking rapidly to try and seduce him. I make sure to say thank you extra loud when he sets down my drink. He gives me the same smile as everyone else, and then leaves me to my interrogators.

"If you haven't finished your applications, why were you doing that tour the other night?" Mom asks slowly.

It takes me a beat too long to remember what she's talking about. The class with Quinn and Mason. "To get an idea of what classes would be like," I say.

"I knew it," she cries. "You're hanging out with Quinn again."

"What? No I'm not," I say, too quickly now.

"You've been on campus multiple times this week, and hanging out in student housing," she says.

"Quinn's roommate was giving Topher and I a tour of campus."

"Not buying it. I told you to stop hanging out with him," Mom says, folding her arms across her chest.

"Hey, let's take a beat," Dad says, grabbing my mom's shoulder.

"No, I will not take a beat. She's running around with that boy again, hanging out at his apartment. He's in college; you're still in high school."

"He's only fifteen months older than me, and I wasn't hanging out with him," I reply.

She widens her eyes, her mouth falling open. "The fact that you know his birthday down to the month isn't helping you. You obviously like him."

"I do not, and he has a girlfriend." I take a long drink of water, hoping it will cool down my face. "Why are you tracking me so much?"

"Because you pretended you're a detective and almost got yourself killed, that's why," she practically shouts.

People are turning around in their seats and looking at us. Mom mouths *sorry*.

"Who's Quinn?" I hear Evan whisper to Dad.

"Later," Dad whispers back.

The waiter returns, balancing a tray of food. I was debating offering him the entire $60 of gas money my dad promised, but he let me down epically right now. A true man would have been there to stop them from interrogating me about Quinn.

Once everyone has their food, Evan enthusiastically starts talking about his roommates at the halfway house, and what some of his former cellmates are doing now. I try to take in as much as possible, but it's like the three of them are speaking another language. My parents recognize the names of everyone he mentions, continuing conversations that they had while he was still away. Evan has an entire life I know nothing about.

I catch a mention of his favorite cellmate being in a gang.

"What happened to him?" I ask.

Everyone looks shocked that I've asked a question.

"I'm not sure. We lost touch a month or so after he got out. It's hard to leave that life," Evan grimaces.

I nod. "I've heard there's been an increase in gang activity in town, so that makes sense."

Both of my parents visibly tense. "Where did you hear that?" Dad asks, slowly.

"Pathfinders," I lie.

"You're still in that?" Evan asks.

If we weren't estranged, I'd give him a high five for changing the subject so quickly. Even so, all I can manage is a, "yep."

"How have the competitions been?"

I wince.

"They closed down the chapter in town, so there's been

a learning curve as all the new teams settle in," Dad says, covering for me.

"Makes sense. I'm proud of you for finding something you love and sticking with it," Evan says with another smile.

Pretty smiles aren't going to fix our relationship. "Thanks."

"We're proud of *you* for finding something you love and working for it too. How many semesters of school do you have left?" Dad asks Evan.

He runs a hand over his beard. "It depends on how many classes I can take a semester. My parole officer warned it'll be an adjustment and not to overwhelm myself."

"Wait, you're in school?" I ask.

"Yeah, I'm getting my degree in social work," Evan says with yet another smile.

"Wow," I manage to say. I never thought my brother would be in school, much less a field devoted to helping others. "Is that okay with your past?" I picture him meeting with people struggling with addictions, and learning new places to get drugs.

"I hope I'll be able to better relate to people because of it," Evan says.

It's a nice idea. Maybe he'll make it work.

Evan asks my parents about the upgrades to the bathroom they're thinking of doing, and I zone out again.

Promise me you'll hit me in the head if I
ever think talking about bathroom remodels
is exciting.

ANIKA

Screw remodels. How's your tragic
brother?

I glance at him, laughing with my parents. He looks healthy. He's going to school. He seems like a completely new person. He could be a terrific actor. But maybe I don't need to panic every single time my parents call me unexpectedly. Maybe he's going to be okay.

Slightly less tragic.

FIFTEEN

Saturday February 4th 10:00AM

Layla stands in front of the paintball arena, sticks in her hands.

"Draw one to see which team you're on," she says, walking in a circle while we all pick. Topher, then DJ, and I draw blue. The three of us high five.

"I think that defeats the purpose of this," Jamie says, pointing to the three of us.

Layla chews on her lip. "You're right. Topher and DJ, you're on the red team. Desirae and I will switch to blue team."

Topher and DJ walk to the other side. I smile at Desirae, hoping she has no idea I finally learned what her name actually is. It was a good call for Jamie to split us up. That way when I win, he can't claim it's because I have my old team members with me.

I stare at his ridiculous face across the field from me. He's wearing his own tactical gear with a padded vest on. It looks brand new. He probably ordered them all on Amazon two days ago, hoping they'd make him better. There's no way he's come here as often as Anika and I have. I'm taking him down today. While the employees go through the safety instructions, I picture the smug look on his face falling off as I hit him on the soft part of his arm where his padded vest isn't covering.

We're let into the course, and the whistle blows.

"Take the tower, and the bus," I command. Layla calls out five names, and they all head toward the bus. I take the remaining five and start running for the tower. If we can get on top, we can take everyone out as they move around below.

The snow has melted, the ground a muddy mess sucking and pulling at our shoes, making it impossible to run. Paint starts whizzing through the air, and two of my team members go down, crying out in pain.

"Duck," I say, pulling at Desirae's hands to help her hide behind a stack of barrels. She narrowly avoids a splatter of blue paint.

The tower is forty feet away, and there's an old car twenty feet diagonal from us where two more of our team members are crouched. Other than that, it's completely open space.

"How good of a shot are you?" I ask Desirae.

"This is my first time playing," she says.

I glance to the side of the barrels, and see someone headed our way. I fire a few pellets, and they let out a scream. "I'm going to the car. Then I'll cover you while you join me."

Desirae nods once, looking nervous. I peek out the side of the barrel, then run as quickly as possible in the mud. I dive behind the bumper as splatters of paint hit the side above me. The two girls waiting there scoot farther down, making room for me.

"Desirae is going to run over here. When she does, you two take the tower. I'll cover you the best I can," I say to them. They crouch into position, trying to find a stable spot to take off from. I motion for Desirae, and she takes off running to join us. I see DJ in the distance, running for her. I fire off two pellets, hitting DJ in the chest with the second one. He yells, holding his hands up in surrender as he walks to join the others who are out. There are four of my teammates over there, and three of theirs. We need to step it up.

Once Desirae is safely behind the car, I cover the girls as they run. No one fires at them. There's a commotion near the school bus everyone is distracted by. I turn to Desirae and tell her I'm headed to the tower.

"I want you to stay back here, so we don't have everyone in the same location. You okay with that?" I ask her.

She's breathing hard, her back pressed to the car. "I guess."

"I'll send someone else to join you if I can. I believe in you," I say, patting her once on the shoulder before I look through the car window. I don't see anyone nearby, or the ends of any barrels, so I make a break for the tower. The sun is starting to dry out the mud, making it easier to run. I swing myself into the doorway of the tower. One of the girls stands on the bottom floor, crouched beneath a window, watching.

"I'm going up top, protect the entrance," I say, then sprint up the stairs.

At the top of the tower, I immediately crouch and join my other teammate to peek between the turrets.

"How many members do we have left?" I ask.

"Six. They have eight," she says. "Layla and Porter are

trying to get over here." She points out in the field, where two of them are crouched behind hay bales. Right then a boy from the opposite team darts out into the field, headed our way. I fire at him, red paint splattering all over his arm.

A different scene plays in my head. Brooke's arm covered in red. Her screaming.

I crouch down, my back against the turret. My head is spinning. I close my eyes, waiting for it to stop.

Someone comes stomping up the stairs. I open my eyes, readying to fire. It's Gage.

"It's only me," he says, putting a hand up. Paint flies through the air, inches above his head. He immediately drops to the ground, crawling over to me. I try to focus my eyes on him, but the world is still wobbling. I need to get out of here.

"You two man the top," I say, bolting toward the stairs. I don't bother trying to cover myself, and paintballs whiz above me.

At the bottom of the stairs, Layla is guarding the entrance and firing out the window. When she hears me coming down, she turns to look at me. In that moment, a ball whizzes through the window and hits her in the shoulder.

"Porter, get him," Layla yells.

Porter runs outside the tower in a crouch. Topher cries out feet away.

"Defend my honor," Layla says to me, holding her hands up in the air as she walks out of the tower so no one else will fire at her.

I crouch in the corner, right under the window. A wave of nausea rolls through me and I clutch my stomach. If I run out of here to find the bathroom, I'll definitely get hit with paintballs, and that pain will make me lose it. I need to pull myself back together, now.

This is a game. Paintball. A paintball gun sounds nothing like a real gun. It was paint on his arm, not blood. Don't think about blood. Anything but blood.

Brooke clutching her arm. Quinn and his neck. Dylan and his lifeless body in the river.

I scream into my folded arms. I hate this. I hate being scared of my thoughts, and where they'll go, and what my body will do in response. I've been doing better. I've talked this out. I started medicine. Why does this keep happening?

Two sets of feet start clomping down the stairs. I don't even try to pretend I'm doing something useful.

"We have two people left, they have three," Desirae says, as she and the other girl head to the waiting area.

Two people. One of them is me. I have to do this. I stand up to go back up the stairs, but my vision goes a little fuzzy around the edges and the earth spins up to meet me. I slide back to the ground, putting me head in-between my knees.

I don't know how long I'm there, ears ringing and eyes shut tight. I hear a muffled noise, and glance up.

"Ha!" Jamie yells from the doorway.

Of course it's him. I close my eyes and brace for the pain of the paint, but it doesn't come.

"Whoa, you okay?" he asks, from somewhere closer.

My body starts shaking. "I will be," I get out through chattering teeth.

"Should I go get Topher?" he asks uncertainly.

"No!" I say, a little too forcefully. He can't see me like this. He'll assume it's because of my investigation.

"The medic? Do you have the flu?" Jamie asks.

"Panic. Attack," I get out between shakes.

It's quiet for a moment, then I hear his boots shuffling. I feel him crouched down on the ground next to me. He pats my back awkwardly.

My nemesis is patting my back. "I don't. Want. Your pity."

"That's good because I don't have any," he says in a deadpan.

I focus on the feeling of his hand on my back, blowing out deep breaths.

"Is this what happened during the competition?" he asks quietly.

My mind starts spiraling right back to what started this. Gunshots. Blood. The shaking increases and I squeeze my arms around my knees tighter, trying to hold myself together.

"Sorry. Should I talk about something else?" Jamie asks.

I give the tiniest nod.

"We got a shipment in of little yogurt cups at work. They were peanut butter and bacon flavored, with these crunchy bits on top. They looked good, so I started to eat one. Turns out they're for dogs."

A huff that slightly resembles a laugh escapes me.

"The worst part is I didn't know until I'd eaten half of it. Angie almost peed her pants laughing at me after she told me."

The shaking is calming down. I keep up with my deep breaths.

"I got my acceptance letter to UCCS this week. I'm excited to move to the Springs, but it's going to be quite the commute for work."

"Isn't it four hours away from here?" I ask.

"Two and a half without traffic," Jamie says. "To think you call yourself a Coloradoan."

"I wish I'd shot you in the arm," I grumble. "Right where your shiny new vest wasn't covering.

"I was going to shoot you in the ass," Jamie says.

I look up at him and he's staring at me, his eyes sparkling. Is he, trying to flirt? Or is he still going to shoot me as soon as I'm feeling better? Not if I have something to say about it. I try to stand up, but immediately go back to sitting. I'm still unsteady.

"How good are you at acting?" Jamie asks.

"I've been told I'm pretty awful at it."

He laughs. I'm shocked he's capable of making such a pleasant sound.

"Of course. Try your best." He stands up, then grabs his gun. He points it at his steel-toed boots and shoots. Purple paint splatters over them. He reaches out a hand to me. I stare at it.

"What are you doing?" I ask. This looks an awful lot like he's helping me.

"Getting you out of here," he says.

"I don't need your pity," I repeat. The panic is ebbing away, my body starting to feel like it's mine again. I hate that he's the one here seeing me like this at my most vulnerable. He already thought the worst of me, what's he going to think now?

"This isn't pity. The game has been going on for too long. It's time to end it," he says. "Come on." He thrusts his hand at me again.

I grab it, standing up. The world wobbles, then rights itself. Jamie walks next to me, then wraps his arm around me, under my arms. I jerk away from him.

He holds his hands up in surrender. "Pretend you twisted your ankle."

I glare at him. "I don't need you for that."

"If we're going to sell this, you have to let me help you. There's no way I would let someone with a broken ankle limp through the mud."

I snort.

He frowns. "You think I would?"

"You have had it out for me since the moment we met."

He stays silent, his face contemplative. "Well, I wouldn't. I want to be an officer to help people."

Sure. I'm sure his obsession with upholding rules has nothing to do with it too. I take a few steps, trying to fake a limp. Am I overdoing it? Or not selling it enough? Now I'm overthinking every movement.

Jamie stands there watching me. "Are you going to take me up on my offer, or do you want everyone to know you're faking the second they see you?"

I peek out the window. It's a pretty far walk from here to the exit. And all of the mud hasn't dried yet. I'm no longer shaking but I'm tired.

"Fine," I grumble. Jamie gingerly wraps an arm around me, and I put mine around his shoulders. His scent surrounds me, a mixture of wood and spice. I take a few extra breaths, breathing it in. I do a tentative hop forward as Jamie leads me. This is so awkward. I try the other foot to see if it's easier.

"Pick a foot," Jamie mutters. Then he drags me to the entrance, and we emerge back into the sun. The referee gives a long blow on his whistle, running over toward us. The rest of the team does too.

"She got me, but I put up a hell of a fight. She twisted her ankle in the process. Looks like you're down a player blue team," Jamie says to them.

I give a little hop forward, trying to keep up with Jamie.

Topher comes running over, holding me up on the other side. "You okay?" he asks.

"Yeah. Had to do what I had to do to win," I add. That's what I would normally say, if Jamie hadn't taken pity on me and helped me out of that building. The two of them lead me over to a bench and I sit down. Layla is standing in front of me, her hands on top of her head.

"We're going to be in so much trouble," she says.

"Is it swelling?" Topher asks, reaching for my boot to look.

"Stop," I say.

Everyone is looking at me.

"Let the actual medic take care of it," Jamie says, pointing to a man walking over with a red vest and a large first aid kit.

"I'm fine, you guys go play," I say to Topher and Layla.

"I can't play again knowing someone got injured," Layla says, her eyes wild.

Topher is watching me carefully. The rest of the team is standing behind them, trying to listen in. Jamie turns around and shoos them all away, saying the medic needs space.

"My ankle's fine, it was a panic attack," I murmur to Topher and Layla, looking at the ground. I don't want to see whatever is in their eyes. Topher places a hand on my shoulder for a second, then disappears.

"You're going down Jamie," Topher yells from where he's rejoined the group.

"We're on the same team," Jamie replies.

Layla is still standing in front of me, her arms folded across her chest, when the medic reaches me.

"My ankle is fine," I start to say as the man lays down the kit next to me.

"I need to check. Protocol," he grunts. He places some pressure on the bottom of my boot, and when I don't scream in pain, starts rolling my ankle around in every way imaginable. Then he makes me slip off my boot, and checks both of my feet. When he's satisfied nothing is wrong, he stands up swiftly.

"If you didn't want to play anymore, there's a picnic area over there," he says, clearly annoyed. Before I can clarify that's not what happened, he's walking away.

"They must have people fake to get out of playing a lot," Layla says. She looks at my face, then backtracks. "Not that that's what happened with you. I mean, you did fake an injury. But it's not because you couldn't handle the game. Well, I guess you can't really play when you feel like you can't breathe, so—"

"I'm sorry," I say, cutting her off.

She sits on the bench next to me, setting her helmet down next to her. "Don't apologize. I'm sorry you had a panic attack. They're a bitch."

I raise an eyebrow. "Do you have them?"

"Yes," she says.

I wait for her to elaborate, but she doesn't.

"And you're still in Pathfinders?"

"Why wouldn't I be?" she asks, her forehead scrunching.

"I keep having them when I'm there. The competition, practice, today. I spend every day worried what thoughts will pop into my head, and what will happen when they do."

"Don't think about pink elephants," Layla says.

I glance at her pupils to see if they're dilated. Did she take a paintball to the head?

"I'm serious. For the next minute, don't think about pink elephants," she repeats.

I stare at her, not sure what to do. Not think about pink elephants. Except as soon as I remember I'm not supposed to think about them, I'm picturing a scene from some show I must have seen as a kid with them bouncing around and shape shifting from bubbles into shadows, then balloons.

"You better not be thinking about them," Layla says again.

"I would if you stopped telling me not to," I snap.

"Exactly," she says, standing up from the bench in excitement. "I'm in AP psych and can't believe that textbook is actually useful. There's this phenomenon where if you tell someone to not think about pink elephants, it's the only thing they can think about. It's why diets don't work, and probably why you keep having panic attacks. You're spending so much time thinking about not having them, that you keep having them."

I stare at her open mouthed. Now that Layla is explaining it, I briefly remember a therapist saying something along those lines. I'd been struggling with so many other things, that I completely forgot about it.

"So what do I do?"

"There wasn't a chapter on that," Layla says. "Maybe do the opposite?"

"Only think about pink elephants?" I laugh.

She smiles. "Exactly. Then you'll want to think about everything else, and they won't be as scary."

"I'll let you know how it goes," I say.

"Please do. Maybe I could get enough extra credit in class for helping you that I wouldn't have to do homework for the next few weeks."

There's a long whistle coming from the field, signaling the end of another game. "You should go play," I say.

She hesitates, so I shove her shoulder toward the field. "Go, you've analyzed me enough for today."

"Fine," she smiles, turning to wrap me in a quick hug. Then she jogs off to the field.

The new game has barely started when I hear shouting from the parking lot. Two men are walking up and down the rows of cars.

"We've checked the whole lot twice. It's gone," one of them yells.

The two of them start walking back to the arena. They pass me on their way to the front office. The medic comes out and greets them.

"My car was stolen!" one of the men yells.

The medic swears. Then he brings them into the office.

I get up from my bench and walk closer to the door to hear what they're saying. I peek into the window. The three men are crowded around a computer. I can't hear what they're saying, but from the way they keep leaning into the screen to look closer, I bet they're watching security footage. The man whose car was stolen stands up and starts talking on his phone.

If I want to stop thinking about panic attacks and pink elephants, stolen cars are the perfect distraction. That man's car was stolen from this lot in broad daylight. I check the lot, and thankfully my car and Topher's truck are still there. It could have easily been us.

I head to the locker area and get my backpack out. I dig through the pockets and find a tiny piece of paper.

ISA MONDRAGON
NEWS EDITOR

303-232-5115

I fell asleep reading her other articles last night, trying to get Evan out of my mind. After breaking the news about the college basketball coach, she also found two players who'd assaulted women, but it was being covered up to keep them playing. When Isa exposes this app, the thefts, and how a literal high schooler has sent this city into a tailspin with all the car thefts, things are going to change. They have to. As much as I hate to admit it, Isa was right. Bad PR will create action.

These thefts are still happening. This story is coming out whether I speak to Isa or not. I can't take that away from Kacey, it's not my place. This is *her* story, and she gets to do what she wants with it. I might not be able to protect Kacey and Isa from the fallout of the story, but maybe getting the police to act will be enough.

> Hey Isa, it's Ellie. I'm ready to talk.

My phone immediately starts ringing.

Breaking News: Rise in Car Thefts Related to Unter App

Isa Mondragon, Editor in Chief
February 6, 2023

Sophomore Kacey Aldaco was running late for her history class when she couldn't find her car. She searched the entire lot, walked around the building, but still couldn't find it. "I'd heard about all the car thefts, but I didn't think it would ever happen to me," Aldaco said.

She filed a police report, and then she waited. "I felt like a number. As I waited, so many others shared their stories with me. How the change in laws during COVID made stealing a car only a misdemeanor in most cases, and thieves weren't even spending time in jail afterwards. There's nothing to stop them."

Aldaco's car, like many other student's, was found days later. When she got it back, she found of all things, someone else's homework inside. "That's when we started digging."

With the help of others, Kacey came face-to-face with the owner of the homework, Ruby Gagnon.

"They told me I'd stolen her car and I was so confused. All I'd done was book one on a carsharing app all my friends are using," Gagnon said.

The app, Unter, is being used by dozens of students on campus. You need an invite code to download it, and you can only invite one friend. The premise is that people on campus aren't using their cars all day, so they can rent them out to the app within certain parameters. The problem is none of the cars are from fellow students; they're all stolen.

Gagnon showed me around the app. She went onto a screen, where she saw where the available cars were. Once she paid, she was given instructions on how to access the vehicle. All of them opened with codes, and Gagnon was instructed to plug in a USB to start the car. "I went to a concert at Red Rocks, then left the car on my street when I was back. I never would have known it was stolen."

An anonymous source who helped Aldaco learn who was in her car kept digging. "These thefts were affecting multiple people in my life, and they felt helpless. After hearing about the app, I found through some basic googling that local high schoolers won an award for developing a similar app last year. If I was able to learn that in a few minutes, what are the police doing?" the anonymous source said.

We reached out to the creators of that app: Mason Wilkins, Devon Burton, and another student from their school. Burton is out of the country and unavailable for comment. Wilkins stated that he helped code an app in high school, but hasn't touched it since the competition. "The Unter app is similar, but has major changes from the version we won the competition with. I have nothing to do with that."

The third student is still a minor, so they will not be named at this time.

"It's sad that we had to do our own investigation, and how much we uncovered in a short amount of time. We have no official resources or power, yet we discovered this stolen car ring on campus. I want to be able to go to bed at night knowing that my car will be there in the morning, and I want the same for everyone else in town," Aldaco said.

The App store said in a statement, "Thousands of apps are added to the app store weekly. We do our best to catch fraudulent apps, but some inevitably slip through the cracks. Unter has been removed and is currently under review."

The Rivers Edge Police department refused to comment when contacted.

SIXTEEN

Tuesday February 7th 2:10PM

Someone grabs my arm while I'm on my way to AP Bio. I twist out of their grip purely from muscle memory before I even see who's grabbing me. Jake is standing there, his chest heaving.

"What. Did. You. Do?" he growls, emphasizing each word.

"What do you mean?" I ask, pretending to have no idea what he's talking about. There's been a buzzing in the halls all day, similar to the frenzy when the list of boys was passed around on the first day of school. Even though the article doesn't mention me by name, I've felt everyone's eyes on me as I go from class to class. Two people straight up asked if I was the anonymous source, but I completely ignored them.

Jake wasn't named in the article either, but everyone has done the same search I did and figured out who the unnamed minor was. Now, the two of us are in the hall together, and people are watching. I stand up straighter. Hopefully the videos of this are more flattering than the last one I was in.

"I know you're the one who went to the reporters," Jake says, his eyes blazing. They're bright red, and he smells faintly of weed. The story broke yesterday. What has he been doing the past 24 hours?

"I have no idea what you're talking about," I say cooly.

"I'm a dead man. You know that right?" he whispers.

That's a little dramatic. "They don't even name you in the article."

"No, but everyone else online has no problem naming me in the comments." He looks up and down the hallway dramatically. I count five phones recording us. Jake motions for me to follow him to a double set of doors that lead outside. We stand in the middle of them. If anyone wants to record us and pick up audio, they'll have to come in here.

"I was working with gang members to run that. The app is gone, and I owe them money. They're going to get me."

I blink. Did I hear that right? He confessed to running the app, *and* told me who's stealing the cars. Can I get him to say it again on tape? I fumble around for my phone.

"Stop it. This is serious. They're going to kill me, and it's all your fault." He shoves my shoulder. I stumble back a step.

"How is it my fault? You shouldn't have started this in the first place."

He runs both hands through his hair, pulling it while groaning. "I hope you're happy," he finally says, throwing the doors open and walking outside.

I watch him as he lurches down the sidewalk to the parking lot. People stop in their tracks when they see him, pulling out their phones. He ignores them, still pulling his hair.

I know it's not my fault. I'm not the one who owes anyone money, or decided that working with a gang was a good idea. But his words leave an uneasy feeling in my chest.

The bell rings and I hurry to Bio.

"You'll never believe what just happened in the hall," I say, sliding onto my lab stool.

Ms. Lions claps her hands together at the front of the room. "Today we're doing a review session for the test tomorrow. It will be our first practice test for the AP exam, which is different from any test you've taken before. How many of you have taken other AP exams?"

Many hands go in the air, including Sandra's. Anika, Topher, and I just look at each other.

"I fully expect you all to fail the test tomorrow. That's just how this goes..." Ms. Lions continues to describe how AP tests are graded.

"What happened?" Anika whispers.

Topher glares at her.

I wait for Ms. Lions to stop talking. Four minutes later, she finally does, grabbing study guides to pass around the room.

"Jake confronted me in the hall about the article. He said that he was working with a gang to steal the cars," I say, my voice low.

"What?" Anika gasps, a little too loud. People stare in our direction. I wait for them to look away.

"That's not the worst part. He said—"

"Shhh," Topher says, elbowing me. Ms. Lions has started talking again.

I share a look with Anika. When did he get so obsessed

with tests? This one won't even count toward our grade, it's practice. Anika shrugs.

I don't get a chance to talk during the rest of the review session. I actually don't remember most of the terms on the board, so I'm scribbling things down as quickly as I can. When the bell rings and I look at my notes, they're nonsense.

"Do you want to study with me at the library?" Sandra asks.

"Yes," Topher says immediately.

Anika looks at me. "I'm down," she says.

I check my phone. I don't work until 5, and it beats heading home to sit. "Me too."

Sandra beams. "Great. Then you can finish telling us your story" she adds.

Have I mentioned lately how much I love Sandra? She's the queen of multi-tasking.

"I'll ride with you," Anika says, grabbing my arm. The four of us walk to the parking lot, then split off for our separate cars. Once Sandra and Topher are out of earshot, I turn to Anika.

"What's wrong with Topher?"

"I was going to ask you that. He's obsessed with his grades now, which makes no sense. He already got into his dream school, and he got multiple scholarships. He's practically full ride," Anika says.

"He got scholarships? Why didn't he tell me that?" It's quiet for a second as we get into my car and I turn the heat all the way up and turn the vents away from me.

Anika turns her vents away too. "We didn't want to make you feel bad," she says.

"Feel bad?" I don't finish my question. How much have

they been hiding from me? I put the car in drive and turn out of the parking lot.

"You two are my best friends. I want to hear the good things happening in your lives. Stop worrying about me," I frown. "So Topher's officially going to CU Boulder?"

"Yep, he accepted the offer. I'm going to MSU, and the dorm I applied for looks nice. Way better than the dorms up here." She pulls out her phone and starts scrolling through pictures, then holds her phone up to show me.

"I'm driving."

"Wait for the light. Then look really fast."

I roll my eyes, but look at the picture. It's a little layout from above of the room. There are two rooms attached to a little sitting room. Each room has two beds, and its own bathroom. "Are you serious? That's nice. You'd think it'd be tiny since it's in Denver."

"Right? You'll have to come stay one night; we can go explore downtown."

"That would be fun," I say, trying to picture it. Maybe we could go to a show, or a club. If I got my act together, I could apply there if I wanted. Even be Anika's roommate. We could string fairy lights across the ceiling, and Anika's walls would be completely covered in posters of her favorite bands. My wall would be covered in... I have no idea what. My room at home is covered in pictures with Anika and Topher over the years. Pathfinder competitions. Trips to the reservoir. Polaroids of us squished together on couches with Red Vine mustaches

What kinds of pictures will my future self take? What moments and people will I want to capture and stare up at on sleepless nights? Will Anika and Topher be a part of them? Or will our friendship be contained to the limits of this city, these versions of ourselves? My chest squeezes and my throat burns.

I won't have a dorm room to decorate unless I finish my college applications. Until I look through all the drop-down menus of majors to study, and lists of classes to take, and choose something. My vision swims and my head spins. I take a deep breath, squeezing my hands on the steering wheel. I'm driving; this is not the time to have a panic attack.

"What about Sophie?" I ask, changing the subject.

She frowns. "She's deciding between MSU and staying in town. The tuition is more expensive here, but she'd save money by living at home. Or, she might take community college classes the first two years, then decide later. Her family doesn't want her to come to MSU because they think it's only to be with me." Anika's voice goes quiet. "Obviously I don't want her to decide her future around me. I hate that her decision revolves around money, and that I don't have to think about that as much as she does. It's not fair. But I don't want to break up yet..."

"Who said you have to break up?" I ask.

She twirls a curl around her finger so tightly, it looks painful. "No one. But it's an hour drive. Best case scenario we can see each other once a week, and I don't want us to spend all our free time traveling to each other. What if she resents me because I got to leave town?"

"Has she said that?" I ask.

"No. If the roles were reversed, I'd resent her a little though."

I glance over and see her eyes misting up. I reach out and squeeze her hand at the stoplight. "I'm sorry. But an hour away isn't that bad, if you meet halfway, it's only thirty minutes."

"Do you know what city is halfway? Frederick. Do you know what there is to do in Frederick? Be a middle-class white family with 2.1 children, a labradoodle, and a Ford F-150," she deadpans.

I burst out laughing. "How do you know that?"

"Google it and tell me that's not the vibe you get." Anika sniffs, rubbing at her nose. "I'm trying to enjoy now, but that deadline is hanging over us."

I pull into a parking spot in front of the library, then grab her hand again, giving another squeeze. "It's only February. You've got time to figure this out."

Anika sighs, covering her face with her hands. She lets out a tiny shriek, then pulls her hands away, a smile plastered to her face. Topher's truck pulls into the spot next to us, and Sandra hops out, holding a bag of snacks. There's a package of Red Vines poking out. My favorite.

"We needed to fuel up," Sandra says, before leading us up the stairs to the second-floor study room we went to last time.

We settle around the table and start digging into the snacks.

"What were you saying about Jake?" Sandra asks, opening up a bag of Takis.

I finish chewing on my Red Vine. "He said he's been working with a gang to steal the cars, that he owes them money, and I'm going to get him killed."

"What is wrong with our school?" Anika asks, covering her mouth with her hand since she's still chewing her Takis.

"I can't wait to leave," Sandra says.

"Same," Topher agrees.

I focus on grabbing another Red Vine, pretending I didn't notice that all their eyes darted to me. I'm the only one without plans to get out of town.

"How did he even find gang members willing to do that for him?" Anika asks. "I wouldn't be able to find one if I tried."

Sandra taps her chin with her pen. "I think there's one that wears purple. I saw a security guard throw a guy out of the library that had a purple bandana peeking out of his pocket."

"A gang member was thrown out of the library?" Anika asks.

I pull out my phone and start searching which gangs wear purple in Colorado. Instead of a simple answer, there are multiple options for that color alone. When the officer who insulted us said there was a rise in gang activity in the area, he wasn't kidding.

"Do you think they'll actually hurt Jake?" I ask, my leg starting to shake under the table.

"That's his problem," Topher says. "Let's get studying." He puts his textbook on the table and starts flipping through it. The rest of us get out our books too, and I grab another Red Vine.

Is it fully his problem? Maybe I could have confronted Jake privately about shutting down the app, and he would have had time to get everyone paid off he needed to.

"He could ask the police for protection, right?" I blurt out, accidentally interrupting Topher and Sandra deciding where to start studying.

"Everything I know about gangs is from tv. And those don't make his odds look great," Anika says.

That's as far as I know too. Gangs have nothing to do with the Pathfinder challenges.

"Maybe we could talk with Officer Ken. I think he's supposed to be back in town—" I start.

"Can we please get back to studying?" Topher asks. "Jake got himself in this mess, but I'm not going to fail because of him."

"Why are you so stressed about this test? It's for practice," I say.

"Practice for the AP test in three months," Topher says slowly.

"So? That doesn't affect your grade either."

"It's one less class I'd have to take in college if I score high enough," he says.

"One less class isn't worth all of this stress. And you've got scholarships," I say.

Topher rubs his hands over his face. "Fine, I'll go study by myself," he says, picking up his books and backpack. "You're welcome to join me Sandra," he says. He grabs the bags of hot Cheetos and gummy bears from the table, and walks toward the librarian. She reaches for her keyring and stands up to unlock a new room for him.

"I promised to show him this new study technique I learned about," Sandra says apologetically. She grabs her stuff and heads over to join Topher.

"What'd I say?" I ask Anika as soon as the door closes.

She shakes her head. "I have no idea. We should do an investigation into whatever his deal is."

"Are you serious?" I ask. "I've got a blank notebook we could use." I can't risk another friendship. Having things strained with Anika was awful enough. There are only three months until the end of the school year; I don't want to spend them fighting with Topher. He told me to leave the car thefts alone. Is that it? He's mad I'm not listening to him? He's not in charge of me, and Anika and Sandra both wanted to know what happened with Jake.

She sighs. "Let's give him some time to cool off. Maybe he's just having a bad day."

I glance at him in the other study room. His back is to me, but I can tell he's talking animatedly with Sandra. She's currently laughing at whatever he said. "Maybe."

SEVENTEEN

Thursday February 9th 6:45 AM

A RED JEEP SITS ON THE CURB OUTSIDE MY HOUSE, clouds of exhaust billowing behind it in the frozen morning air. I stop walking halfway down the driveway as the driver's door opens. Quinn gets out.

"Morning," he says with a tight smile.

"Good morning?" It comes out as a question. "Have you been sitting outside my house for a while?"

He runs a hand through his hair. Why does it look even better now that he's messed it up?

"This is creepy, I should have called."

"Well you're here now." My heart is racing, my mind spinning with possibilities. I meet him at the bottom of the driveway.

"Can we go inside?" Quinn asks, taking a step toward my house.

"No," I snap, holding my arms up to block him from coming any closer. "You need to get out of here." Both of my

155

parents are still inside. If my mom sees him here, she's going to lose it. It'll prove her theory that I've been sneaking around to hang out with Quinn.

"Why?" Quinn looks up and down the street, probably searching for danger.

"Because my mom doesn't like you," I say. "And she'll be leaving any second."

His expression changes rapidly: amused, then serious again. He lets out a tight breath. "I was going to do this gently, but there's no time. Jake Peters was found dead. They're suspecting foul play."

A siren sounds in the distance. There's a gust of wind that whips my hair around my face. A few strands stick to my chapstick. I carefully unstick them and pull my hood over my head.

"Ellie?" Quinn asks.

Oh yeah. He's here. "Hmm?"

"I just told you that Jake Peters, your classmate who was running the Unter app, is dead."

"No," I say stretching out the word. His words aren't computing. He's wrong. "I saw him at school yesterday. He was alive. Flipped me off, but alive."

"It happened after school," he says.

I shake my head. "I don't believe you. He's fine." I walk past him to my car. There's only a thin layer of ice on the windshield, and if I blast the defrost for a few minutes, it should take care of most of it. I lean in the door and start the engine.

Quinn followed and is standing next to me. "What are you doing?"

"I'm going to be late for school," I say simply.

"You're going?" he asks incredulously.

"It's Thursday, why wouldn't I?"

He blinks. "I thought that you might be feeling, I don't know, shaken up to hear about the death of another classmate."

"I'm fine. Because you're wrong."

He raises his brows. "Ellie, I was there when they brought him in. Its him. The kid who made the app."

"You keep telling yourself that," I say. When he continues to stand there, I ask," Need anything else?"

He puts both of his hands on the back of his head. "I guess not," he says as he starts walking backward to his Jeep. "Text me if *you* need anything."

"Have a good one," I say. The majority of the ice has melted off the windshield, so I climb into my car. The wipers swish back and forth, removing the last of the sludgy bits, so I can clearly see Quinn get into his Jeep and pull away.

I drive to school, my mind repeating what he said. Jake is dead. Jake. Is. Dead. No matter how many times I turn the words over, the sentence doesn't make sense. He can't be. I saw him yesterday. That was only a few hours ago. I'm going to see him today if I want, right outside Sandra's math class. He'll flip me off again, and it'll be great.

I park and Topher pulls up next to me with his truck. I fiddle with my backpack on the passenger seat, pretending I'm fixing something. Things were awkward between us yesterday after the library fiasco. If he's going to be weird, this is the perfect opportunity to walk off without me. He gets out of his truck and stands there, clearly waiting for me. I stop pretending to look for something and climb out of my car into the cold.

"How's it going?" I ask automatically.

"No complaints yet. You?"

"Same."

Actually, I have a few. For starters, there's the fact that Quinn showed up at my house and tried to ruin my day. Then there's the fact that I can't tell one of my best friends about this because he gets weird whenever I mention stolen cars. Thinking about going through the entire school day with whatever this is between Topher and I makes me want to scream.

I hold it in and walk in silence with him, focusing intently on my feet. Not all of the snow has melted off the sidewalks and I'd hate to trip and actually hurt my ankle.

When we approach our spot near the computer lab, I'm relieved to see Sophie and Anika already there. They're hugging and Sophie whispers something in Anika's ear before kissing her on the cheek. Anika grabs Sophie's face and pulls her in for a longer kiss. Topher and I slow down.

"Do we interrupt, or walk incredibly slow until they finish?" Topher asks.

I pretend to seriously think about it. "Interrupt for sure."

"Agreed. It's five feet away, how long can it take to get there?" He clears his throat loudly.

Some of the tightness in my chest eases. This is the Topher I know and love. Maybe things are fine between us.

Anika and Sophie pull apart, Sophie's cheeks quickly turning bright red.

"Sorry," Sophie says.

"Don't apologize for our love," Anika says, bumping her head against Sophie's shoulder. Sophie pulls her in closer.

"I don't want to make anyone uncomfortable," Sophie says.

"I live for it," Anika says, wiggling her eyebrows.

Sophie reaches toward Anika's stomach, about to tickle her.

"Don't you dare. I will flip you on your ass in this hall-way," Anika warns.

"She really will," Topher says.

Sophie looks at me. "Ellie, can you teach me to fight back?"

"Absolutely," I grin.

"You can try. But I've got five years of practice already," Anika taunts.

"I'm a quick learner," Sophie says.

The warning bell goes off and we all scramble in opposite directions to get to class. I was so distracted by my friends that I don't remember Jake until we're well into the lesson. I can't go check to see if he's here now, so I pull out my phone.

Is Jake in class today?

SANDRA

No. Why?

Are you sure?

Yeah... Do you know something?

Jake isn't here today.

Quinn works in the coroner's office. Why would he come over to lie straight to my face? He genuinely wanted to make sure I was okay when I heard the news.

Oh no.

No, no, no.

I'm sweating and my stomach flips. I run to the trashcan in the front of the room, holding my hair back, ready to wretch. The classroom goes instantly quiet. My mouth fills with so much saliva I spit it into the trashcan. I keep standing there, waiting for something to happen.

"Ellie?" Ms. Tigris says, putting a hand gently on my back. "Are you okay?"

I shake my head. "I need to go home."

"Here's a pass for the nurse." She hands me a paper and my backpack. I take both of them, then run out of there. I skip the nurse, going straight outside to the parking lot. The cold air is a shock to the system in the best way possible. The feeling of nausea starts to disappear, along with the sweat.

Inside my car, I stare at the road in front of me. Where do I go? It's 7:30 in the morning on a school day.

There's the obvious choice. I could go to Quinn's and find out as many details as possible about Jake's death. But the thought of that makes my stomach twist again.

I could start driving and not stop until I make it to Vegas, or California. I could go to the beach and start a new life. Except, I don't have enough in my bank account for the drive there, much less food or hotels. I should talk to Angie about a raise so running away is an option in the future.

There's a dean walking toward the parking lot, checking to see if kids are doing drugs in their cars. I start driving, not sure where I'm going. I drive home on autopilot. My dad's car is still in the garage, but if I'm lucky he'll be in a meeting and I can sneak upstairs. I open the front door quietly as possible. It's pointless; my dad is standing in the kitchen looking right at me.

"Hey kiddo, what's going on?" he asks.

"My period is killing me," I say, wrapping my arms around my stomach.

He opens up a cabinet and pulls out some medicine. "Do you need a heating pad?"

Why does my dad have to be one of the cool men who aren't disturbed by periods?

I sigh. "No. That's not what's wrong," I say.

He frowns. "Okay? What is?"

"Do you promise not to get mad?" I ask. After Evan was arrested, they told me I could say that whenever and they'd just listen. I'm sure they meant about drinking, or being pregnant, not what I've done.

A few emotions flit across his face before he smooths it into something neutral. This is the first time he's had to do this. "Of course."

He walks over from the kitchen into the living room, sitting down on the couch. He crosses his leg onto his knee, and his foot is shaking. I sit in the armchair, pulling my legs up to my chest and wrapping my arms around them. We sit in the quiet as I try to figure out where to start.

"Sophie kept having stolen cars show up in front of her house, and my friend Kacey's car got stolen, so I told them I'd help look for it, and in the process, I uncovered that a kid at my school was running a car sharing app with stolen cars, and it ended up in the newspaper, and he was murdered last night because he didn't give a gang money."

My dad blinks a few times. Then he takes a swig out of his mug. "Which one is Sophie again? The one from Biology, or Anika's girlfriend?"

I can't help it. I burst out laughing. After everything that I said, that's the first detail he wants clarification on?

"Anika's girlfriend."

"I thought so, but you have so many friends with 'S' names I had to check. Let me message my boss that I'm taking the day off, and you can tell me all the details again."

He runs off to the office, types furiously for a minute, then comes back to his spot on the couch. I start at my birthday with Sophie's request and tell him everything. Well, almost everything. I downplay how much I chose to investigate things, leave out that my sleepover at Sophie's was actually a planned stakeout, and that a gun was pointed at me. In this version, I simply happened to be in the right place at the right time.

"He's dead, and it's all my fault," I finish, my voice cracking.

My dad leans back into the couch, crossing his arms.

"You're not the one who killed him, right?" he asks.

"Dad!" I shriek. How could he ask me that?

He holds his hands up. "Having heard the whole story, I don't see how you could think this is your fault unless you actually did it."

"This car theft ring was going on and the police were leaving it alone. I uncovered it, then talked to a reporter. Jake told me I was going to get him killed, and now he's dead."

"But he's the one who decided to work with the gangs, and short them money. You should talk to Evan; he has stories of people being killed for less. Even if the story hadn't come out, he probably would have gotten hurt anyway."

"I sped it up though. I should have gone to the police, or given him an ultimatum so he could have paid them, or..."

He scratches his arm. "Sure, you could have done that, but the police might have ignored you, and Jake wouldn't have had the money."

"What if I helped the wrong side? I didn't give the police that chance. I went with journalism, and now he's dead."

He frowns. "Who said anything about sides? Do you think you have to be either team police or team journalism?"

"It sems like it." How many times at Pathfinders were we reminded to never talk to the press if they approached us about something? How many times did I hear Officer Ken grumble about meddlesome reporters? My own life was a circus for a while thanks to reporters. But I believed in Isa and took a chance. She wrote her story, and now Jake's dead.

He leans forward, resting his elbows on his knees so he's closer to me. "In a perfect world journalists hold people, especially those in power, accountable. They uncover the facts, and systems are supposed to change because of them. From my view it sounds like the car thefts in town are out of control, and whether it's understaffing, burnout, or maybe even looking the other way, this app has been able to fly under the radar. That journalist, with your help, is holding those systems accountable."

"Why do officers seem to despise journalists then?" I ask.

"They call police out on their mistakes with the benefit of hindsight. The police do things that require discretion, and then you have some reporters who are creating clickbait and can twist words to get more views. Of course they're going to butt heads. That doesn't mean what you did was wrong, or that you're responsible for what happened. I'm proud of you."

That catches me off guard. "You're proud of me?"

He looks me straight in the eyes. "Do I love that you're running off looking into potentially dangerous things? Not at all. Yet I've seen you learn and grow and try more new things in the past year than I have since Evan was arrested. I've worried that *that* moment would be your defining one. That it was the driving force of why you wanted to be an officer, and you were giving everything to Pathfinders to try and get there quicker. I'm proud of you for exploring and learning that the world isn't black and white, it's so many shades of grey."

"You're not mad that I've been investigating things again?"

"I'd rather you not, but I'm not delusional enough to think I can stop you. You need to remember you're only eighteen. Yes, you've been in Pathfinders and know more than most people about safety, but that doesn't mean you can pretend that you're an actual detective and do whatever you want. You need to be smart and stay safe. No more running off to save the day, deal?"

"Deal," I say. "What about mom?"

"It's been a hard few months for us all. She wants what's best for you, and for you to be happy."

I look down at the floor. "I'm not trying to make anyone worry. I just notice things everyone else has missed. And I'm decent at digging on the internet."

"Sounds exactly like what journalists do," he says with a smile. "Maybe that's something you want to look into."

I scrunch my nose. "I absolutely hate writing."

He shrugs. "Fair. And that's a tough job market right now. Let's keep having these talks. If you keep us in the loop, we won't be as worried coming up with our own worst-case scenarios."

"I'm not doing drugs, I'm not pregnant, and I'm not joining a gang. Any other fears I can put to rest?"

"Are you having thoughts of hurting yourself?" my dad asks.

I stare at the floor again, letting out a breath. I shake my head no.

"It's okay if you are. Remember what the doctor said?"

The ER doctor I saw that night in November.

"I haven't had any. Promise."

"Then I think we're good." He gets up from the couch and comes over to my chair, holding his arms out. I get up and let him wrap me in a hug. It doesn't bring Jake back to life, or completely erase the feelings of guilt, but it's a start.

EIGHTEEN

Friday February 10th 10:00AM

Detective Zhao opens up her filing cabinet, papers exploding everywhere.

"There's a method to the mess," she says, rifling through them. Whatever she's looking for isn't in there, so she opens the next drawer and starts over.

"I believe you," I say, only partially lying.

I swivel in the chair she offered me, looking around her small space. I thought as a detective, she'd have her own office filled with bookshelves and décor. There would have been a large wooden desk in the middle of the room and I would sit opposite from her like I was in the principal's office. Instead she has a cubicle. There's barely enough room for her to put her legs underneath her desk because she has filing cabinets underneath, each of them probably as stuffed with things as the one she's currently digging through.

Maybe this is why she has teenagers solving her cases.

She has all the information she needs; she just can't find where she put it.

She closes the drawer she was looking through, then opens the one above it.

"Aha," she says, pulling out a notebook and manilla folder. Then she opens up a tiny set of Sterlite drawers on her desk and grabs a tape recorder.

Someone burps loudly from somewhere else in the cubicles. Detective Zhao rolls her eyes, then stands up. "Let's go somewhere else to talk." She starts off through the maze of cubicles to the door.

"I thought Detectives would have their own offices," I say, following after. All of my daydreams of becoming a detective did not include listening to other people burp.

"There's two on this floor, and you get them in order of seniority. Only three more people need to retire or get promoted until I get one," she adds.

How young are the people ahead of her? That might never happen.

"Happy belated birthday," Detective Zhao says as we turn into the hallway.

"Thanks." The only reason I'm alone with her right now is because I'm eighteen, and both my parents had work things they couldn't get out of. My phone keeps buzzing in my pocket with texts from both of them asking if I'm okay and demanding updates. If they have this much time to text, how are they getting any work done?

"How are you enjoying your new Pathfinders team?" she asks.

I hesitate, trying to think of the right thing to say. Something nice, but technically true. "They have more resources and members than we ever did."

She nods. "I went through the academy with Lieutenant Sanders. She's one of the best."

Interesting. Have they been talking about me? Has Lieutenant Sanders told her about all my issues? If she has, Detective Zhao doesn't mention it. Instead she opens up a small room with a circular table and vending machine. She settles down and I sit across from her. This is much less intimidating than the interview room we spoke in last year.

Detective Zhao readjusts her ponytail as I get settled in my chair. Then she flips her notebook open and turns on the tape recorder.

"It's February 10th at 10:00 in the morning. Do I have your permission to record this conversation, Ellie? I want to reiterate that you aren't under investigation and are here of your own choice. You are free to leave at any time."

"That's fine," I say.

"Thank you. Are you aware that one of your classmates, Jake Peters, was recently found deceased?" Detective Zhao asks.

"I heard." Social media was buzzing with the news last night, so Quinn can't get in trouble for letting me know earlier in the day.

"I wondered what you thought about it."

"Why are you asking me?" Dread crawls up my spine. I didn't murder Jake. Dad kept reiterating yesterday his death is not my fault. But is that how Detective Zhao will see it?

"After the events of last year, I would be remiss if I didn't ask if you have any insights," Detective Zhao says. Her expression and tone are neutral and do nothing to make me feel better.

"I don't know much about Jake," I say honestly. The only things I knew were about his illegal app and expensive shoes. I scrolled through everyone's memorial posts with pictures and videos of him last night. Apparently, he liked cats, soccer, and played the trumpet in middle school.

"I recently read an in-depth article into an app that Jake was allegedly running," Detective Zhao says. "It was written by a feisty college reporter, Isa Mondragon. You should meet her; she reminds me of you."

Is that her trying to figure out if I helped Isa with the article? Isa promised she wouldn't out me. I try to keep my face in what I hope is a neutral expression. "She sounds great."

Detective Zhao pauses. "That article showed how my colleagues have dropped the ball when it comes to these car thefts. I'm not working with them. I'm here to find out the truth of what happened to Jake so his family can have peace."

I look her in the eyes. I *want* to trust her. Before Isa approached me, I fully planned on bringing her everything I'd found. She's not the one who's been ignoring Sophie's family, and not returning Kacey's calls.

She *is* the one who had no problem stomping into my living room and telling my parents everything I'd been up to, and getting me grounded.

"Didn't the article say that Jake built the original app with two other friends? Have you looked into them?" I ask carefully. Maybe I can steer her in the right direction without revealing too much.

"I'm aware of his other partners. Do you know of anyone else I should be looking into?" she asks, expertly dodging my question.

"Did their alibis clear?" I ask, curious.

She raises a brow. "Anyone else?"

I stare at her, trying to think of an indirect way to tell

her the rest. I'm drawing a blank. How would Quinn play this? He's always saying things in an easily deniable way.

"I may or may not have asked Jake about his app, and noticed that he had a lot of expensive accessories. After the article came out, he told me I was going to get him killed because he was working with a gang and owed them money."

Detective Zhao starts scribbling in her notebook furiously. "Did he mention which gang?"

"Which one? Are there multiple in town?" I ask.

"Of course there are," she says, looking puzzled. "Was Jake wearing a lot of items in a particular color?"

"Not that I noticed." I close my eyes and try to picture him that last day. All I can see is the fear and anger on his face.

"Maybe purples, or greens?" she asks.

I try harder to remember. Now all of his features are blurring in my memory. "I don't know."

"That's okay. Anything else?"

"No." If she already knows about Jake's app partners, then she doesn't need to know the strange path I took to find out about the app, and that I've already talked with Mason.

"If you think of something, anything, let me know. You've already been extremely helpful," she says, tapping on her notebook with her pen. She starts to get up from the table.

My chest squeezes. The first time I met Detective Zhao, I wanted to be her. I wanted to sit down and interview her for hours on how she got where she is in her career, and what I could do to make my path easier. Anika and Topher's lives are falling into place to start their futures, while mine feels completely uncertain.

"How did you know you could handle being an officer?" I blurt out.

Detective Zhao slides back down into the chair, and turns off the tape recorder. She studies my face for a long moment. "What do you mean? Are you worried about the academy?"

"No, I'm confident I can do all of the physical elements, and the tests. But..." I trail off.

"You can tell me," she says.

I let out a deep breath. "I keep having flashbacks. I learned how to breathe and stuff, but it hasn't gone away. I dread Pathfinders. How am I supposed to be an officer when I already hate it?"

"Do you still want to be an officer?" she asks.

I pick at the edge of a hangnail. "I don't know. I've always wanted to be a detective, and that's the only way to get there. But it feels like I'm broken and that's not even an option anymore."

"You're not broken," she says immediately. Then she drums her fingers on the edge of the table, staring at a spot on the wall. "I see awful things every day. However, my first few cases as a rookie are still the most prevalent in my mind. I think it's because it's the first time you see how cruel life can be, so it's the most shocking."

"Did you have panic attacks?" I ask.

"I've had them before, yes. Usually on my drive home after the adrenaline has worn off."

"How am I supposed to keep my partner safe or be a reliable officer if I have anxiety?"

"That's what your training is for. It's months and months of rigorous repetition so that when the time comes, you don't have to think. You just do."

That's what Officer Ken said over and over. I know that.

But it doesn't make me feel any better. I've had that training, but I'm still a mess.

Detective Zhao leans closer to me across the table. "Listen to me. The Pathfinder program is not the same as the training to become an officer. That is all day, every day for months. It's more intense, and it's made to get you ready. Not everyone can make it through.

"You not only had to fire a gun, but on someone you knew. That is something that the majority of officers don't have to do during their career. Officer Ken never did, and I haven't either. It makes sense that you're shaken up. It doesn't mean you can't still become an officer if that's what you want to do. The fact that you're even thinking about these things shows you've put more thought into this than a lot of people I know."

She knows all the details of what I went through last year. I shared a glimmer into my secret shame, and she still thinks I'm capable. And while I did have a rough time at paintball, I was fine when I was mere feet from an actual gun. Maybe there is still a way for me to keep on my dream.

"I'm always here to talk. We need more people like you on the force," Detective Zhao says, reaching over and squeezing my hand. "Now let me remind you, it's my job to figure out what happened to Jake, not yours. If you hear anything, let me know immediately. Stay safe out there," she says, standing up from the table.

"I will," I say. As I walk out of the station, exhaustion overwhelms me. I spent all day yesterday in bed, watching movies and trying not to think about Jake's words to me. Talking with Detective Zhao zapped any energy I had left. Even if I wanted to look into Jake's death, I can't right now. Here's hoping Detective Zhao can piece everything together despite that mess of papers in her cubicle.

NINETEEN

Saturday February 11th 7:00PM

Anika and Topher are standing in my doorway. Anika is in a red dress, leather jacket, and knock off Doc Martins. Her cheeks glitter in the light from my lamp. Topher looks equally nice in a chunky maroon sweater and jeans.

"Hey," I say, clutching my ratty blanket to my chest. I haven't left my room at all today, and I'm still in my pajamas.

"Get dressed. We're going to a party," Anika says.

I snort. "No, we're not."

"Yes, we are. I'm not going to let you sit here and mope about some kid you didn't even know." She walks into my room and tries to yank my blanket away. I hold on tight, barely keeping it on.

"Mom!" I yell.

She appears next to Topher, poking her head in the doorway.

"Anika's trying to force me to do something I don't want to do," I whine, still fighting for the blanket.

"Because I asked her to. It's senior year and you've spent too much of it in your room," Mom says.

"They're taking me to a party. There could be drinking, and drugs, and untold things there," I say.

"I know you'll stay away from them. Hurry up and get dressed." With that she disappears into the hall.

"The two of us are stronger than you. Don't embarrass yourself," Topher says.

I give a dramatic sigh and let go of the blanket. Anika almost falls over due to the sudden lack of tension.

"Whose party is this?" I ask, walking over to my closet.

"A friend of Sophie's," Anika says.

"Do we trust them?"

"Of course. They're in band," she says.

I flip through my hangers. "What does that mean?"

"How wild can people from band be?" she asks, perching on my bed. Topher sits down next to her.

"Playing an instrument doesn't define someone," I say.

"I've heard things about band parties. They're not on the same level as theater kid parties, but pretty close," Topher says.

I peek out of my closet. "What happens at theater kid parties?"

Anika groans, whacking Topher in the chest. "Stop it. Let's just go, and if the party sucks, we can leave. Please?"

"I agreed when I picked you up," Topher says.

I pull out two random shirts. "Should I try on everything I own for a proper makeover montage?" I ask.

"Definitely not. We're already late," Anika says.

"Isn't it cool to be late?" I ask.

"Not when your girlfriend is already there and you haven't made out in a day," Topher says.

Anika blushes. Then she pulls out a navy-blue striped sweater I forgot I had and throws it at me, along with my favorite jeans. Both her and Topher turn around as I wriggle into my clothes. I stop at my dresser and swipe some mascara on, along with ChapStick. Anika grabs my lone perfume bottle and spritzes me with it.

"Let's do this," she says, eyes glittering.

We run down the stairs and out to Topher's truck. I call shotgun first, but Anika shoves me out of the way. I grab her around the middle and try to move her. She tries to fight back, but is at a disadvantage because of her dress.

"Get in already," Topher yells. Anika huffs, then climbs into the back. I take my spot in shotgun, immediately regretting it. Topher's head is straight ahead, not looking at me. The air feels tense between us again.

It's probably nothing. You're imagining it.

I hope I am.

When Topher pulls up at the house Anika directed us to, we all look around.

"Are you sure this is the right place?" I ask. There are no lights on inside. Topher rolls his window down and we listen. There's no distinctive thumping of bass.

"Sophie says she's in there. Look, there's a bunch of cars parked down there," Anika points farther down the street. There's an open space of untamed weeds with seven cars parked in a row. Topher whistles at a classic orange Ford Mustang at the end of the row, parked next to a grey Dodge Challenger with a black racing stripe up the hood.

"I can't believe they parked those in the weeds," Anika says.

Topher parks next to the Dodge, making sure to leave plenty of room between his truck and theirs.

"Park much?" Anika comments.

"I don't want anyone accusing me of scratching it. People with cars like those get aggressive," Topher says.

We walk silently down the street, our boots crunching in the snow. Anika climbs up the stairs of the house and tries the door. It's unlocked and we follow her inside. The only light is from a rainbow strobe in the middle of the room.

A door opens further in the house, and light and sound spill into the room. The door is to the basement, which sounds like it's full of people. The light illuminates the front room enough that I see four people crowded on a couch only feet away from me, making out furiously. Bodies and limbs are tangled and I can't tell where one person starts and the other ends. I take a step away from them, as if I might get sucked in.

We practically run to the basement steps and head down, the music and voices growing louder. There's a turn in the stairs, and another couple is pressed against the wall, furiously kissing.

"Told you you were wrong about the band kids," Topher says.

"I wonder if they're better kissers because of all that mouth work," Anika muses.

"I'm telling Sophie you said that," I say.

Anika hits me in the arm as we reach the bottom step.

It's warm and muggy down here. There's a foosball table in the middle of the room, and an animated game is happening. Music is blasting, another strobe light is going, and there's a keg in the corner. People are setting up a card table with red solo cups for a game of beer pong a few feet away.

"Anika!" a voice calls, and Sophie makes her way through the crowd to us. Anika tips her head back and kisses Sophie in greeting.

"Thanks for coming," Sophie says to Topher and I.

We both nod. It's awkward for a beat, then Anika grabs Sophie's hand and they join the people dancing in the far corner. Looks like it's just Topher and me.

"So," I say, drawing the word out.

Topher doesn't say anything before walking across the room to the keg. I follow after him, unsure what we're doing. He grabs a solo cup that's already been filled, and brings it to his lips. He makes a disgusted face, but swallows.

"Want to try some?" he asks, holding the cup out to me.

The sour smell crinkles my nose. How do people learn to like this stuff? I shake my head. He shrugs and takes another sip.

"Who wants to play beer pong?" someone yells.

"Me," Topher says, walking up to the table. He gets teamed up with a girl I've seen around school, but can't remember her name. I look around the rest of the room. Anika and Sophie are still dancing, kissing every few seconds. I don't want to stand there next to them, nor do I want to stand and watch Topher. I'm not naïve. I know a lot of people in my school drink. This is just the first time I've seen Topher do it. It's a new line he's crossed that I'm not ready to, at least not tonight with cheap beer.

I wish I was at Quinn's apartment. The party that DJ and I crashed was more fun than this, and it ended in the ER. The lights were on, there was a cookoff, and people were playing videogames. It wasn't a humid room reeking of body odor and spilled beer.

I need fresh air. I try to tell Topher where I'm going, but he's intently watching the other team take their first shot. Whatever. I head up the basement stairs and turn on my phone flashlight at the top. To the right is the kitchen with a sliding door outside. The backyard is lit with twinkling lights strung across a pergola, and solar powered stakes all along the perimeter. A variety of camping chairs have been set up on the patio around a tiny firepit.

That's exactly what drunk teenagers need, an open fire.

Two couples are making out, and a group is vaping in the corner. In the middle of the yard ladder toss is set up. It's so random, but it's something. I cross through the snow and grab the three sets of balls.

"Want to play?" a voice asks from behind me.

I turn around and see a boy standing there. He's about 5'10". From the flickering light of the fire, his blue eyes and earrings sparkle. His beanie is pulled low so I can't see his hair, but he's cute.

"Sure." It's only a game, and if he's weird, I can leave. I've been alone the past two days and wouldn't mind company.

He grabs the other set of balls, then stands by the ladder I'm aiming for.

"What's your name again?" I ask, in case I've met him before.

"Marco," he says, then tosses the first set of balls. They land on the middle ladder rung. "What's yours?"

"Ellie." I toss the balls. It looks like they're going to fly over the ladder completely, but then they miraculously wrap around the top rung.

"What instrument do you play?" Marco asks. His next throw whacks the ladder, but lands on the ground.

"I'm not in the band. My best friend's girlfriend's friend is I think." I throw the balls, and they land on the bottom rung.

He laughs and my cheeks flush with warmth at the sound. "My best friend's girlfriend is in the band too. They dragged me here, then went to make out." His final toss lands on the middle rung.

"Hey, my friends abandoned me too," I say as if that's something to be proud of. His answering grin makes it worth it. I toss my last set and they land on the middle rung.

"You won. Want to—"

Whatever he was going to say is cut off by a girl running over and launching herself into his arms. "Marco, I missssed you," she slurs, lengthening the word.

A guy follows after her. He looks me up and down, then turns to Marco. "You done playing with balls?"

Marco rolls his eyes. In that moment he becomes even more attractive.

"I wanna see your car," the girl says to Marco.

"Later," Marco says.

The other guy walks over and wraps his arm around the girl, pulling her off of Marco. "They're ready, let's go."

"I'll meet you at the cars," Marco says. His friend looks at him a beat too long, then leaves with the girl.

"We're going to Sonic; you want to come?" he asks.

"Sonic? The soda place?" I haven't been there in years.

"Yeah, there's no food here. A bunch of us are going, it should be fun."

He's right about there being no food. I imagine a burger and fries, maybe a shake. It's that, or I can stand in the corner of the muggy basement and wait for my friends to stop sucking each other's faces. "I'll come."

Marco smiles. He holds out a hand. I stare at him. A cute boy has invited me to go to Sonic with him, and now he wants to hold my hand. Is this night real? I've never held hands before, and I'm about to with a guy I just met, who wants to drive me somewhere. This is giving off a few red flags. I could easily take him down if I need too though. I wrap my hand in his. His fingers are freezing against mine.

"Sorry," he apologizes, squeezing his hand tighter around mine.

"It's fine, we'll warm up," I say.

He smiles down at me, and gives my hand a squeeze. Butterflies erupt in my stomach as he leads me back to the house.

When we're inside, the light from the bathroom down the hall illuminates the kitchen. It hits Marco's face, and I take in all his features. His earrings are purple, sparkling again in the faint light. His eyes are blue, and he has dirty blond hair curling out the bottom of his beanie. His face is angular, his cheekbones sharp.

Loud voices come from the bathroom.

"It makes no sense!" Sophie yells.

"I'm sorry," Anika cries. The door closes, and their voices are muffled. We keep walking through the house, passing the lit basement stairs. Topher is standing in the bend of the staircase, making out furiously with someone. I walk faster with Marco, eager to get out of here.

We hurry down the sidewalk to the makeshift parking lot in the open space. Marco leads me to the end of the row, slowing down in front of the last few. The engine of the orange Mustang is running, the headlights lighting our path. Marco's friend from earlier is sitting inside with the girl.

Marco keeps walking, stopping in front of the grey Dodge Challenger Topher parked next to.

"What do you think?" Marco asks, gesturing to the car with our interlocked hands.

I try to respond, but I'm drowned out by the sound of the Mustang revving its engine. The exhaust has been modified and the engine is obnoxiously loud.

The sound reminds me of ride-alongs in Officer Ken's car. There were so many nights we'd be out on patrol, and we'd pass street racers.

"They like to meet up at Sonic and show off their cars, then go out racing," Officer Ken had said.

Marco is about to take me street racing. I drop his hand immediately. I need to get out of here. I search for an escape, but the Mustang's brights flick on and the light makes my eyes water. I look down at the ground, focusing on Marco's shoes. They're purple and black vans, with fraying purple laces.

Was Jake wearing more of a particular color? Maybe green or purple?

I take in all of the details of Marco. The edge of his shirt peeking out of his hoodie is purple. The drawstring of his hoodie is purple too. Either Marco is obsessed with purple, or he's in a gang.

I squint in the light, trying to see his friend better. He has a single dark earring in his ear. It matches Marco's. What are the odds that purple is both of their favorite colors?

You've got to be kidding me. Anika and Topher dragged me out of the house to forget about Jake's death. Yet here I am, with people who might be able to give me some answers.

I start calculating. I don't know these people. Street

racing can turn deadly. I promised everyone that I'd stay safe and stick to research only. Figuring out who killed Jake is not my responsibility.

You're going to get me killed. Jake knew this was coming, and he blamed it on me. My stomach twists into the familiar knot it's been in since I learned about his death. I can walk away right now. Say I left something in the house and not come back. Beg Anika and Topher to take me home, where I'll sit in my room and feel guilty for Jake's death. Wait for Detective Zhao to dig through all of her papers and figure it out.

Or I can try and find him justice.

"It's gorgeous," I say to Marco, grabbing his hand again. He smiles, then leads me to the passenger door which he opens for me. I slide into the leather seat, readying myself.

"What kind of car is this?" I ask when he sits next to me. I know what it is. When I was fourteen, I made a game out of learning makes and models of car, to try and be better at identifying them for police reports. The easily impression-able Ellie who's going to get information wouldn't know that though.

"2009 Dodge Challenger. I've made some modifica-tions." He turns the key in the engine, then hits the gas even though it's still in park. The engine roars.

"Wow," I say, trying to act impressed and not terrified. Images of horrific car accidents I've seen flash in my mind. I double check the seatbelt to see if it locks. The nylon belt pins me in so I can barely move. I reset it, then rub my sweating hands on my thighs.

"Hope you like to go fast," Marco says. He puts the car in drive, then shoots forward. His friend in the Mustang moves so he's right next to us. Marco rolls down his window.

"Ready?" Marco yells over the engines. They both rev

them. Then Marco shoots forward on the wrong side of the road. The Mustang is keeping pace with him.

"Do you do this a lot?" I ask.

"Oh yeah." When we're at the end of the street and the Mustang hugs the turn, Marco is forced to move behind him.

"How do you afford this car? I can barely afford gas."

"I work, a lot."

"I'll have to apply wherever you are," I say.

Marco gives me a crooked grin, then swerves into the next lane, barely missing the Mustang. "I'll let you know if they're hiring."

"What's the name? I can check their website."

Marco frowns, then swerves around a minivan, racing to get in front of it. As soon as he gets back into the original lane, the light turns red and there's no way for him to run it without getting hit, so he stops. So much for his fancy maneuvering getting him ahead.

I need to stop pushing on where he works. What's another vague question I can ask to get information on Jake?

"Are you having fun?" Marco asks.

"Oh yeah," I lie. I absolutely love being in a stranger's car while they drive like a maniac. When can I do it again?

The light turns green and Marco shoots forward, switching lanes in the intersection.

"You shouldn't do that," I warn. Then I cover my mouth. Am I really going to tell him that was an illegal lane switch, while he's *street racing?*

"It's okay to be nervous." He reaches a hand over to rest on my thigh. I move my leg away from his touch. I see the neon Sonic sign down the street. Only two more lights to get through, and I can get out of here. Two more intersections that we could crash in.

"Do you go to Rivers Edge?" I finally ask. I've never seen him around school.

"Yeah, have we met before?"

"I don't think so. It's a wild school, so many people keep dying."

"I know. Although it sounds like a lot of them deserved it," Marco says.

"Did you hear about Jake Peters?" I ask.

The Mustang appears and cuts us off so Marco slams on the brakes. I shoot forward, the seatbelt locking to stop me. Marco swings into the right lane to get around them, but it's a right turn only, so he has to stop suddenly when there's nowhere for him to go. He swerves back into the left lane, cutting someone else off. They honk aggressively.

"I bet this is how Jake Peters died," I try again. I know I'm pushing it. But we're almost to Sonic and my one-on-one time with Marco is almost over.

"Who?" Marco asks.

"Jake Peters. The kid with the stolen cars app."

Marco's jaw twitches, and I swear his hands tighten on the steering wheel. "Never heard of him."

Sure he hasn't. I'm not a lie detector, but his body is practically screaming *liar*.

The Sonic is up on the right, but Marco doesn't turn. I'm instantly on alert.

"You missed it," I say, pointing. Maybe it was a simple mistake.

"I want to go in the back way," he says, still going forward.

I tense. Is he taking me somewhere else? I glance at the doors. They're locked, but there is a button next to my window controls. As long as he doesn't have the child locks on, I should be able to get out of the car at the next light. If that doesn't work, I have my keys in my hoodie pocket, and I could stab him in the eyes with those while reaching over to turn off the locks. Or maybe I should go for the groin...

Marco finally turns right, then right again. He slows down as we approach another entrance into the Sonic parking lot. My body instantly relaxes. He was telling the truth. As he approaches, he keeps revving the engine, and other engines rev in response. He finally turns into the parking lot, all of the cars coming into view.

"Wow," I let out.

"I knew you'd appreciate it," Marco says.

He assumed a lot about me from one game of ladder ball.

I eye all of the cars in the stalls. LED lights glow from undercarriages. Spinner wheels with black and chrome rims whirl. Some cars are bright neon, while others have classic paint jobs like Marco's. I search all of the cars, noting purple accents on quite a few of them. If this is indeed the gang that wears purple like I suspect it is, they are doing a horrible job flying under the radar.

Marco pulls into the row of parking spots at the end of the lot. His friend's Mustang is already there. People are perched on the hoods of their cars, watching us arrive with interest. Marco backs slowly into the spot. My hands are sweating again. I'm about to walk out into potential gang territory, and I have no way to get out of here.

He keeps the engine running, revving it once more. People from the other cars start walking over and he rolls down the window as they approach.

"That car distracts from your ugly face," someone yells.

Marco laughs, then flips them off. He finally pulls the key from the ignition and the door locks click. I can't get my door open fast enough, accidently bumping his friend standing next to me. He frowns.

"I'm so sorry," I start apologizing.

Marco is out of the car and on my side. He reaches his hand out to help me from the car and I reluctantly grab it. Funny how quickly holding hands went from thrilling to repulsive.

"What's your name?" his friend asks, still frowning at me.

"This is Ellie," Marco says.

I should have lied to him back at the party, but I hadn't exactly expected to be going undercover when Marco asked for my name.

His friend takes a step back. "Ellie *Garcia?*"

"Is that your last name?" Marco asks me.

"That's me," I say, trying to act cool. Like it's not something they should be worried about.

Marco's friend does a little head nod to Marco.

"Why don't you go order some food? I'll be right there," Marco says. He points to a couple of picnic tables in the middle of the lot surrounding a menu where you can order.

"Sounds great," I say, smiling extra wide. I walk to the picnic tables, pretending to admire all of the cars on my way. I'm surveying everyone else, assessing whether they might be a threat. None of them look my way, focused solely on the cars.

At the table I look at the menu, positioning myself so I can see Marco out of kylhe corner of my eye. He and his friend are arguing animatedly. They look my way, and I look up and down dramatically at the menu. This is not good. I shake my arms out, loosening up for whatever is next. There's no way I could take them one-on-one with this many potential allies for Marco. I could call the police, but nothing's happened yet. By the time I would need to call, I'm not sure if I'd last long enough for them to get here.

There's always running. Halfway down the block there are backyards with chain link fences facing this way. I could easily hop one of them and then disappear into the dark.

Engines start revving again. I look back toward Marco and his friend. They're not standing where they last were. The headlights of their cars turn on at the same time, and then they peal out of the parking lot. Everyone looks their way as they leave.

They left me here. My legs feel weak. I won't have to fight them, or run for my life. But how am I going to get out of here?

I flip through my contacts. I can't call Anika or Topher. Topher's been drinking, and Anika is busy. My parents are too far away. I don't want to wait here for the twenty plus minutes it would take them to get their shoes on and reach me. I look up and down the street for somewhere safer I could wait. I'm on the edge of the college campus. It's 9:45 on a Saturday night. There's no way any of those places are still open. But I do have two friends who live nearby in student housing.

I dial Kacey and wait for it to ring.

TWENTY

A RED JEEP PULLS UP NEXT TO THE PICNIC TABLES AND rolls the window down.

"Get in loser," Quinn says.

I've never been so relieved to see his face. I jump into the car and slam the door behind me, then press the lock button. "Get out of here."

Quinn goes without question, turning out onto the main road. I turn around, checking to see if anyone follows us. They don't. I slump into the seat, letting myself relax as the heat blows onto my face.

"Where's Kacey?" I finally ask.

"I already had my boots on, so she sent me," Quinn says.

He did get here extraordinarily fast. "Thank you."

"What happened back there?" he asks.

"Can we get some food first? It's been a night."

He drives to McDonalds and orders a small feast for us. Then he parks in the lot under the street light. I take a few bites of my burger before I tell him that my friends abandoned me at the party, everyone was making out, and I was bored and hungry so I accepted a ride to Sonic except it turned out to be a group of street racers. He's quiet, slowly sipping on his chocolate shake the entire time. When I finish, he grabs a few fries and chews them while looking out the front window.

"You have nothing to say?" I finally ask.

"That's what you get for going to a band kid party when you're not in the band," he replies.

"What?" I laugh.

"Band kids are extremely horny, and sometimes nerdy, of course it was going to be an awkward make-out fest. Everyone knows that."

"I didn't, and I'm pretty sure Topher and Anika didn't either," I protest. "Were you in band?"

"What do you think?" he asks, waggling his eyebrows.

"Eww."

He laughs. "I wasn't. One of my sisters was though, and she blacklisted me from all band parties."

"She didn't want you to see her making out with everyone?"

"Don't remind me," he shudders. "So how are these street racers connected to Jake's death?"

I choke on the sip of shake I was taking. "What do you mean?" I rasp once I catch my breath.

He tilts his head and raises his eyebrows. "There's no way you wouldn't have known exactly what those guys were the second you saw their cars and heard where they were going."

"Maybe Marco was super-hot and I wanted to go make out with him," I shoot back.

The corner of his mouth twitches. "If that was the case you wouldn't be with me right now."

"Maybe I'm on a self-destructive streak. Not everything I do is an investigation," I huff.

His face hardens. "Are you?" he asks quietly.

"No, of course not."

He looks out the window. "What have the past three months been like? You wouldn't say the other night, and I can't stop thinking about it."

"Why?" Why would he have been thinking about me that much?

He's still looking out the window. "I feel guilty for disappearing when you were going through something."

Ahh. He doesn't have secret feelings for me. He's just a good guy. "I'm fine now. I'm not trying to get hurt. I was trying to get information on Jake's death, and I thought Marco might be able to give me some."

I see the reflection of his lips twitching into a smile in the window. What could he possibly find funny?

He finally turns to look at me. "I'll tell you what I know about Jake's death if you tell me."

He was smiling because he thought of a way to bribe me for the information he wants. Of course. "What about the neck beard pictures?" I tease.

"You can see those too."

I haven't told anyone all of the details, not even Anika or Topher. They've both been so worried about me. And, I don't think they'd get it. Anika was there that day, but she didn't see everything. She didn't have to make the decisions I did, or wait to hear someone scream in pain, desperately hoping it wasn't Quinn. Whenever people ask about the confrontation at the river, it's an exciting story for her to tell.

Her eyes light up and she starts talking animatedly, ready to entertain and explain how she drove in and saved us all. Which is true.

I do everything in my power not to think about that day, or what's happened afterwards. Shoving it down hasn't been working. Maybe telling one person, one who will truly get it because he was there, will take away some of its power.

Quinn rests his hand on mine. Unlike when Marco tried to in his car, I let him.

"You don't have to tell me. I'll tell you what you want to know, and I'll even show you the neck beard pictures."

"No. I want to tell someone. It's just, heavy." I roll my shoulders back and get comfier in my seat.

"I was fine at first. Then the panic attacks started. I've had anxiety my whole life, but these were something else. I'd wake up in the middle of the night and feel like I was dying. Like I'd never be able to breathe again. Some nights I'd wake up shaking like I had a fever, or feel so sick I'd spend the whole night in the bathroom.

"They started getting more frequent, and not only at night time. I never knew when one was coming, and it felt like I was crawling through every day, looking over my shoulder for the next one. I tried to act normal, to keep pretending nothing was different. Then there was the Pathfinder competition."

I can feel Quinn's gaze on me, but I don't look at him. If I'm going to get this out, I can't get distracted by whatever expression is on his face. I focus on the flickering streetlamp outside the front window.

"We were in the middle of the SWAT scenario. Our team was doing great, when I heard a faint popping in the distance. There was a shooting competition going on in a different part of the building. I knew that in the back of my mind; I've competed in it before. But in that moment, something took over me and I was right back at the riverbank. I panicked and took off running in the wrong direction. Everyone who was behind me followed after me, and it caused mass confusion. We lost the competition and everyone was furious with me, but I didn't even care."

My chest is tight and my heart is starting to race. I close my eyes and take a deep breath, noticing my feet on the floor of the Jeep. I'm not there. I'm safe. I'm here with Quinn. He squeezes my hand in his, his fingers warm against my freezing ones.

"Something inside me broke that day. I spent the majority of last summer planning for the Pathfinders competitions. I almost got my entire team suspended from school for doing a practice SWAT scenario there. I'd been trying *so* hard to get back to normal, but failing that competition so badly, it felt like I was never going to get there. That all of my plans for the future were ruined. For the first time I felt hopeless. And then this thought popped in my head, that it'd be better if I wasn't here. Then I wouldn't have to feel like this anymore."

Quinn makes a sound in his throat, and his fingers squeeze mine even tighter.

I keep going. It's almost all out. "I went straight to my parents. Those thoughts terrified me. They took me to the ER, and I did this long assessment with a social worker. They said those were intrusive thoughts based on the fact they scared me and were unwanted. They had me set up an appointment with a psychiatrist later that week, and I started an anti-anxiety medication. I started seeing a different therapist, but with waitlists I can only go every few weeks.

"I've slowly started crawling out of that dark place and feeling like a human again. I'm still having panic attacks; mostly at Pathfinders. Oh, and one at your apartment. But looking into these stolen cars is the first time I've felt like myself in a while."

It's out. All of it.

I glance at Quinn out of the corner of my eyes. He's staring out the windshield, running his free hand through his hair. His other is still tightly holding mine.

"Thank you for sharing that with me," he finally says.

"Please don't pity me, or look at me different—" I start.

He turns to look at me, his eyes and mouth wide. "Why would I pity you? You went through all of that, and kept going. When it felt like you couldn't anymore, you were brave enough to ask for help. I, I don't have words."

Hearing that from someone who didn't birth me hits different. I squeeze his hand back.

"You're so strong, and the world better watch out for you."

I snort.

"Too cheesy?" he asks.

"Definitely. Now hand over the neck beard."

He pulls his phone out and starts scrolling through it, then passes it to me. I stare at the photo of him in his bathroom, leaning over the sink to get closer to the mirror. He actually has some decent scruff on his face, but his neck is covered in a patchy monstrosity of different lengths. It all surrounds the red scar in the middle of his neck, just below his Adam's apple. I scroll through the next photos, seeing the beard from different angles. From closer up, I can see the puckered skin of the scar.

"Did she cut you more than once?" I ask him. The scar isn't one clean slice.

He inhales sharply. "Yeah, she was moving it around while she was talking."

I nod, checking in with my body. Just the sight of that healed scar had me panicking weeks ago. What will learning more details about it do? This conversation has been removing a scab and waiting to see if the wound will start bleeding again. Or, if it's healed enough to stay closed.

I wait one breath. Two. Nothing happens. I feel tired, but also lighter. I'm not going to have a panic attack.

I hand Quinn his phone back, my own buzzing in my pocket. I ignore it.

Quinn studies me. "Jake was shot multiple times in the chest sometime between 5 and 7pm on February 8th. It was a .22 caliber bullet."

Now I'm the one with my mouth open wide. When he said he was going to tell me what he knew, I figured he'd give one of his vague, 'it may or may not be,' hints. Not all of these details.

"February 8th, between 5 and 7pm, with a .22 caliber," I repeat.

"Patty is going to kill me," Quinn groans, looking up at the roof of his car.

I pat his hand. "She'll never find out. I learned from my mistakes, remember?"

"You won't be jumping out of cars to confront suspects?" he says with a smirk.

I put a hand to my chest. "I would never."

My phone starts buzzing incessantly in my back pocket. It makes a grating noise pressed against the worn leather seats of the Jeep. I pull it out, Anika's picture staring at me on the screen.

"Hello?" I answer.

"Ellie?" her voice shakes. Then she sniffles. "Where are you? I can't find you."

"What's wrong?" It sounds like she's been crying, which she rarely does. This is serious.

"I need you," she sobs.

TWENTY-ONE

Saturday February 11th 10:50PM

Topher's truck is waiting on the curb in front of my house. Quinn parks in front of it. When I approach, Anika hops out of the driver's seat of the truck. In the streetlight, I can see her mascara-stained cheeks covered in tear tracks.

"What happened?" I ask. She wouldn't elaborate on the phone.

She shakes her head. "We've got to get him out of here." She points to the backseat of the truck. I lean through the open door and see Topher slumped over; his seatbelt twisted around him awkwardly.

"Topher, wake up," I say.

He moans into the seat. At least we know he's conscious.

"Come on, get up," I try.

"Go away," Topher says, the words blending into each other.

I step back and look at Anika, and Quinn, who's joined us. Quinn peeks into the car.

"Topher, you okay?" he asks.

The sound of Quinn's voice does something to Topher. He starts making a choking sound. I'm about to hop in and start the Heimlich when Topher sits himself up enough that the sound changes into laughter.

"Of course you're here," he slurs.

"I missed you," Quinn says. "Let's get you out of there." He reaches into the car for Topher, awkwardly grabbing his shoulders, then his hand, as he navigates Topher out of the back seat. Topher has to climb up past the driver's seat to get out, banging his head on the horn twice. He almost falls to the ground, and Quinn and I both catch him, lowering him to the sidewalk where he sits.

"How did you get him in here?" I ask Anika.

"You don't want to know," she sniffs.

I really do, though. The mechanics of it aren't adding up.

"Now what?" Quinn asks.

I glance at my house. "We see how serious my parents were when they said I could come to them with anything."

The nice thing about having a brother who just got out of jail for manslaughter? This is nothing in comparison. I'm not even the one who's drunk. I reach down for Topher's hand to help him back to his feet.

"I don't want to," he says. "I'm mad at you."

"For what?" I ask.

Quinn puts a hand on my arm. "He's drunk, don't listen to him."

I ignore Quinn. If this is what it takes for Topher to finally tell me why he's been so weird lately, I'll take it. I sit down on the curb next to him, the smell of stale beer and sweat overpowering me.

"Why are you mad at me?" I ask.

"Everything snot about you," he says. His head is swaying, but he looks me directly in the eyes as he says it.

"I know it's not," I say. Is that what he really thinks about me? Is that how I act?

"He's drunk," Quinn warns again.

"I'm not going to make it in college," Topher says, putting his hands over his face. Anika settles down on the curb on Topher's other side. She's sniffling and wiping her eyes.

"Of course you are. I heard you got a pretty big scholarship to CU Boulder. That's impressive," I say.

Topher makes a strangled noise. "I failed a pop quiz in high school. I'm going to fail college and they'll take the money back and I'll have to be a cop like my dad," Topher says solemnly, pausing in between every two words.

"No you won't," Anika says.

"Lieutenant Sssanders keeps telling me that I'm a natural and they could use someone like me. I have to."

"No, you don't. You deserve to do what makes you happy. So go to Boulder and try. You can't give up already," I say.

"You think I can do it?" Topher asks, head wobbling between Anika and me.

"Yes, you can do anything," I say, reaching for his hand to squeeze.

"You've got this Topher," Anika adds, grabbing his other hand.

Topher looks back and forth between the two of us. He pulls his hands out from ours, then wraps his arms around us in a hug.

"I'm going to misssssss you. It's all ending," he whispers.

Anika starts crying again. I lean forward and wrap my free arm around her so we're all in a group hug on the curb. I squeeze them to me, holding tight. Everything is going to change, but we're still here now.

"Topher, you smell," Anika finally says, pulling out of the hug.

"You suck," Topher says, trying to lightly punch her in the arm. She easily dodges it.

Topher looks around, spotting Quinn. He points at him. "You."

"It's me," Quinn says.

"Ellie was soooo sad. Now she's getting happy again. I don't want you to ruin it," Topher says.

"That's not going to happen, I promise," Quinn says.

Topher stares at Quinn with glassy eyes. Then he looks back at me.

"What is going on out here?" my mom's voice comes from behind us. Her and my dad are standing on the driveway, wrapping their robes around themselves like this is a teen movie. The motion activated light on the garage turns on, burning all of our eyes.

"Nothing," I say, my voice cracking.

My parents start shuffling down the driveway, joining us.

"Is he drunk?" my dad asks, pointing to Topher.

"Noooooo," Topher slurs, super convincingly.

"Why are you here?" my mom asks, her eyes narrowing at Quinn.

"I wanted to leave the party and I called Kacey, but then Quinn already had his shoes on, so he came—"

"Who is Kacey?" my mom asks.

"You're in college. You shouldn't be hanging out with high schoolers," my dad says to Quinn.

"I wasn't sir, I was just trying to help," Quinn stammers.

"Can we go inside? I'm freezing," Anika says.

"Of course." My mom wraps her arm around Anika, and starts leading her to the house. My dad and Quinn are helping Topher off the sidewalk. I go into the house, the warmth inside a welcome relief.

"I need to know so we can best help. Who was drinking?" my mom asks.

"Only Topher," Anika says. "I tried a sip of beer but I hated it," she adds when my mom doesn't immediately answer.

"Thank you. And you, Ellie?" she asks, focusing on me now.

"I didn't have anything. Everyone was drinking and making out, and I was bored, which is why I was trying to leave."

That answer must satisfy her, because she moves on. "How much did Topher drink?"

"No idea. I wasn't paying attention to him," Anika says, her voice cracking on the last word. She covers her face with her hands and starts crying again. My mom walks through the house, flipping on all the lights as she looks for tissues. I lead Anika to the couch, and wrap a blanket around her.

My dad, Quinn, and Topher stumble through the doorway. They deposit Topher on the other couch, and Topher immediately lies down.

"How much did you drink?" Dad asks Topher.

"I'm bad at beer pong," he laughs. Then keeps on laughing. My best friends are going through the entire spectrum of emotions, feet apart from each other.

Mom returns with the tissues, and a glass of something. It's bright pink.

"Drink this," she says to Topher, handing him the glass. "It has electrolytes in it to help prevent a hangover."

"Should we be worried about alcohol poisoning?" Dad asks her in a hushed tone.

"I can't remember the symptoms," she whispers back, loudly.

"He's still conscious, hasn't vomited, and his breathing looks fine," Quinn says from his spot near the door.

My parents both look at him.

"Thank you," Mom says at the same time Dad says, "I'm slightly worried that you know that off the top of your head."

"He works for the coroner," Mom replies.

"And he's underage in college," Dad hisses. "Do you like him or not, make up your mind."

My cheeks flame. My sorta-kinda-I-should-give-it-up crush is standing here in my living room. With my parents in their pajamas. While they argue about him. "Let me walk you out," I say to Quinn.

"You stay here," Dad snaps.

"I've got it. See you later, Ellie. Anika, Topher. Mr. and Mrs. Garcia." Quinn ducks his head, then walks out the door. I go over and lock it.

"What was that?" I say, completely exasperated. "That was so embarrassing! We could all hear you."

"Sorry. This is the first time we've dealt with this," Mom says, waving her hands to gesture to the living room. Anika is still crying, and Topher is making faces as he slowly sips at his pink drink.

"We have to call his parents," Dad says. "I don't want them coming after me if they find out we covered this up."

Topher moans. "Please, let me stay."

My parents share a look. "Sorry Topher. It'll be okay." Mom grabs my hand and pulls me away from everyone else.

"What's going on with Anika? Is she hurt?" Mom whispers.

I glance at Anika, remembering Sophie's raised voice in the kitchen. "I think she got into an argument with Sophie."

Mom digests that. "She can stay the night then. Why don't you two go upstairs? We'll take care of Topher."

I pick at my fingernail. I don't want to abandon him.

"Oh no," Topher groans, then starts stumbling to the bathroom.

He doesn't need me to hold his hair back. I grab Anika's hand and lead her up the staircase.

I get Anika pajamas and an extra toothbrush. She locks herself in the bathroom and comes out a few minutes later looking slightly better. The mascara is off her cheeks, but her eyes are still red and puffy from all the crying. She jumps up on my bed and I settle in next to her, pulling the blankets up to my chin. It's been forever since we've had a sleepover just the two of us.

"Spill," I command.

Anika pulls the blanket over her head. "Sophie thinks I'm embarrassed to be dating her," she says, her voice muffled.

"Why would she think that?"

"Because I haven't told my parents about her yet."

"It's only been a week, right?"

"Exactly!" Anika says, pulling the blanket off her head. "She thinks that's a red flag though."

"Maybe if you were hiding it from everyone, but you're not."

"I said that too. This is why we're best friends," she says.

I smile back. "Why haven't you told your family?"

She twirls the loose threads on my quilt. "Our family lost so many people last year. I don't want to introduce them to her, and then lose her if we can't make it work."

"Did you tell her that?"

She swipes at her eyes. "I tried. But she didn't believe me." She sighs. "I think she's going to break up with me."

"If she does, she's ridiculous. You're amazing, loving, feisty, kind, silly, a musical connoisseur."

She gives a small smile.

"Gorgeous, loyal, passionate. Do I need to keep going?"

She whacks me with a pillow. "I get it. Thank you."

Voices sound from downstairs. I recognize the deep tone of Topher's dad. There's no yelling, so that's good.

"Do you think he'll forgive us?" I ask.

Anika snorts. "He's the one who kept going with the beers. If you're going to drink that much your first time, don't be mad when we can't cover for you."

"True. I'm glad he finally told us what's wrong though."

"It breaks my heart he feels like he shouldn't go for his dreams," Anika says.

"Space isn't going to know what hit it," I say.

"Let's hope it doesn't throw meteorites at us in retaliation," Anika says.

"You are so strange; do you know that?"

"It's part of why you love me," she says, tossing her hair over her shoulder. "So, why were you with Quinn?"

I tell her about my short-lived experience with street racing. She sits up on her knees, practically bouncing.

"You were out with a *gang*? That's amazing."

I squint at her. "That's not how I would have described it."

She waves a hand at that. "This is great. Now you have more leads into Jake's death."

"I never said I was investigating that."

Anika rolls her eyes. "I'm going to help you. Let's make a murder board."

"No. I'm not letting anyone else get hurt."

She snorts. "So you're going to do it all by yourself?" When I don't respond, she snorts again. "You actually think you can do this alone? This has been a group project since day one. Sophie told you about it, Kacey got you involved, Sandra connected you with Jake, Quinn's girlfriend helped you find the thieves, need I go on? You can't pretend to be all noble and insist that no one else can help you."

I open my mouth to argue, but she puts a finger on my lips.

"Shhh. We're not going to war. We're writing things on a piece of paper and googling stuff. Let me have this."

I pick at the side of my fingernail again. Then I get up from the bed and grab a fresh notebook.

THINGS WE KNOW

Jake is dead

He said that he owed a gang money and they were going to hurt him

He was shot on 2/8/23 between 5 and 7pm

He was shot with a .22 caliber bullet (potentially a rifle)

He was working with Mason and Devon.

Mason claims he wasn't involved with the app.

Devon is out of the country

Detective Zhao wanted leads that weren't them

Detective Zhao asked about Jake wearing green or purple

There are two gangs in town—the Serpents (green) and Royals (purple)

There is a street racing crew that meets up at Sonic

A lot of them wear the color purple which may hint they are Royals

Marco had a nice car, and was cryptic about how he paid for it

"We can work with this," Anika grins. "Now let's plan next steps."

TWENTY-TWO

Sunday February 12th 4:00PM

Burnt cauliflower is one of the most disgusting smells I've been forced to experience, and I've smelt corpses. I'm opening all the windows on the first floor of the house while my parents argue about grabbing more cauliflower to try again. They're so wrapped up in that riveting debate, they don't hear the knock at the door. It's Evan. Normally I'd yell at them to get it, but I'm already on shaky ground with the events of last night, so I suck it up and open it.

Evan is standing there with flowers in one hand and a Tupperware container in the other. He's wearing an ivory sweater and nice jeans, his hair gelled back. When he walks in, I'm hit with the smell of cedar and musk. Why's he wearing cologne and dressed so nicely? It's the *Superbowl*. I peer behind him into the dark, expecting a date to appear. He's alone.

"What'd they burn?" he asks as he shrugs out of his coat and hangs it up.

"Buffalo cauliflower. Why are you dressed so nice?"

"Because I can. Here's some buffalo cauliflower I made," he says, shaking his container.

"Dad, you don't have to go to the store," I yell.

My parents walk out of the kitchen and come into view. They see Evan and practically run over to him. When Evan hands Mom the flowers, she gasps and immediately tears up.

"You didn't have to bring me flowers," she says.

"I know, I'm catching up on all the times I couldn't."

She wipes at the corner of her eye before returning to the kitchen in search of a vase.

"I made buffalo cauliflower," Evan says, handing the container to Dad.

"Oh thank goodness," Dad claps Evan on the back before taking the container into the kitchen. We follow after him.

"This all looks amazing," Evan says. "What can I help with?"

Mom is back with her flowers in a vase. "We grabbed most of it at the new bougie grocery store. We were up late last night and too tired to cook."

"Out partying?" Evan teases.

"Ellie was," Dad says. "And then she showed up with her drunk friends and Quinn."

My cheeks heat up. "Only Topher was drunk," I mumble.

"That's nice they felt safe coming here," Evan says.

"True, but..." Dad starts.

"Why don't you two go watch the game?" Mom interrupts.

"It's not on yet," I say.

Mom widens her eyes and tilts her head dramatically. It takes me a second to realize she's trying to get me out of this awkward conversation about the party last. Would I rather hear what my dad has to say, or hang out alone with Evan? I've already been forced to listen to play-by-play updates of how Topher's first hangover has been as Dad texts with Topher's dads. Spoiler alert- there's been lots of vomiting. With the burnt cauliflower smell still in the house, I can't stomach to hear any more. Hanging out with Evan it is.

Maybe the commercials will have started.

I grab a few of my jalapeño poppers, chips, dip, and a single piece of the buffalo cauliflower before settling on one of the couches. Evan grabs the armchair, his own plate completely full of the vegan appetizers we found.

We chew in silence as sports commentators talk about statistics. The commercials haven't even started yet.

"I start a new job next week. It's in a restaurant," Evan says finally.

"Will you be okay with that and your values?" I ask. Then I want to hit myself in the face. Why can't I make normal conversation with him?

He smirks. "Am I really the first vegan you've met?"

"No. There are two who get into yelling matches over whether honey is an animal product or not, and then hand out pamphlets about how smart pigs are."

"Sounds intense," Evan says. "The restaurant I got a job at is vegan, so I guess I'll have to find somewhere else to hand out my flyers on the health benefits of the lifestyle." His face is completely serious. Then the corner of his mouth twitches upwards.

"Shut up," I laugh.

"Maybe I'll be able to give Mom and Dad some cooking tips next time I'm here," Evan says with a smile.

I roll my eyes. "I doubt restaurants use air fryers."

"What?" he asks.

"I forgot; you weren't here when those came out." I give him a rundown on air fryers, and instant pots, even though those are dying out. He stares at me wide-eyed the entire time.

"If I had those, I'd never go out to eat," he says in awe.

"That's what Mom and Dad said too. And yet this is their second time using it."

Evan laughs. I try the buffalo cauliflower he made. At first, it's delightful. A crunch, the buffalo sauce. But then the aftertaste of the cauliflower hits. It still tastes like cauliflower. I chew it as quickly as I can, then get rid of the taste with a jalapeño popper.

"What's the weirdest thing you didn't expect since getting out?" I ask. I'm ready for him to say TikTok.

"How overwhelming the grocery store is," he says.

"What?"

"There's so many options and it makes my head spin. I have to make a million different choices for every single item on my list."

"You should try grocery pickup," I suggest.

"Isn't that expensive?" he asks.

"No, it's free if you go there. Delivery costs money."

He looks wary.

"Give me your phone, I'll help you make an account."

He moves onto the couch next to me and hands it over. It doesn't take long until he's set up, with items in his cart to grab tomorrow.

"Thank you. Truly. I hate how much I don't know," he says quietly.

"No problem, it was easy."

"If I can repay the favor, let me know."

I laugh, thinking there's no way he'll be able to teach me something. Unless... Anika and I brainstormed next steps. If we can find Marco at school tomorrow, we'll try to get information out of him. We'll only approach him if we're in the school, in a public area, for our safety. The odds of us randomly finding him under those circumstances are slim.

Evan has been in jail the last five years though, and he mentioned that his cellmate was in a gang. Maybe he can help me.

"I ended up abandoned at Sonic last night," I say.

"Wait, what?"

"I went to a party with Topher and Anika, but they went off with other people. I met this guy and he invited me to go to Sonic with him and his friends. They seemed nice and I was hungry and bored so I went with them. But then he and his friends left me there."

Evan turns on the couch, facing me. "You could have gotten hurt. Why would you do that?"

I wave a hand. "I was fine. I can handle myself."

"Maybe things have changed, but on Saturday nights all the street racers go to Sonic to hang out."

"That explains all the nice cars," I say, pretending I didn't already know that. Supposed female incompetence makes a great weapon.

Evan looks around, checking on where my parents are. They're still far away in the kitchen. "Not all of them are, but some of those racers are gang members. Promise me you'll never do that again."

"None of them looked like gang members," I say.

Evan sighs. "You probably didn't know what to look for."

"What should I look for?" I ask.

"Don't go in cars with strangers, and you won't have to worry about it," he says.

I pretend to be thinking really hard about something. "They said that kid who died at my school was using a gang to steal cars. Do you think those are the people who were doing it?"

"Who knows. There are multiple in this city, and their territories have been shifting because of housing going up."

"Yeah, I heard there's the Royals, and the Serpents. Which one do you think would have been more likely to help with stealing cars?"

Evan's eyes immediately narrow. That was too specific of a question. He's onto me.

"Wow," he says, leaning into the back of the couch, away from me. "I can't believe I fell for it."

"Fell for what?" I ask. If I keep denying, I can get out of this.

"For a second, I thought that we were getting somewhere. But all you want is information from your screwup brother."

Guilt slithers into the pit of my stomach. "No, I didn't say that."

"I'm not an idiot. You didn't randomly happen to get stranded at Sonic; you were investigating that kid's death, weren't you? And you're hoping that I have inside knowledge about the gangs so you can keep digging." He turns so he's facing me again, getting closer to my face. "I know you solved the killings last year, but that was different. You know nothing about the world you're stepping into. These aren't the type of people you mess with and get to just walk away."

I scoot backwards on the couch, putting distance

between us. "It's partially my fault Jake was killed. I'm the one who went digging, who uncovered the app he was running, and then talked to a journalist. He told me I was going to get him killed, and then he was. I need to find out who did it, and if you have insights into whether the Royals or the Serpents would have worked with him, that would help."

He shakes his head. "I'm not helping you get yourself killed."

I look up at the ceiling, blowing out a breath. "Stop being so dramatic. You have no idea what I'm capable of."

"And you have no idea what you're asking about. Sorry, your degenerate of a brother isn't helping you." He stands up suddenly and goes off into the kitchen. I hear dishes clanging in the sink and water turning on.

"You don't have to do that, we'll get it later," I hear Mom saying.

"No, I've got it." His voice is clipped and hard. He's furious.

My parents walk out of the kitchen. I can feel their eyes on me, trying to figure out what's going on.

"Did something happen?" Dad asks in a low voice.

"Nope," I say, staring straight ahead.

Mom joins Evan in the kitchen, talking to him softly. I can't hear him answering. Dad looks between the living room and the kitchen, trying to decide where to go. Does he sit with the kid he can see every day, or the one he just got back?

"I have a paper I need to write," I say, making the decision for him. "Thanks for the food." I rush up the stairs, getting away from it all. From the look of hurt I put on Evan's face. From knowing which of us my parents would rather be with. From that tiny glimpse of having a relation-ship with my brother I just destroyed.

TWENTY-THREE

Monday February 13th 1:10PM

"I THINK HE'S ALONE," I SAY, SCANNING THE LIBRARY once more.

"Mission is a go," Anika whispers.

All day we've been taking opposite sides of the school, trying to find Marco. I wondered if he'd lied about actually going here, until I checked the parking lot. His Dodge Charger was parked in the very back of the farthest lot, next to the orange Mustang. It was only a matter of time until we found him. Unless he spent his whole day in the boy's bathroom.

Anika finally spotted Marco leaving the cafeteria, so we both ditched sixth period and followed him all the way here, to the library. He's settled in a circular chair, his legs draped over the side, laughing at something on his phone. He's still wearing the purple earrings, shoes, and hoodie drawstring. There's no one else around him as he keeps scrolling on his phone and laughing.

Evan's warnings echo in my head, but I ignore them. Marco's scrolling in the school library. He can't so much as speak too loudly in here without getting in trouble. I scan his body for any suspicious bulges that might be a weapon. If he has a knife hidden in his pockets, it'll take him a moment to reach it from the way he's sitting. By then I'll have dragged Anika through the shelves back to the exit.

I can do this. I think.

Anika starts walking to him, and I force my legs to follow her. Marco looks up as we approach, and swings his legs so his feet are back on the ground.

"Where are you going?" Anika asks.

"I've got class," Marco says, starting to stand.

"We need to talk," I say.

He's standing now. "I've got to go."

I press down on his shoulder, shoving him easily back into the chair. "You left me at Sonic, at night, in the middle of winter. You owe me a conversation."

His eyes flare with emotion and he's about to stand up again. I take a step closer to him, crossing my arms over my chest and glaring. Anika does the same, creating a human shield between him and the rest of the library. His eyes flit between Anika and I. Then he sighs dramatically, settling back into the chair. His amethyst earrings shimmer with the movement.

"What?" he spits out.

I can't believe I thought he was cute for a few minutes. I blame it on the loneliness and the dark. "Why'd you leave me like that?"

"Why'd you lie about who you were?" he shoots back.

"I didn't. I told you my name is Ellie."

He snorts. "You left out the part where you're a wanna-be cop."

"Why would you be so worried about that? We were just playing ladder toss and then getting some food."

He wraps his arms across his chest. "Come on. You were practically interrogating me in the car."

"I didn't know we were going street racing when you invited me to get fries. I was hungry." It's the truth. I had no idea until I saw the cars.

He simply glares at me.

Anika places a hand on my arm. "Look, you both didn't say much to each other, and then went for a drive. Not the smartest thing to do. I know Ellie didn't agree to go with you initially because she thought she could get information from you. She thought you were cute and wanted a chance to get to know you better."

I nudge her in the ribs with my elbow. Telling him that was *not* part of the plan. He raises an eyebrow like he's not buying it.

"And then she realized you might know a thing or two about something she was interested in. But you could have easily killed her street racing, and it was a jerk move to desert her in the dark. You owe her," Anika finishes.

"I don't owe you anything," Marco says. He leans forward to grab his backpack from the ground.

"Just one question. Please? Then I promise to pretend I have no idea who you are," I say.

He doesn't say anything, slowly slipping on his backpack straps. He hasn't left yet.

Anika suddenly ducks to the ground.

"What are you doing?" I hiss.

"My sociology class is walking in here," she whispers.

I look to the doorway, and sure enough, her teacher is walking in along with the rest of her class. They're filing toward the bank of computers on the back wall. Anika starts crawling on the floor to hide behind some shelves.

Marco is shaking his head, getting up to leave for real now that we're distracted.

"Were the Royals helping Jake steal cars?" I ask in a rush.

Marco freezes, his expression turning angry. "We would never jack cars for that idiot."

"Do you know who would?" I ask.

He finally stands all the way up from the chair, towering over me. He seems taller than he did a few minutes ago when Anika was still standing next to me. "You better watch yourself," he says, his voice low.

"Or what?" I challenge.

He leans down, his face inches from mine. His energy-drink-breath reeks. "You don't want to know." He jumps toward me, trying to be intimidating.

I barely stifle a laugh. The jump was too much. I place a hand on his chest and push him out of my way. I head down the rows of stacks to where Anika disappeared.

I know Marco alone isn't what's dangerous. It's him and any other gang members together. If I angered him enough right now, he could ask them all to go after me. But I can't take him seriously with that wannabe scary behavior. If that puts a bigger target on my back, then it is what it is.

TWENTY-FOUR

Monday February 13th 6:10PM

"What is the first step of a traffic stop?" Lieutenant Sanders asks.

We're standing in the middle of a football field. Except, instead of the grass being surrounded by a track, it has a ring of asphalt painted like a road. An old police cruiser is parked across from us. Farther down the road is a beaten up 90's Ford Taurus. I bounce up and down on my tiptoes, looking between the cars. I'm going to drive the cruiser and do a real traffic stop. This never would have been a possibility with my old Pathfinders team, but the Loveland office has access to resources we didn't.

I glance around the group, my eyes landing on Topher. I smile at him, and he gives me a small one in return. He's finally feeling better today, and had a long talk with his dads once he sobered up. He seems like a weight has lifted, and I'm relieved.

I catch Jamie's eye while looking around, and he quickly looks away from me.

"You report the car's information to dispatch," Layla says, answering Lieutenant Sanders' question. "You want a record of all the vehicles you interact with in case it becomes a dangerous situation." She starts going over the details, and I zone out again. I just want to drive already.

"Jamie and Layla, can you demonstrate for the group how we're going to do the traffic stop?" Officer Sanders asks.

Without even talking to each other, Jamie starts walking to the cruiser while Layla goes to the Taurus farther down the loop. Jamie winks at me when he passes. I don't know what he's so smug about; I'll get to drive the cruiser right after him. He turns on the lights, and then the sirens moments later. We all take a step backward in the grass, even though we're nowhere near the asphalt.

He zooms past us, and then stops a good distance behind the Taurus. He turns the tires so they're facing the left. The sirens stop blaring, but the lights are still flashing. The brights come on, exposing the slight mist in the evening air.

The radio on Lieutenant Sanders hip starts talking. Jamie is saying the license plate number of the vehicle. Lieutenant Sanders replies that there are no warrants, and he's clear to approach.

Jamie gets out of the car and starts walking toward the Taurus where Layla is sitting, pretending to be the driver. He walks outside of the light of the high beams, so the driver won't be able to see him coming. He reaches the car and raps on the window, standing slightly behind so he can get a look inside to see if there are any visible weapons. Layla hands him her wallet, and then Jamie starts walking back toward the cruiser. Lieutenant Sanders calls for them to come back and join the group.

"Great job. Did you notice that he turned the tires outwards so if he needs to pull into traffic quickly to pursue a fleeing suspect, he can? The tires can also act as a sort of a barricade if someone were to start firing at him," Lieutenant Sanders explains.

I raise my hand in the air.

"Ellie?" Lieutenant Sanders asks.

"It's also a good idea to touch a few places on the vehicle like the trunk and side so that if the car were to flee, there would be some fingerprint evidence that he had been there," I say.

Jamie narrows his eyes at me. I give a neutral look back. If he doesn't want me to correct him, he shouldn't have made a mistake.

"Very good, thank you Ellie," Lieutenant Sanders says, looking slightly amused.

Layla gives instructions on how we're going to simulate traffic stops. When we aren't in the cars, there's an obstacle course in the middle of the grass field for us to practice on. "Ellie, Topher, you two go in the cruiser first," she finishes.

"Did Jamie say something he likes about me?" I ask. She said we'd be partners on everything until we could say something we liked about the other.

Layla smirks. "No. You both have never done this before so Lieutenant Sanders wanted to show you together. Why? Do you have something you'd like to report?"

I mean, he was pretty nice at paintball. But I'm not going to be the first one to break.

Lieutenant Sanders asks to look at our licenses one last time, and walks with Topher and I to the cruiser.

"Ellie, why don't you go first, and then Topher." She hops into the passenger seat, and Topher is forced to sit in the back. I wasn't expecting to have her sitting there, watching my every move, but it'll have to do. I'm going to *drive* a real cruiser, not simply sit inside one. I rub my hands up and down on the steering wheel. Pieces of old cracked leather peel away, and I let go. I can't break anything today. I look around the controls, locating where the lights and sirens are in this vehicle. I adjust the mirrors and seat, double checking them. With nothing else to adjust, it's time to do this.

"Pull up over there," Lieutenant Sanders points.

"Of course." I put the car in gear, but not enough, so it's in neutral. I try again, the car jerking slightly until I get the shifter in the right gear. I swear softly. I have to get this. I can't give anyone ammo to say I'm not cut out for this, or make a sexist joke. I can practically hear Jamie's remarks in my head.

"Don't worry about anyone else. This is your first time," Lieutenant Sanders soothes.

I move the shifter back to park, then start over. Finally in drive, I approach the Taurus slowly. I stop a good forty feet behind the Taurus, trying to get the tires facing out. My first attempt leaves me so I'd be blocking two lanes of traffic which isn't ideal. I back up and try again until I'm completely out of the other lanes, with angled tires. Perfect. I reach for my seatbelt, about to get out of the car.

"Don't forget to call in the plate," Topher says from the back.

"Oh, right." The radio clatters to the floor when I reach for it, so I pull it back up with the coiled cord. I call in the plate, and Officer Sanders gives me the okay to approach over the radio from right next to me. My cheeks are hot, and it's a relief to get out of the car. Topher's door opens from behind me.

"You can wait in the cruiser," I say.

He shakes his head and keeps walking with me. Maybe Lieutenant Sanders told him to follow. Did I mess up so badly she thinks I need a chaperone to grab Jamie's license and registration?

I'm about to rap on the driver's side window when Topher calls out, "weapon!"

I blink, and then I see it. Jamie's plastic gun plainly visible on the passenger seat. How did I miss that? These practice traffic stop scenarios are to train us to anticipate whatever the refs have come up with that day for the competition.

I reach for the plastic weapon on my utility belt and point it at the vehicle.

"Hands on the wheel," Topher and I yell in unison.

The car door starts to open.

"Stay in the vehicle," we yell.

The door opens and Jamie comes out, holding his gun.

"Why would I stay in the car for an officer that can't even park?" he says.

"Hands above your head, hands up," I start yelling, slowly backing up to give us some space. Why did it have to be Jamie in the car? Anyone else would just comply and let me practice running their papers. Jamie has to make this as dramatic as possible.

He starts to put his hands above his head, but then quickly reaches for his back. I know that we're supposed to pretend to fire at him. To shoot to kill.

I've had enough of Jamie.

I barrel straight into him, tackling him to the ground. Then I flip him onto his stomach and sit on him.

He rolls over, and then shoves me. I fall backwards a bit, landing on his legs. He gets out from under me and pushes me again to the ground. I roll over, getting away from him. We both scramble to our feet and he charges at me. I feign to the left, then grab him from behind. I'm holding onto his back, and he's carrying me, trying to fling me off. I hold on tighter.

My face is right in his ear. I say the first thing that pops into my head. "You smell good."

He freezes and I slide off his back. Instead of continuing the fight, he walks away from me.

"Break it up, break it up," Lieutenant Sanders is yelling, running to us.

I hold my hands up in surrender, just like Jamie was supposed to. "He was going to fire at me. I was deescalating," I say.

Lieutenant Sanders puts a hand on her hip. "Seriously?"

Jamie is looking around with wild eyes, anywhere but at me.

"Let's do it again, this time with Topher driving," Lieutenant Sanders says.

I go to climb into the cruiser, but Layla steps forward. "I'll be his partner this time," she says.

That's fine with me. I walk over to the crowd in the grass where the rest of the team is watching the traffic stops. No one is doing the obstacle course. I stand next to DJ. He takes a step away from me, staring at me with wary eyes.

"What was that for?" I ask.

He holds his hands up. "I don't want to get on your bad side."

"Excuse me?"

"You got into a full-on fight with Jamie for no reason."

I scoff, about to list off all the ways that Jamie was asking for that. "That wasn't a full-on fight," I say instead.

DJ shivers dramatically. I catch another group of our teammates staring at me. My cheeks flame. I walk over to the obstacle course in the middle of the grass. No one is doing it, so I might as well. I glance at the track, pretending not to feel everyone's eyes on me. Topher is perfectly parking the cruiser with the wheels out. I'm proud, but slightly jealous.

I focus on my feet, weaving in and out of the tires on the ground. In and out. *Why does Jamie get under my skin so easily?* Next is a rope ladder. The ropes burn against my fading calluses as I climb. *I hurt my brother.* At the top I swing my legs over to the other side to climb down. *My teammates are scared of me.*

I reach the ground, then lower myself to my stomach to shimmy under a net. *It's partially my fault Jake is dead.* I shove that one away, focusing on my arms, hips, and knees. I get into a familiar rhythm and army crawl across the cold ground. I make it to the other side and take off into a sprint, jumping over different pallets of wood that are supposed to mimic fences.

My mind is quiet as I dodge, weave, and climb. I swing off the final set of monkey bars and land over the finish line. I push the strands of hair that escaped out of my ponytail out of my face, and catch Jamie watching me, an odd expression on his face. He looks away when our eyes meet.

I circle back to the beginning of the course and do it again. And again.

We have to bring the smaller parts of the obstacle course back to the equipment shed at the end of practice. My arms are jello and my legs burn with every step as I awkwardly shuffle with two jumbo orange cones across the grass. When

I finally reach the shed, I throw the cones down on the floor. They tip to the side, knocking off a box from one of the metal shelves. I right the cones, and shove the box back in place.

There's a loud crash from farther inside the shed. I jump up and yelp, knocking over another box. Ping-pong balls spill out of it, bouncing all over the floor.

"You've got to be kidding me," Jamie says, annoyed.

"Why do you have so many ping-pong balls?" I cry out. They're everywhere, pinging as they bounce over and over. I grab the box they fell from and start scooping them back into it.

"It was a perfectly fine amount until you messed with them," Jamie grumbles. To my relief he leans down and starts helping.

We're both reaching into the box at the same time and his skin brushes mine. Butterflies flutter in my stomach. I freeze and look up at him. What is happening right now?

Jamie is staring at me. His hair is a mess but his eyes are burning.

"What's your problem?" he asks, breaking the moment.

"What's yours?" I shoot back.

He rolls his eyes. "Oh I don't know, you tackled me for no reason earlier."

"You were going to pull a weapon."

"That's not how you're supposed to respond," he says, exasperated.

"You're just mad that I took you down."

He leans in closer to me. "You. Are. Ridiculous." He emphasizes each word.

"And you like it," I say back.

He doesn't respond. He's staring back at me, but his eyes flit down my face multiple times. Is he looking at my lips? Is he thinking about kissing me? I look at his lips too. He's so close. He's breathing hard.

An indescribable sensation comes over me. Almost a hunger. I want to kiss him. I need to. Right here, right now.

"I'm going to kiss you," I say.

"Do it," he says back.

I lean forward at the same moment he does. The cardboard box is still between us. We both hesitate, inches apart. Is he waiting for me? I was the one who said I was going to kiss him. I close the distance and press my lips to his.

It's slightly wet. But that's it.

I pull away from him, my foot sliding on a ping-pong ball, and I fall backward. Jamie shoots to his feet, reaching out a hand. I grab on and stand, my cheeks on fire.

I need to get out of here. I finally had my first kiss, with a boy I can't stand, and *it was awful*. I waited all of that time for a kiss, and *that's* what it was? A little bit of wet pressure. I head for the front of the shed.

"Wait," Jamie says, his hand grabbing onto my forearm. It's gentle; he's not forcing me to stay.

"I've got to go, lots of homework," I stammer. I don't even bother turning toward him.

"Hold on," he says. He steps closer to me, and then his hand slides up my arm, to my neck. I shiver. With his other hand, he turns my face until I'm facing him.

"Let's try again," he says softly. He pauses, waiting for an answer. I give the tiniest of nods. He steps closer, holding me still as he kisses me.

His lips press firmer against mine, again and again. Softer, then harder. I grab his arms, holding myself steady. His hand moves to the back of my neck and I shiver. I move my lips against his, matching what he does. It's a dance and

I'm copying each of his steps. Then throwing in a few of my own.

He finally pulls away, out of breath. His eyes are lit up, and he smiles. My heart is hammering in my chest, and I feel more alive than I have in months.

"Jamie, you okay?" Layla calls out in the distance.

"Shit," he says. He takes a step to leave, but now *his* foot slips on a ping pong ball. I catch him, both of us bumping into the metal shelves. A giggle escapes me.

I lean down to scoop up the rest of the ping-pong balls.

"Just leave them," he hisses.

The two of us emerge from the closet to where Layla is standing, feet away.

"What took you so long?" Layla asks.

"She somehow spilled an entire box of ping-pong balls," Jamie says with an eye roll.

"I wouldn't have spilled them if you hadn't scared me," I retort.

"Don't be so jumpy and we wouldn't have a problem," Jamie says.

Layla looks between the two of us, and sighs. Good. She has no idea what happened in there. Jamie walks with her, looking over his shoulder once with an unreadable expression. When he turns around, I press my fingers to my lips, the ghost of the kiss still there.

TWENTY-FIVE

Tuesday February 14th 7:05 AM

I'VE NEVER SEEN ANIKA THIS ANXIOUS. SHE'S PACING IN a small circle in our meeting spot outside the fishbowl classroom. A pink heart balloon floats above her head, and she's squeezing an adorable Squishmallow otter in one arm, a large bouquet of flowers in the other. I spot the price sticker and balk, then help her remove it so Sophie won't see it.

"There are chocolates in my backpack. Can you grab them and shove them in my elbow?" she asks.

I struggle with the zipper on her bag, the giant heart box barely contained in her bag. It takes a little rearranging, but I successfully shove the box underneath the otter.

"She's usually here by now," Anika says, starting to pace again. I look up and down the hallways, searching for Sophie.

An announcement over the speakers reminds us that there are flowers and chocolate for sale in the gym, for those of us who didn't spend $40 on flowers already.

"Do you think this is enough?" Anika asks.

"It's perfect. If she doesn't like it, then she's not worth it."

Anika glares at me. "Yes, she is. I'm trying to make up for our fight too. Things are still a little weird."

"I'm sorry." I search the halls, desperate to find Sophie and end Anika's misery. When I spy her coming down the hall with Topher, I want to hug her in gratitude. I get a good look at what she's carrying, and snort. She has the exact same balloon, bouquet, and otter as Anika. The two of them take each other in and start laughing.

"Should we even bother trading?" Sophie asks.

"Of course. I want the ones you picked out for me," Anika says.

I help them swap their items, since both of their arms are full. Then I take multiple photos of them squeezing as close together as they can with their loot, their smiles contagious.

When we separate for class, I glance at my phone. Still no texts. I barely slept last night, replaying my kisses with Jamie over and over. Around 2AM, I realized that we kissed the day before Valentine's Day. What's the protocol for this? He's the one who initiated the second, better, kiss. Which makes me think he wanted to kiss me. Yet, when we left, he'd seamlessly gone back to the Jamie who wants nothing to do with me. Was that an act for Layla, or was the kiss the fluke?

I open up a message to him, then close it. What would I even say? *I still don't know how I feel about that kiss. I mean, I liked it. A lot. But it's *Jamie*. My nemesis.

When the bell rings after school, I'm so focused on my phone and the lack of texts, that it takes me a second to realize my engine isn't starting when I turn the key. I pull it out, then try again. Still nothing.

I go to the front and try to pop the hood open. It doesn't budge. A quick google later I'm searching for the hood release button. I finally find it near the floor, along with the latch in the middle of the hood. I stare inside, as if I have any idea what's wrong.

There are two cables sticking out that look like they're unattached. I type my car's make and model back into google, looking for a video that might help me know where to put them.

"You need some help?" a voice asks. A guy wearing a black hoodie is approaching me. He's 5'11", white, with brown eyes. Although he has acne on his jaw, he looks older than high school. The sunlight glints off an emerald earring in his ear. I tense. Is he a member of the Serpents?

I look around the parking lot. Everyone cleared out quickly, probably to go make out with their Valentines. There are a few random cars left, but no one outside right now. I could run to the school, but the path is covered in snow and stubborn patches of ice that won't melt. There's a good risk of hurting myself, and he could potentially catch me. I reach backwards to the side pocket of my backpack. There's a container of mace in there. I wrap my fingers around it and slip it up the sleeve of my jacket.

"I've got it," I say.

He keeps approaching. I stagger my feet to give me more leverage if I need to fight him. As he walks closer, he cranes his neck to look at my engine.

"Your battery cables are disconnected, that's all," he says. "May I?"

I hate this. I'm vulnerable and have no idea if he's telling the truth. I want him to go away, but, if it is that simple of a fix... it'd be much faster than calling my parents and waiting for one of them to get here.

He reaches the front of my car and waits for my answer to his question. He didn't just assume, which is a good sign, right? What's the worst thing that can happen? He reattaches the cables, and the car still doesn't start? Or sparks a bit? Versus him knowing what he's talking about and I get to leave right now. The reward is outweighing the risk here.

"Sure," I say, my voice pitchy.

He reconnects the cables quickly while I watch. It doesn't look like something that would naturally disconnect. Has someone messed with my car?

"How do you think they came disconnected?" I ask.

He doesn't look at me, only closes the hood of my car. "It should start now."

I lean in the open door, and turn my key in the ignition. Sure enough, the engine starts. I wait to make sure nothing sparks. It doesn't.

"Thanks. What's your name?" I ask. Maybe I judged him too quickly.

He looks up from the hood of my car, his eyes boring into mine. "I heard you've been digging into who killed Jake Peters."

The back of my neck tingles. I straighten up.

"I don't know what you're talking about," I say carefully.

"He wasn't killed by the Serpents, or the Royals."

"How do you know that?" I ask, my eyes focusing on his earring.

"You'll have to trust me. I'm here as a favor for your brother. It wasn't either of us. So stop digging into the gangs, or you're going to get hurt." With that he starts to walk away toward the baseball field.

"Do you know who did it then?" I ask, following after him, picking through the slippery spots on the asphalt.

"Only who didn't," he says. He keeps walking and I have to run to keep up with him.

"How are you sure? What else do you know?"

He stops walking suddenly and I almost bump into him.

"That you shouldn't chase cars after midnight." He stares at me for a long moment, then starts jogging across the baseball field. I track him as he crosses the grass to the other side. There's a parking lot over there with a lone black SUV. Exactly like the one I chased after during the stakeout at Sophie's house.

I try to remember the face in the car from that night. Was he the one who pointed a gun at me through the window? My legs are weak, and I stumble back to my own car, locking the doors as soon as I'm inside. I rest my head on the back of my seat. I'm in perfect view of the rearview mirror. Someone has drawn two x's and a straight-line underneath it with green marker. A dead face. I furiously wipe at it, but it's not coming off.

Not only did a member of the Serpents unplug my battery, but he was inside my car. I whip around, searching the back seat, fully expecting someone to be sitting there. It's empty, except for a few receipts and straw wrappers. My head is pounding, and I scan the parking lot again. Everyone is gone.

I pull out my phone and scroll to Evan's name. He answers on the third ring.

"Hello?" he says quietly. I hear people talking in the background.

"I hope you're happy" I spit.

"I'm in the fridge at work, could I call you back later?"

"No need. I received your message loud and clear."

"What are you talking about?" he hisses.

"Your Serpent friend unhooked my battery, drew a dead smiley face inside my car, and threatened me."

"What?!" Evan yells. "What did he say? What'd he look like? Are you okay?"

I roll my eyes, even though he can't see. "Why are you pretending to care? He said he was there as a favor for you."

"You have to listen to me. I would never tell someone to do that. I asked my old roommate a few questions after our conversation Sunday, but that's it, I swear. It must have gotten lost in translation."

"What got lost in translation?"

"That I was worried about you!" he yells. "That I think you're being reckless playing detective. You could have died last year, and now you're digging into something dangerous."

My blood boils. This is his fault. "I'm not a little girl anymore. I'm an adult."

"Then act like one. I didn't tell anyone to threaten you. I've got to go." He hangs up.

I look up from my phone, my eyes landing on the green x's again. I scream, banging on the steering wheel. First, I pissed off the Royals and am constantly checking in the halls to make sure Marco and his friends aren't going to jump me. Now, the Serpents know what I'm doing, and have made it clear they can easily get to me. If they don't like what they see, will they cut my brakes? Or something worse?

But if what that Serpent said is true—that they had nothing to do with Jake's death—then why would they care if I kept looking into it? Was he lying? Or just trying to scare me like Evan wanted?

Cautiously, I put the car in drive. I test the brakes, and jerk forward with the sudden stop. I drive home, staying under the speed limit and in the right lane in case I need to suddenly veer off the road because my car is malfunctioning. I'm shocked when I make it home safely. I run straight to my room and pull out the notebook Anika and I were working in, flipping to a fresh page.

Serpent claims the Serpents didn't kill Jake,
and neither did the Royals
Royals claim they didn't work with Jake
Serpents were the ones stealing the cars for
Jake?

I stare at the list, chewing on my thumbnail. There's the possibility that everything he said was a lie. Why would someone who's stealing cars and willing to kill over it tell me the truth? Yet, it seemed like everything the Serpent said was specifically worded to give me information, but not too much.

I flip back to my page with Anika, trying to see how this fits in. If what the Serpent said is true, then I can ignore the gang angle as it's related to Jake's death.

I open up Threadlit, wondering if there are new leads on there I don't know about. It's a waste of time. The only theories on there that I haven't tried looking into are that a car theft victim got revenge on Jake, or that I did it. The idea of tracking down all of the victims of Unter is daunting, and I know it wasn't me.

I need to go back to the beginning. I start with the first article I found about the app that led me to Jake Peters, Mason Wilkins, and Devon Burton. Then I'm on back on Mason's Instagram. There are still the same pictures of computer guts, memes, and thirteen-year-old selfies. The GoFundMe link in his bio is still broken.

I still can't find any social media pages for Jake, but searching his name pulls up everyone's memorial posts for him. I've seen most of them, and no one left any clues about who his murderer was in their captions.

I check on Devon again. All I find is the same Facebook page as before. His last post is from three weeks ago, and written in Spanish. I scroll through all the religious posts he's made in the past six months. Before that, he's only tagged in other people's posts. There are graduation pictures, track meets, and some from the business competition. I keep scrolling and freeze, my breath whooshing out of me.

There's a post for Devon's eighteenth birthday, and in the very last picture he's holding a rifle. It's not a semi-automatic. If I was the betting type, I'd bet it was a .22.

There are lots of .22 caliber weapons out there, and I know guns can be a common gift. Devon is out of the country... but this feels like too much of a coincidence.

I call Anika, but she immediately sends me to voicemail. Of course she did, it's Valentine's Day and she's out with Sophie. She actually has a normal relationship, meanwhile I've spent way too much time today wondering if I should text the guy I kissed yesterday.

Anika would probably have some good insight into what

I should do with this Jamie situation. Again, it's Valentine's Day, and she's busy.

Things are better with Topher. Do I risk pushing it by telling him what I just found out about Devon Burton? Would he have any tips about Jamie? Do I even want him to know about what happened in that storage closet?

Are you busy? Want to go get some food?

He doesn't respond for ten minutes.

Topher

Sorry… on a date. Tomorrow

With who?!

I wait fifteen minutes, then call it. He's too busy, which is fine. I don't feel guilty at all for not telling him about my kiss. Is he out with whoever he was kissing on the stairs at the party? Or maybe Sandra? He's going to have some explaining to do tomorrow.

I'm happy for Anika and Topher. They deserve to have a good Valentine's Day. I'm not going to mope that I'm home alone, and I have no idea what Jamie thinks about me. No, I'm going to solve Jake's murder instead. I keep scrolling father back on Devon Burton's page, making sure there isn't anything else I've missed.

TWENTY-SIX

Wednesday February 15th 4:30PM

"Wʜᴀᴛ's ʏᴏᴜʀ ᴘʀᴏʙʟᴇᴍ?" I ғɪɴᴀʟʟʏ ᴀsᴋ.

Jamie looks up from where he's furiously scrubbing the wall. "Nothing."

"You've destroyed three magic erasers." I point to the pile of crumbled sponge all over the floor where he's been at work. "It's not nothing."

"These stains have been here for years. Someone needs to get them."

Fine. If he's going to stress clean and pretend that nothing happened between us, two can play that game. I go back to my phone and keep reading the blog of Devon Burton's mom. She was the one who tagged Devon in the birthday pictures with the rifle. I went on her social media and found a link to her blog. I stayed up all night reading it, wondering if she might casually mention that her son has been lying about being out of the country, or maybe his rifle has gone missing lately.

Instead its weekly updates of the funny things her kids say, letters that Devon has written to her, along with her weekly meal plans. I've read two years back at this point, and there have been a few mentions of Devon, Jake, and Mason working on their app, but I haven't learned anything helpful. Except for a few instant pot recipes that look good if I ever want to find where my parents put that thing.

Jamie grabs a new magic eraser and keeps scrubbing the wall near the bathroom. He's as far away from me as possible while still being in the shop. When I see the next blog post is another recipe, I turn off my phone and sigh dramatically. Jamie glances at me for a millisecond, then goes back to his scrubbing. I roll my eyes.

"No one's here. We can talk about Monday."

"There's nothing to talk about," Jamie grumbles.

Ouch. I know it was my first kiss, and it wasn't the best when I initiated it. But I thought the second one was better. I guess not.

"Got it. Well I'm sorry then," I say, my cheeks flaming. I might need to quit after this. I can't work with someone who knows how bad of a kisser I am.

He turns around quickly. "Sorry? For what?"

"For kissing you in the first place."

He rubs a hand over his face. "That's not what's wrong."

"Then what is it? Because we're coworkers and co-assistant team leads. You can't act like this every time I'm around."

"That's the thing, we *are* co-assistant team leads and coworkers. We can't do this," he says, waving to the space between us.

There's the tiniest twinge of, something. But he's right. "Of course," I say. "I won't mention it again."

"Me either. Purely professional from now on."

"Sounds good." He goes back to scrubbing the wall, the sponge making a squeaking noise. "So, to be clear, it wasn't that I'm an awful kisser?" I ask.

He glances at me over his shoulder, his brow scrunched. "What?"

"I need to know if I'm a bad kisser, for the future. If there are things I can do to improve, I don't know. Forget I said anything." I cover my face with my hands.

The sponge starts squeaking against the wall again.

I'm going to quit. I'm pretty sure it's against the Geneva Conventions to be forced to spend this much time with someone who thinks you're a bad kisser.

"No, it wasn't bad," he says so quietly, I'm sure I've imagined it. I peek between my fingers. He's still scrubbing the wall. "I couldn't stop thinking about it."

I pull my hands off my face. "Really?"

"Yes," he groans.

"Me either," I admit. "As much as I didn't want to."

He turns around and stares at me. My cheeks heat again. The bell over the door jingles, and a guy walks in with three younger kids. Jamie turns back to his disintegrated sponges, and grabs the broom to sweep them up.

I glance at the family who just interrupted our moment. Then look again. The guy looks familiar. I tense, searching for any purple or green on him. No earrings, arm bands, or covertly tucked in bandanas. If he was here to threaten me, would he bring three kids with him? I hope not, but it would be a good way to give a false sense of comfort.

He must feel me staring at him because he looks over at me. I give him a small smile and he gives a quick one back. If he knows me, he doesn't acknowledge it. Normally, vaguely recognizing someone wouldn't be a big deal. But when you're on two gangs' radar, it is.

I covertly watch him out of the corner of my eye as I stuff the spoon containers with as many as possible. I accidentally catch his eye again as he's helping the kids pick out toppings. He instantly looks away and tells the kids they need to hurry up. They start whining and he murmurs something to them that I can't hear.

If I don't know him, why would he seem so bothered that an employee was watching him? I turn the tablet we use for checkout toward me. If he uses a card, I can get a quick glance at his name and see if I recognize it.

He finally comes over to pay. He keeps his eyes down, not looking at me.

"What color spoons do you want?" I ask, looking at the younger kids with him. I put the container down so they can clearly see the two options. They stand up on their tiptoes, heads whipping back and forth between the green spoons and pink spoons. I tell the guy the total and he digs around in his wallet, flipping through the bills in the pocket.

No. Not cash.

He pauses for a long moment, then finally pulls out a credit card. I grab the card and bring it to the reader, glancing at the front.

Devon Burton.

I do a double take.

No. Way.

Devon Burton is standing in front of me right now. Buying frozen yogurt with his siblings. I should have recognized them all from his mom's blog.

I hand the card back, trying to stay calm.

"Let's go," Devon says to the kids.

"No, I want to eat here," one starts to whine.

"We've got to get home," Devon says sharply. When the youngest kid doesn't move, one of the older ones pulls on their arm.

"Come on, Devon probably doesn't feel good, remember?" she says.

Devon's face turns bright red, and he wraps his arms around all of them and herds them to the door. The bell jingles as they leave.

Devon is here. This changes everything. I pull out my phone, scrolling through my contacts. I'm not making the same mistake as last time. I skip Quinn and go down to Detective Zhao's number. It goes straight to voicemail.

"This is Ellie. I just saw Devon Burton in my frozen yogurt shop. He's back in the country, who knows how long he's been here. Call me back."

I hang up, then dial again in case she accidentally ignored my first call. Voicemail, again.

"What was that?" Jamie asks as he dumps the sponge bits into the trashcan behind the counter.

"Nothing," I say quickly. I go back to my messages, opening my thread with Anika.

> JUST SAW DEVON. HE COULD HAVE BEEN HERE THE WHOLE TIME.

I wait for the dots to appear, but they don't. She's busy volunteering. I drum my fingers on the countertop. I need to talk this out with someone. I could try Topher, but he refused to tell Anika and me who he went on a date with yesterday. Apparently, it was awful and not worth repeating. Anika tried to steal his phone from him so we could go through his messages, and he was *not* happy. I'm not going to push it by texting him about this right now.

There's Quinn, but again, I don't want a repeat of the last time I messaged him a theory in a hurry. I need more information. I scroll through my contacts again, pausing on Mason. I still have his number from our conversation in his math class.

> Hey Mason, this is Ellie, we talked in your math class about Unter. I have one more question. When was the last time you heard from Devon?

Three dots immediately appear.

MASON

> He sent an email in October trying to convert me to his church, but that's it

> Why

I hesitate. From my conversation with Detective Zhao, I'm pretty sure Mason had an alibi the night of Jake's death. Devon's has fallen through.

> I just saw him. Here.

> Are you sure

> Absolutely.

The three dots appear over and over, then go away. Then appear again.

> Why would he pretend that he's still out of
> the country

I send back a thinking face. No dots appear.

"I don't like this pretending I don't exist thing either," Jamie says.

I look up at him, confused at what we're talking about. "Huh?"

He stares at my phone. "You're calling people so you don't have to look at me."

It takes a second to get out of investigator mode and remember what we were talking about before Devon showed up. Kissing. And how it *wasn't* bad. "No, that's not what I was doing, I thought I saw—"

He opens the swinging door and comes behind the counter. For a millisecond I think he's going to attack me. But then he's kissing me, his hands in my hair. I step backward, knocking a box to the ground. My eyes fly open to see what it is, but Jamie presses me into the wall, kissing me harder. Whatever fell can wait. I close my eyes and focus on moving my mouth against his.

When he finally pulls away minutes later, I'm gasping for air. Jamie is staring back at me, breathing hard. There's a clump of his hair sticking up from where I pulled on it.

"Was that okay for you?" I ask shyly.

"Okay? That was incredible," Jamie grins. Then he sees the box that fell over while we were kissing. The spoons I was restocking are everywhere.

"We really need to stop doing that," he points to the mess.

I laugh, and we both crouch down to collect the now useless spoons. I'm warm all over with him so close. His leg brushes against mine.

"Maybe we could keep this between us. Then it wouldn't interfere with work and Pathfinders," he says, still picking up spoons.

I instantly pull away. I've seen enough about relationship red flags to know that wanting to keep a relationship a secret is a huge one.

"No. I'm not going to be your secret little hookup. If you want to be with me, you can't be embarrassed about it."

His eyes go wide. "That's not what I meant. I didn't even think about it like that."

My phone starts ringing. It's probably Detective Zhao.

"I need to get this," I say.

"Ellie," Jamie says, reaching toward me.

I run to the bathroom, locking the door behind me. I answer the call on the last ring.

"I know this is weird, but I didn't know who else to call," a male voice says.

I pull the phone away from my ear, looking at the contact. It's Mason, not Detective Zhao.

"What's going on?" I ask.

"I talked to Devon."

"Why would you do that?" I screech.

"Because I had to know if you were telling the truth. You weren't his friend; you might have mistaken him as someone else. He picked up though."

"What'd he say?"

"I asked him when he came back to the country and

why he didn't reach out, and he immediately broke down. He admitted he did it."

"Did what?" I ask slowly.

"Killed Jake."

What? How could he go from buying frozen yogurt with his siblings, to admitting to murder minutes later?

Mason continues talking. "Now he's thinking of hurting himself. I need you to help me talk him out of it."

"You should call the police," I say.

"He's in a bad place and he's not going to walk out of there. But with you, he might."

"What are you talking about?"

"You stopped a serial killer. I've heard about how you talked them down. You can do this. Get Devon to calm down and turn himself in. Jake's family deserves justice, not a sad story about Devon dying too."

"Hold on, I *just* saw him. He was with his siblings. Where are they? Is this a hostage situation?" I ask.

"No, no. He was alone in his car; he'd dropped them off. The guilt is eating him up and he wanted to tell someone what he did. I told him to turn himself in, that I'd go with him to do it, but he started freaking out. Now he's feeling hopeless."

"Then where is he?"

"He's going up to a spot on the reservoir we all used to hike to when we were stuck coding. He's going to hurt himself. Please, I can't lose someone else. At least if we talk him out of this, he'll be behind bars."

"Let's call the police—"

"No," Mason says firmly. "He'll start shooting. If I'm there with you, we can stop anyone else from getting hurt. Please, Ellie."

I close my eyes, trying to think this through. Devon is

heading up to the reservoir right now. Mason knows exactly where he's going. If we call the police, this will most likely end with Devon dead. The images of his family on their blog pop into my head. His mom writes all of those posts with so much love. I remember all the parents at the memorials, absolutely devastated over the loss of their boys who had done such awful things.

There's my own parents who've been through hell and back with my brother. Who have been so happy at their second chance to have a relationship with him.

I've felt a taste of that hopelessness Devon is feeling right now. I was lucky to be able to get out of that place. Devon may have murdered someone, but everyone else who loves him doesn't deserve to lose him forever over this moment.

My confrontation with Brooke at the riverbank has been this presence looming in the back of my mind for months. It's effected all aspect of my life, and made me question everything about my future. I'm finally getting myself back together. Will going up there and trying to help Devon ruin all of that progress?

I haven't had a single panic attack related to my investigation into Unter and Jake's death. Not when a real gun was pulled on me. Not when I was trapped at Sonic with gang members, or when two threatened me. When I'm investigating things, I'm strong. I'm capable.

It's time to prove it to myself.

"Where are we going?" I ask.

"Up near the reservoir. I'll send you a pin of the spot."

"I'll be right there."

"Thank you, Ellie. Thank you," Mason says, his voice breaking. Then he hangs up. A few seconds later, my phone buzzes with the spot.

I swing the bathroom door open, and Jamie's standing right there.

"I misspoke earlier. Let me explain."

"I've got to go. Family emergency," I say. I run to the back room and grab my coat and backpack.

"Are you okay? What happened?" Jamie asks.

"Don't worry about it. It's going to be slow; you can handle the shop."

"If this is about what I said earlier," he starts.

I don't let him finish, and push open the door, the bell jingling as I leave.

TWENTY-SEVEN

Wednesday February 15th 5:15PM

THE SNOW FALLS FASTER, AND I READJUST MY windshield wiper speed. Again. Then I turn off the heater. I'm burning up in the emergency snowpants I keep in my trunk that I slipped over my jeans, and the hoodie I threw on underneath my coat. If I'm going to be talking Devon off a literal cliff in a snowstorm, I don't want to be distracted by the cold. I'll just sweat to death before I get there. And keep being impaled by whatever random things I've stored in these coat pockets over the years.

My tires slide in the falling snow, and I loosen my grip on the wheel, letting the car try to right itself. I should turn back and go home. I can hear all the voices of people telling me to stop. Evan, my parents, Detective Zhao, Quinn, Topher.

I picture myself huddled in corners, holding myself together during panic attacks. At Pathfinders. The competition.

No. I'm not going home. I'm not going to sit in my room, feeling sorry for myself, wondering what I could have done. According to the map, I have three big curves left until I reach the spot Mason said Devon would be waiting. I'm not giving up when I'm literal feet away from helping someone.

The second curve is next to a steep drop off. Thankfully there's a guardrail. I glance at the dark expanse of nothing on the other side of the rails. My heart speeds up, and I focus on the road in front of me. Just one more curve and I'll be there.

An SUV comes racing up from behind, going into the other lane to pass me. Slush sprays up, completely covering my window. I can't see at all. I hit the brakes reflexively, harder than I should. My tires skid on the snow, snow crunching as they slide. I yank the wheel away from the guardrail and drop-off, but it only makes me slide that way faster. I close my eyes and brace for impact.

It doesn't come.

I peek out the window. My right-side mirror is less than an inch away from the guardrail. I didn't crash. I'm still on the road. I'm okay. I slowly turn the wheel, barely tapping the gas as I nudge my car back onto the road. I'm so focused on not sliding again, that I barely see the truck.

It slams into my bumper and my car goes spinning. My heart slams into my chest and I can't breathe. The back of the car bangs into the guardrail. I'm flung forward, then immediately backward as the airbag deploys. The screeching of scraping metal fills my head.

The car stops moving. Slowly, I open my eyes. I'm facing the opposite direction. The guardrail is on my side of the car now, next to my window. If I crane my neck slightly, I can see the side of the drop-off. It's steep and rocky. The bottom is covered in snow, but I can't tell how far down it is.

I'm alive. I'm still up here.

There's a rap on the passenger window that makes me jump. Someone is peering down into my car. I stare at the control panel next to me, knowing I'm supposed to do something with it, but not sure what. I press all the buttons until the passenger window rolls down. A familiar-ish face leans inside.

"Ellie? Are you okay?" Mason asks.

Mason. We were on our way to Devon.

"I think so," I say. When I open my lips, they're wet. I wipe it away, then look at my hand. It's covered in blood. I make a noise.

"Don't move, your nose is bleeding," Mason says, sounding worried.

I nod, immediately regretting it. My neck feels strange. I need to worry about my neck being injured, not my nose.

"I'm calling for help, stay here," Mason says. Then he disappears.

I keep my head against the headrest, trying not to hyperfocus on every sensation running through me. I know what to do. Well, I know what to do from the other side of this scenario. I need to stay calm. Help will come. If it can get up here. A wave of dizziness goes through me.

What have I done?

Stop it. I need to focus on something else. I close my eyes, and hear the sound of an engine. The crunching of snow. The smell of iron and diesel. The engine is getting louder. I open my eyes just in time to see Mason ramming his truck into my car for the second time.

I'm slammed forward into the airbag again. The metal of the guardrail groans as my car pushes against it, bending it.

Pulling my face out of the airbag, I see the hood of my

car completely crumpled in front of me. I turn around, seeing Mason's expressionless face as he backs his truck away. For a fraction of a second, I think it might have been an accident. He was trying to get help, and his tires slipped.

His engine revs as he goes to do it again.

I fumble with my seatbelt. I'm trapped in my seat by the locked nylon. I push against the button, but nothing happens. I strain for my keys in the ignition. There's a seatbelt cutter on there. I've gotten the keys in my hand when the truck rams into the car again.

When I get my face out of the airbag, the guardrail is bent up and over the ledge. It's created an opening to the drop below, and my car is sitting precariously on top of it, teetering back and forth.

The truck backs up again, getting ready for a final hit. My fingers close on the seatbelt cutter, starting to cut. As I move my arms, I feel the car start rocking back and forth slowly. I glance in the rearview mirror. Even if I cut my seatbelt off, there's no guarantee I'll get out of the car before Mason hits me again. Or, that I'll be able to get out without sending the car over the cliff myself.

I've seen and heard of miracles during the years at Pathfinders. People walking out of wrecks every day they shouldn't have survived, and seatbelts helping with that. I set the cutter down. I need to stay as limp as possible and not tense up. That's why drunk drivers fare better in crashes. I close my eyes and take deep steadying breaths as the truck rams into me one final time, sending me over the cliff.

TWENTY-EIGHT

Wednesday February 15th Sometime Later

It's freezing. Did I leave the window open in my room? I try to sit up in bed to close it, but can't. Something is holding me down. I feel along my body. When I move my left arm, pain radiates through my chest, knocking the breath out of me. I gingerly test my right arm. It's stiff, but otherwise okay.

I pat down, finding a belt across my chest. I slide my fingers down until I find the release button. It takes three tries to get it to click, the belt finally loosening. It whips across my body, whacking my left shoulder. The pain turns my stomach. I breathe until it lessens, then carefully remove the belt from my shoulder with my right hand. Finally free, I look around. Where am I?

It takes a moment for my eyes to adjust to the dark. Slowly, the details of my car come into focus. There's an airbag inches from my face. The windows are all shattered.

Around me snow glitters in the dark, even though there are no lights.

I reach up to my face. It's wet in some places, and crusty in others. I swallow and taste metal in my mouth. Blood. I gag. I need water. I need my phone. I reach up to turn on the overhead light, ignoring the tightness in my neck. Nothing happens. I push it again, and again. I pat my pockets, feeling for my phone. It's not there. I gingerly feel underneath me and next to my seat on the floor.

I'm forced to take a break to catch my breath. Each movement sends pain in new directions. How did I get here? *Where* is here? On my right is a large clearing of snow, and then a forest of trees. On my left is a dark wall of... it looks like rock. The longer I look, I can make out giant boulders. I lean closer so I can see how high it is. High enough it hurts my neck to look, but not so high I can't see the top of the cliff. And the giant pieces of metal hanging in the air like tentacles.

It starts coming back. Driving in the snow. Something hitting me. Again, and again. The screeching and groaning of metal bending. Soaring. A boom. Rolling. Then, nothing.

Someone drove me off a cliff.

Someone tried to kill me.

Mason.

I lean to the right, cradling my left arm against my chest, desperately searching for my phone. My fingers brush against glass shards, receipts, and granola bar wrappers. I'm still fumbling in the dark when I hear a roaring noise. A ball of light shoots toward me. It lands feet away from the passenger door.

Is that, a bottle, on fire?

It's then that I smell the gasoline.

The majority of car crashes don't end in fire, but if there was a *literal* Molotov cocktail thrown at a wreck with leaking fluids, it would. I sit up and scramble for the door handle, struggling to open it. I need to get out of here, now.

The door is smashed and won't move. I bring my legs up and kick against it, as hard as I can. It doesn't budge. The fire outside the car gets brighter and the bottle shatters. I look around. There are too many jagged pieces of glass on the front and back windows to climb out. My window is almost completely gone. I kick out the last pieces of glass. Then I climb through.

The fire begins to roar as I land awkwardly in the snow. Every inch of my body is screaming in protest. I can't even isolate where the pain is coming from; it's everywhere. The heat of the fire is hot against my back, and smoke curls into my lungs. I start coughing and can't stop. I push myself up, the snow stinging my cut hand, and stumble away from the car. I fall down into the snow after a few steps, then have to get back up all over again.

I reach the boulders and sit on one, thankful for a break. The fire has engulfed the entire car now, and smoke furls into the sky. Hopefully someone will see it soon and call 911. I just need to stay alive until they get here.

I pull the hood of my hoodie up, and then my coat. I find the extra pair of gloves in my snow pants and shove them on. I wiggle my toes in my boots. My feet are still dry. Thank you, past-Ellie for dressing warm, anticipating a long night in the snow talking someone into going to the police. These extra layers give me a better chance of getting out of here. I stand up from the boulder and start pacing from side to side to keep my body moving.

This is the perfect time to focus on how much of an idiot I

am. Devon never called Mason. I knew the timing didn't make sense, so soon after seeing Devon in the shop. Mason lied to me, convinced me to drive up a winding road to the middle of nowhere in a snow storm, and then drove me over a cliff.

I stare at the hunk of metal and glass that used to be my car. I only had it for a month, but it put up a hell of a fight. I'm going to miss it.

If Mason had been able to get my car over the cliff on the first hit, it would have been perfect. A simple car accident on a slippery road. Instead, he battered my car over and over. There will be significant damage on his truck too, which will back up my statement to the police. He's going down.

"Ellie, are you okay?" a voice calls out from above. I step behind the boulder and press myself as close to the rock wall as I can. A flashlight beam shines down the rocks, not quite reaching me.

"Where are you, Ellie? Let me get you help."

It's definitely Mason up there. Red hot anger courses through me. How delusional does he think I am that I would believe that he wants to help me right now?

There's an explosion. It shakes the world around me, and I let out a scream, curling into a ball. When it's over, I sit up and glance at the car. It's still there, completely on fire. One of the back tires exploded. Who knows how long there is until the rest of them blow.

"I know you're down there Ellie," Mason yells. I can see his form at the edge of the cliff, looking down at me.

Any chances I had of hiding are gone after the scream I let out. "If you wanted anyone to think this was an accident, you shouldn't have thrown a Molotov cocktail down here!" I yell.

A gunshot shoots into the boulders, chipping off pieces of rock.

Pure rage courses through me. He rammed me over a cliff. He set my car on fire. And now he's shooting at me? If he's trying to kill me and get away with it, he's doing a horrible job. "You're only making it easier for the police to trace this back to you," I scream.

"Then I better make it worth it," Mason yells back. More gunshots ricochet off the rocks around me. I search for an escape. The only place to go is the forest.

Another tire explodes. I don't scream in surprise this time, I roar. I start running in a serpentine pattern through the snow toward the forest. The gunshots ping into the drifts around me as I keep moving, stumbling into the snow. I push back up with my right arm and keep going. I need to reach the tree line. Then he won't be able to see me, and I'll be safe. The fire will attract attention, and someone will come save me. I just need to reach the trees.

I stumble again, jarring my left arm. The pain in my chest makes the edges of my vision go fuzzy. I collapse into the snow, struggling to breathe. It's over. I can't do this. I'm injured, running through snow drifts, and he has a gun. Bullets keep ringing out around me. I squeeze my eyes closed, not wanting to watch the end.

A bullet whizzes into the snow near me. I peek through my eyes at where it made a small tunnel through the snow drift. He missed me by a good ten feet, when I was lying completely still. He's a horrible shot.

No.

I push myself up again, my right arm shaking. I'm not going down like this, not to an opponent as unskilled as he is. I'm Ellie Garcia, and I'm not done. I've practiced and trained over the years. I can do this.

I start running again and reach the edge of the forest as the third tire explodes. I stumble into a tree and wrap my right arm around the trunk to steady myself. The snow drifts are higher and uneven, tugging against my legs as I make my way around the tree until I'm hidden from the clearing. Finally covered, I rest my back against the trunk, trying to catch my breath.

Rocks crash and tumble in the distance. I lean around the trunk and see an erratic flashlight beam as Mason makes his way down the rock wall. It's a steep decline, but he's doing it, rocks tumbling around him. I groan. He won't give up. I can fight him, or I can run.

I test out my body. The adrenaline is wearing off, and the pain is creeping back into my limbs. He has a gun, and isn't injured. I have better fighting skills than him, but he could potentially take me out from farther away. Potentially. He's a horrible shot, but with enough tries he might get lucky once. I need to run.

I push off from the tree too quickly and I'm immediately dizzy. The edges of my vision get black again. I stay completely still, waiting for it to pass. It mostly does, and I take a step. Then immediately fall into another snow drift. Of course I'm running for my life during one of the snowiest winters in years.

There's a scream of pain in the distance. I look behind me, but all I can see are my footprints and imprints in the snow from my falls. Hiding isn't an option. I'm going to pass out if I run. And he's not going to stop. Driving me over a cliff wasn't enough for him. He set my car on fire, shot at me, and followed me all the way down here.

One of us isn't walking away from this.

I pat my coat pockets. Maybe I stored something useful in here. Extra gloves, hand warmers, an old granola bar, wadded up tissues, and zip-ties? Really, Ellie? How about a knife, or a stun gun?

I look around for some sort of weapon. There are fallen tree branches everywhere, old limbs that couldn't stand up to the weight of all the snow this winter. The ones closest to me are too small to do any damage. I trudge through the drifts, checking on the fallen branches of the next tree. A little thicker, but not enough to be helpful.

I see one. I fight through the snow, falling to my knees. I'm struggling to stand when I hear an animalistic scream. It's Mason. I don't see him among the trees. Maybe he hurt himself again coming down the cliff. That will work in my favor. I get up and scramble for the thick branch laying on top of the snow. It catches on my glove when I pick it up. It's still sharp on one end where it snapped from the tree. I couldn't have asked for a better stick.

I search for the best place to make my attack. Some-where the snow is relatively flat, so I won't have to fight against it. There's a spot near the front of the forest that could be considered a distant cousin of flat ground. I maneuver to it. Each time I lift my leg, it gets harder to do it again. I'm so tired.

You're almost done.

Finish this.

I reach the clearing and start walking in a tiny circle, slowly widening it. The snow compacts beneath my boots. On one of my rotations, I catch a glimpse of Mason. He's barely past my flaming car, struggling through the snow with a heavy limp. The barrel of the rifle he's holding is swinging all over the place and I cringe. He obviously has no training on gun safety. He's only wearing a hoodie with no signs of extra clips of bullets. If he reloaded before coming down here, he maybe has ten shots. He's injured, cold, and probably tired. My odds are getting better.

My fighting ground flat enough, I rest against the trunk of a tree where I can still see Mason, but he can't see me. I test the weight of the branch in my right hand. It'll have to do. Shivers wrack through me and my eyelids droop. The fetal position has never seemed more desirable. But this isn't over.

Mason is almost here. He's swearing every time he lifts his right leg from the snow. Perfect. I stand still, bouncing up and down between my feet. I tuck my left arm in close, and tighten my grip on the stick.

I wait for Mason to take three steps into my flattened arena. Then I jump out from behind my tree, kicking into his right leg. He immediately crumples to the ground. I whack his right arm that's holding the rifle, and he lets go of it. I squat down to throw it out of his reach, but that means letting go of my branch. Mason comes to his senses, and grabs the rifle again, hitting me in the face. It isn't that hard, but my face has taken a beating already. Blood starts gushing out of my nose again.

I stumble backwards, tripping over the tree branch and falling into the snow. Mason is standing, pointing the gun at me. I roll to the side, screaming as the pain in my shoulder flares through me. A bullet pings into the snow inches from me. The kickback from the rifle sends Mason back to the ground.

I scramble to my knees, grasping the tree branch. I use it as a cane, pushing myself back up. Mason starts moving toward the rifle. I lean forward and stomp on his right ankle. He shrieks. I snatch the rifle from the ground and ignore the pain in my left shoulder. I try to disable it, but I can't remember how. Mason's moving toward me again, so I throw it into the trees as far as I can. Blinding pain shoots through my arm at the movement, the black spreading in my vision. Mason grabs onto my legs with a scream, pulling me into the snow.

He's on top of me and something sharp digs into my stomach. I knee him blindly, getting a lucky shot in the crotch. He screams and I roll, pushing him off of me. I pat down my stomach, checking for signs of a wound. There's nothing but my coat. He's scrambling toward me, trying to grab me again. I jump up, vision swimming. I can barely make out the shape of him and I kick. My boot collides with something and he roars. His injured leg is right in front of me. I kick again, and again, until something crunches. He's howling in agony.

The black edges in my vision aren't leaving. I lean against a tree trunk, bending at the knees to try to help the blood get back to my head. If I pass out, he'll kill me once the pain in his leg stops. I could kick him in the head to try and knock him out, but I don't want to risk killing him.

I shift my weight and feel something prod me in the stomach again. I pat each of my pockets, pulling out a long piece of plastic from the hidden one inside my coat. The zip-tie.

A faint laugh escapes me. Past Ellie, you're amazing. I walk back to Mason, each step taking a herculean effort. I sink to my knees in the snow. Mason is panting, sweat dripping down his face despite the cold.

"Give me your hands," I pant.

He tries to fight against me. I place the tiniest bit of pressure on his ankle, and he screams.

"Wrists together," I order, my hand hovering over his ankle.

Whimpering, he puts his wrists together and holds

them out for me. I grit my teeth against my own pain and quickly zip-tie his wrists together. I pull as hard as I can, the blackness creeping farther and farther in. When the clicking stops and Mason hisses, there's only a pinhole of light left. Panting, I start to crawl in the snow. I need to get as far away from him as possible. I barely move as the world starts tilting, and then fades to complete darkness.

TWENTY-NINE

Wednesday February 15th Who Cares PM

"Ellie! Come on, wake up. Come on."

There's pressure on my chest. I try to open my eyes, but they're so heavy.

"Come back to me. Come back."

I want to keep sleeping. I'm so tired. I just need a little longer.

Pain goes down my chest, jolting me completely awake. I gasp and my eyes fly open.

"There you are," a voice says.

"Is she conscious?" a tinny voice asks.

"Yes, her eyes are open and she's breathing," the voice says. They're hovering over me, barely visible in the faint light of a flashlight.

"Good. Now, I want you to. . ." the tinny voice trails off. I'm still so tired. I close my eyes again, the voices fading in and out.

I jolt, fire burning through my veins. I try to get away from it, but I'm strapped down. There are lights and faces all around me.

"You're safe. Try not to struggle, we have you restrained until we know your spine is okay," a face says to me.

I blink, the features on the face swimming in and out of my vision. It's so bright, and the fire keeps racing through my veins. There's something pressing painfully against my face.

"Deep breaths," another voice says. I try to see where it came from, realizing there's a mask on me. It fogs up with my shallow breaths. My eyes dart around the room, trying to figure out where I am. It's claustrophobic in here with equipment crammed all along the walls. I feel a bump underneath me. We're moving.

"Ambulance?" I rasp.

"Yes, we're taking you to the hospital right now. Do you know your name?" the first face asks. She has red hair and blue eyes.

I give the tiniest nod since there's a neck brace on me.

"You have to say it," a third, familiar voice says.

My eyes struggle to find where it came from since I can't turn my head. There's movement in the ambulance, and Quinn appears on my left side. He's covered in blood, giving me a stern look. Seeing him instantly makes me want to sob. I try to reach for his hand, but I'm still strapped down. He must figure out what I want because he grabs my hand and gives it a squeeze.

"You know, if you wanted to go snowshoeing, you could have just asked."

Snowshoeing? Were we going to go? What is he talking about?

The redhaired paramedic asks me if I know my name again, and takes the mask off my face as I rattle off my full name, birthday, and address. Quinn catches my eyes and gives me a smile.

"Are you okay?" I ask. The sight of the blood is unsettling.

"I'm great. Why?"

"Your face," I croak.

He wipes his face, then looks at the crusted blood. "Oh, this is yours."

Why is my blood on his face? I glance down my body, trying to find the source of the bleeding. I'm covered in an aluminum space blanket so I can't see anything.

"How?"

"You were unresponsive when I first found you, so I started CPR. But then you decided to start breathing on your own, thankfully."

The pain in my chest. I feel it now, trying to rub at it, but can't. I huff in frustration.

"It's a good thing you were unconscious for most of your rescue, I'm sure you would have been critiquing everyone's technique," Quinn says with a smirk.

Rescue. An image of the cliff flashes in my mind. I look around the ambulance again, my eyes landing on Red Hair and a bald paramedic. What did these people have to do in the snow to get me into this ambulance? Alarms start going off behind me, and the oxygen mask is put back on.

"Ellie, we need you to take some deep breaths," Red Hair says calmly. "Keep it light or stop talking," she says to Quinn in a stern voice.

Quinn is running his hands through his hair, eyes

darting between me and the beeping monitors. "Do you want to talk about Hawaiian haystacks instead?"

"Hawaiian haystacks?" Bald Man asks.

"It's where you put cream of chicken soup on rice with pineapple and other toppings," Quinn starts.

An image of the rec center flashes in my mind. The smell of chlorine, the humidity of the basement. Going up the stairs with Quinn, and sitting on the floor. The feel of his hands on my face. And then the rush of disappointment that the kiss wasn't real.

"There's that look of annoyance I know," Quinn says. "You have a real problem with midwestern buffet dishes."

I shake my head slightly, the brace rubbing against my neck.

"Try to stay still," Bald Man warns.

I'm tired of people saying that. "No!"

Everyone stares at me in surprise.

"No what?" Quinn finally asks.

"Maybe we should stay quiet the rest of our ride," Red Hair suggests. "We're almost there."

"I want to hear her opinion," Quinn says.

"I liked you better when you were crying," Bald Man mumbles.

The restraints rubbing against my wrists, my knotted hair plastered to the back of my neck in the brace, the liquid fire running through my veins, and the walls of the ambulance are closing in. I *need* to move my arms. I want to crawl out of my skin.

"Let me go, I need to get out," I pant. The monitors behind me start to beep again in warning. The oxygen mask gets cloudy again.

Red Hair is saying something to me, but it's another language for all I know. She grabs my hand and the feeling is too much. I start crying. Red Hair and Bald Man start talking to each other quicky, drawers opening and closing.

Quinn's face appears in front of mine again. "Hey, you're okay. We're almost there." He reaches out a hand and sweeps a piece of hair off my face. His touch sends tingles through my scalp.

"Get it off my neck," I sob.

Red Hair and Bald Man are still talking in the background, but my focus goes to Quinn's gentle fingers reaching for my hair and freeing it from the neck brace. Each section he gets out sends a small wave of relief through me.

"What are you doing?" Red Hair snaps.

He frees the last section of my hair and I shudder in absolute relief. Having that sensation gone makes the ambulance instantly feel bigger.

"Her hair was bothering her," Quinn says. "I don't think she needs to be sedated, she's fine now, right Ellie?" He grabs my hand in his, the feeling of his skin on mine sending warm tingles through me.

I glance to Red Hair and see that she's holding a syringe and a vial. She's looking between the monitors and me.

"I'm okay." I focus on the feeling of Quinn's skin against mine. I close my eyes and sigh. His touch isn't overwhelming like Red Hair's. "You're good at holding hands," I mumble.

Quinn laughs. "Thanks. I've been practicing."

"You should have," I start, my eyes still closed. I'm so tired, my mind wanders.

"I should have what?" Quinn asks.

A spiral staircase. Chlorine. His thumbs on my lips. "Kissed me," I get out.

It's completely silent in the ambulance except for my heartrate monitor.

"I should have kissed you?" Quinn asks. "I did."

I try to shake my head no. That was not a kiss. I want a real one. When I'm not so tired.

"If that's the one thing she's trying to tell you right now, it must have been pretty bad," Red Hair says.

Bald Man snickers.

"We were pretending that we weren't eavesdropping on an important conversation, so I pretended to kiss her so we had an excuse to be there," Quinn says. "And then she got mad at me for doing that, so obviously it was a bad idea."

"Sounds like she was mad that it wasn't the real thing," Red Hair says. "Don't you guys agree?"

There are two yeses, one from Bald Man, and the other from the driver seat behind me. The ambulance stops moving and I open my eyes.

"Keep us posted on what you two decide, I'm invested now," Red Hair says to me. Then the back door of the ambulance opens up, and there are new faces staring in at me. Nurses from the hospital.

Quinn's hand lets go of mine, and he hops out of the vehicle. There are clicking noises, and my stretcher starts to move. Then there's a commotion.

"Get back," a voice booms.

"That's our daughter," a voice that sounds eerily like my dad's yells.

I search for him, but can't see his face.

"This is the emergency loading zone; you can't be back here," the booming voice says.

"My baby," someone who sounds like my mom wails.

"We're here too," Anika says, out of view.

"Ellie!" Topher's voice calls out.

"This is a hospital. All of you can go to the waiting room," Bald Man says.

They wait as more people start talking. Finally, Red Hair and Bald Man unload my stretcher from the ambulance. Security guards are standing on my sides, their arms held up, shielding me from my family and friends behind them.

"I need to say something," someone yells.

Everyone stops moving.

"I like Ellie, and we've been secretly making out," Jamie's voice says from somewhere out of view.

Red Hair yells from behind my head, "There's a chaplain inside if anyone else needs to make a confession." Then she pushes me through the emergency room doors. As we get inside, she leans down close to my face. "You are one interesting person."

THIRTY

Thursday February 16th 8:00AM

WHEN I WAKE UP, IT'S TO SOMETHING SQUEEZING MY arm painfully.

"Oww," I cry out. I pull the blanket off me and see a blood pressure cuff there. I try to shift it on my arm, but I can't. My left arm is in a sling. There's no cast underneath it, and I can still wiggle my fingers. I reach for where the sling is tied on to undo it.

"You probably don't want to take that off," a voice says.

I startle and see Evan sitting in a hospital chair next to my bed.

"What are you doing here?" I ask.

"I offered to give Mom and Dad a break so they could freshen up. You should pretend to dramatically wake up when they get back because you heard mom's voice, that would get you some brownie points."

I moan, thinking about how upset they're going to be, and put my good hand over my face. A tube pulls at the skin on my hand. There's an IV hooked up there. I look around. How many monitors are on me?

"What's wrong with me?" I ask.

"Fractured collarbone, broken nose, some bruised ribs, a concussion, and a touch of hypothermia. They're going to monitor you for at least another day to make sure there's no lasting damage from that."

Oh. So the sling is actually necessary. I twist slightly, and immediately wince. There are the ribs. The room spins a little, so I lay back on my pillow.

"What happened to Mason?" I ask.

Evan makes a face. "All I know is his hypothermia was worse because he wasn't dressed for the cold, and he broke something."

"Is he alive?"

"As far as I know," Evan says. He places his ankle on his knee and leans forward. "What the hell were you thinking?"

I glare at him. "When I actually kill someone, then you can lecture me."

He frowns. "Seriously? I didn't willingly put myself into danger again, and get myself driven off a cliff."

Anger courses through me. I just woke up. I feel awful. I don't need this, *especially* from him. "You don't get to walk back into my life and pretend to be the overprotective big brother. I know you were dealing with your own stuff when we were younger, and that you've changed. But you're practically a stranger to me."

"A stranger who got the Serpents to put out a warning to everyone not to hurt you," Evan says flatly. "*And* got you information you wanted so you'd feel better. Not for you to then get yourself almost killed by some computer nerd."

I blink at him. "You what?"

He folds his arms across his chest. "The Serpents know to leave you alone. Don't push it."

"How? Did you have to make a deal with them?"

His jaw ticks. "Let's just say they owed me a favor, and I called it in."

What could he have possibly done that would leave them in his debt? Was it while he was in jail? From before then? "But they disconnected my battery cables," I say.

"As a warning." He sighs. "I know I haven't been the older brother you deserve. You're right, I have just reappeared, but you're my little sister. I would love a chance at getting to know you; if you'll let me."

I stare at my brother. Do I want to get to know him? "It's going to take time. And you can't boss me around. I'm an adult now."

He gives a tiny smile. "That's fair. And you can't use me for information on your investigations. I'm more than my mistakes."

"Deal," I say. "Let's start over."

He smiles, and I give a tiny one in return.

There's a knock at the door. It swings open, and I sigh in relief. It's not my parents. It's Detective Zhao. With a bouquet of flowers.

"I heard talking from the hallway and thought I'd see how you're doing," she says, setting the flowers down on the counter.

"I've been better," I say.

"She just woke up; the nurse should check in," Evan says, glaring at Detective Zhao.

"Of course. Why don't you call her?" Detective Zhao suggests.

Evan glares at her, pushing the call button. A staticky voice tells him someone will be right in.

"How've you been, Evan?" Detective Zhao asks while we wait.

"Fine," he says flatly.

I glance between the two of them. "You already know each other?"

"Evan's case was one of my first investigations," Detective Zhao says.

Talk about awkward. I'm shocked this is the first I'm learning about it. Detective Zhao is pleasantly smiling at Evan as he glares back at her. Having been through one of her official interviews for something I didn't do, I can't imagine what it was like when Evan had to talk with her.

The nurse arrives and both Detective Zhao and Evan go to wait in the hall while I'm examined. After they shine a light in my eyes and I take some Tylenol, Detective Zhao enters my room again. I hear voices right outside the door.

"Your parents are here. If you want, I can interview you with both of them in the room so you only have to tell the story once. Or, they can wait out there. It's up to you."

I glance between Detective Zhao and the door. A wave of exhaustion washes over me. It's going to be painful enough to tell this once. There's no way I'll make it through twice.

"Let them in. Let's get this over with."

THIRTY-ONE

Friday February 17th 10:30AM

There's a knock at the door, and I brace myself. *Please don't let it be my parents, again.* I don't think I can make it through another one of their sobbing guilt trips. I'll take another police interview; thank you very much.

Anika and Topher's heads peek in. I press the button on my bed and move so I'm sitting up. Topher is holding a bouquet of flowers in a plastic water bottle, and sets it down next to the others. Anika comes straight to my bed, crushing me in a hug. I groan.

She immediately leaps up and away. "What's broken?"

"Just my nose. And my left collarbone. And my ribs are bruised. Oh, and a concussion. But I'm great," I give her a thumbs up with my good hand.

Anika folds her arm across her chest. "If you weren't already broken, I'd punch you for scaring us all so bad."

"I'm sorry," I say. I've been saying that a lot. To my

273

parents. Detective Zhao. The firefighters who rescued me in dangerous conditions. All because I fell for Mason's trap. Maybe I should make merch for my apology tour.

She rolls her eyes. "Whatever. Also, you're welcome. I sent out the search party for you, and Quinn happened to find you in time."

"Thank you." I reach out to grab her hand, my left shoulder still twinging in pain from the movement. She squeezes it back.

"Now spill. Don't leave anything out. We ditched school for this," she demands.

I suppress a sigh. All I've done the past two days is retell this story, and sleep. But the doctors, and Detective Zhao, have made it clear that Anika's quick acting is why I'm alive. If I'd been left in the cold much longer with my injuries, things could have gone very badly.

I stumble through the story, having to backtrack multiple times because I left something important out. I finally reach the part where I zip-tied Mason, and then woke up in the ambulance.

"Thank you for saving me," I say to Anika.

"If I'm honest it wasn't only me. Jamie was worried when you stormed out of the shop, and then he texted Topher, and we got the text chain going from there."

Wait, Jamie was involved too? My head feels like it's spinning again. A memory flashes.

"Was, was Jamie in the ambulance bay?" I ask.

Anika starts cackling. Topher stomps on her foot. Anika climbs into my bed on my right side, snuggling in close. Topher perches on the left side of my bed, careful of my sling.

"So when were you going to tell us you were sucking face with the enemy?" Anika asks.

"I could have told you that," Topher mumbles.

I turn to him. "Excuse me? We kissed for the first time on Monday."

Topher raises his eyebrows. "Right after you two were publicly rolling all over each other?"

"Ellie," Anika shrieks. "You've been holding out on me."

"The next day was Valentine's Day and you were busy. When we kissed again, he told me he wanted to keep it a secret, and then I was run off a cliff."

Anika winces.

"He did the opposite of keeping it a secret and shouted it to the world," Topher says.

"Now my parents know," I groan. "I thought I hallucinated him doing that."

Anika pats my hand. "There, there. I think they're more upset about you almost dying than Jamie sticking his tongue in your mouth."

I whack her. She cackles again.

"It's on," Topher says, glancing at his phone.

Anika reaches for the TV remote attached to the bed, then starts flipping through the channels. She stops on the local news. It's a police press conference. The chief of police is standing at a podium inside somewhere. Anika fumbles with the bed remote to get the volume up. As she does, the chief leaves the podium, and Detective Zhao shuffles forward.

"That's our lady," Anika squeals.

Detective Zhao reaches the microphone and takes a moment to adjust it.

"Good afternoon. My name is Detective Zhao, and I am the lead detective investigating the death of Jake Peters. Jake Peters was a student at Rivers Edge High School, and found deceased on February 8th. I'm here to announce we have taken Mason Wilkins in custody and he has been charged with the murder of Jake Peters. The greater community is not at risk."

"Is it true Wilkins killed Peters over the Unter app?" a reporter asks.

"The murder appears to be financially motivated," Detective Zhao says.

I look between my friends. "Can you go on his Instagram?" I ask.

Topher pulls out his phone and gets to the screen. I look at the broken Go Fund Me link again. Looking through the jumble of words, I see the name Doreen.

Anika is already typing on her own phone. "Look, Doreen Wilkins," she says, shoving the screen in my face.

It's a Facebook account for an older woman. She's lying in a hospital bed with a beanie on her head, holding up two thumbs up as a Denver Broncos player poses next to her. There are already dozens of messages on her page asking her what happened to her grandson, and offering up prayers. There's a link for a meal train site, saying that the last thing Doreen needs to worry about right now is feeding herself.

"I could be remembering wrong, but I'm pretty sure Mason mentioned he was taking care of his sick grandma when we asked if he was still coding," I say.

Anika keeps scrolling through Doreen's Facebook. "There are multiple Go Fund Me's on here. If she was sick and he was taking care of her, I'm sure hearing that Jake was making a lot of money using their app did not go over well."

"Shh, listen," Topher says, pointing back to the TV.

Detective Zhao tilts her head. "Could you repeat your question?"

"Is it true that the weapon used to kill Peters was stolen from their third app partner?" a reporter says.

"The murder weapon used was registered to a mutual friend of Wilkins and Burton. That friend was out of the country at the time of the murder. We believe Wilkins knew where the weapon was stored and stole it."

"Was the other app partner actually out of the country?" another reporter asks.

"The third partner was flying internationally on February 8th and 9th, and was accounted for at the time of the murder."

Devon Burton returned from his mission trip the day that Jake was killed? What awful timing.

"Why is Wilkins being charged with one count of attempted murder?" another reporter asks.

"Wilkins was involved in a separate attempted murder where he endured significant injuries. He's currently stable and expected to make a full recovery. That's all I can share at this time," Detective Zhao says.

"Was it Ellie Garcia?" a voice yells from the crowd. My heart stops beating as I watch Detective Zhao. She stares for a beat.

"That's all the questions we have time for today. Thank you." She walks away from the podium.

My heart starts beating again.

"She's got your back," Topher says.

My throat tightens. I don't know why Detective Zhao refusing to answer a question about me has me close to tears, but it does. I want to know who was asking about me, but my head is starting to pound again. There's a rap at the door, and a nurse peeks her head in.

"Rest up. You're going to need it," Anika says, before giving me a quick hug.

Topher hugs me as well, and then my bed is empty. The nurse tells me it's time for more medicine and I feel cold rushing down my veins. I'm drifting off to sleep before I can wonder what Anika thinks I'll need my strength for.

THIRTY-TWO

Saturday February 18th 9:00AM

"ARE YOU SURE YOU HAVE EVERYTHING?" DAD ASKS. HE squats to the ground, checking under the hospital bed. Again.

I pat my pockets looking for my phone, then remember once again I don't have one. They weren't able to salvage it from the crash. The only things I have are the pajamas and toiletries my parents brought me. "I'm sure."

There's a knock on and door. The nurse is finally here with my discharge paperwork. I'm aching everywhere and want my own bed and pillows. And for monitors to stop beeping at me.

It isn't a nurse at the door. It's Quinn.

"Is it okay if I drop in really quick?" he asks, looking between my dad and me.

"Of course," I say.

My dad looks awkwardly between the two of us. "I'll go see if I can find that paperwork," he finally says.

Quinn gives him a smile and presses against the wall so

my dad can pass him. Once my dad is gone, he approaches my bed, standing at the end with his arms folded.

"So this is what this looks like from the other side."

"What do you mean?"

He settles in the chair next to me, leaning back in it. "You don't remember the time you heroically saved me from my own stupidity?"

"Which time are you referring to?" I ask. My mind still feels foggy, and the memory doesn't come back right away.

"You really took a hit to the head, didn't you?" he asks.

I sigh dramatically. "Everyone's freaking out about my head. I'm fine."

He snorts. "Have you seen yourself?"

"Don't remind me," I groan. My face is a mess of colorful bruises, swelling, and cuts. Every time I'm unfortunate enough to see my reflection, I feel woozy. "You can leave."

"You don't get off that easy. I have to milk this for all I can," Quinn teases.

I sigh again. "I'm reckless and stupid, I fell for Mason's trap, and people had to risk their lives because of my actions. Happy?"

He tips back in the chair. "Not really. What did Mason say to get you up there?"

"Devon was going to hurt himself, and that if we approached him together, I'd be able to talk him down. I know, I should have just called the police," I say when I see Quinn about to speak. Everyone has reacted right here.

"There was a chance to get justice for Jake's death, and I wanted Devon Burton behind bars. I..."

I haven't told this part to anyone else. Everyone has bought the story that I went up there purely to get justice for Jake.

"I had a glimpse into not wanting to be alive anymore. If I could help someone else out of there—even if I did think they were a murderer—I wanted to."

The feet of the chair slam into the ground as Quinn stops tipping. He lets out a long breath, looking out the window. For a moment, his eyes look shiny. Then he blinks it away, shaking his head.

"I know, I'm pathetic and naïve, and I should be dead right now," I say, gesturing to my battered and bruised body.

The chair makes a grating noise as Quinn scoots it closer to my bed. He rests his elbows on his knees, and holds his face in his hands. He's only a few inches from me.

"No you're not. You're someone who had a friend get wrapped up in something over her head and couldn't see a way out. You're someone whose brother had to fight for his life. You're someone who's learned that the world isn't black and white, and you didn't know why Devon might have done what you thought, but still wanted to give him a chance.

"I see someone who, if this happened to anyone else, wouldn't be alive right now. You survived a car crash over a cliff, ran away from an attacker in a snowstorm, managed to zip-tie him, and caught a killer. That's the farthest thing from pathetic and naïve in my book."

Tears spring to my eyes. I've been trying to hold them in the past day because the salt burns as it hits the various cuts on my face. Too late now. "You're just saying that."

Quinn rolls his eyes. "No, I'm not. You should have heard everyone on the rescue team talking about you. They were all shocked that you were alive."

"Thanks to you," I say, reaching out and grabbing his hand. He squeezes it back.

"How'd you find me?" I ask.

His expression changes rapidly. It settles on a smirk. "That guy you've been making out with said he heard you say something about the reservoir."

I cover my face with my good hand and groan. My heart races and the heartrate monitor chirps in warning.

Quinn barks out a laugh. "I want to hear all about *that* later."

I kick him in the side since he's on my left and I can't punch him. He swats at my foot, laughing. Then he immediately sobers up.

"I saw the smoke from the fire, then the guardrail. I can't even describe what I felt looking down the cliff and seeing the smashed remains of your car, on fire. I..." He swallows. "I was on the phone with the 911 operator and they kept telling me to wait. I couldn't though. I found a spot farther down the road that wasn't as steep and climbed down.

He swallows again. "I followed the blood trail and bullet casings through the snow, and I found him first. If you hadn't been only feet away, I'd have stomped on his broken ankle until he told me where you were."

"Then what?" I ask. He's the only one who can tell me what happened. Detective Zhao gave me a few details from when she showed up on the scene, but he was there first.

"You were unresponsive, so I started CPR, and after two rounds you started breathing on your own."

I place my hand on my chest over my sore ribs. The skin is bruised there, but nowhere near as beat up as the rest of me.

"Sorry about that," he says with a wince.

"This is nothing. You should see my bruised ribs from the crash," I say, reassuring him. "Keep going."

He presses his lips together, then continues. "The rescue team wasn't far behind. They lifted you up the side of the rocks with ropes and harnesses. It was pretty cool; I wish you could have seen it. Detective Zhao straight up laughed when she saw the zip-ties on Mason." He smiles. "What is your thing with zip-ties?"

"Okay first, I'm putting them in all my pockets as soon as I get home. You never know when you'll need them. Second, did she really?" I ask in disbelief. "She was *pissed* when she interviewed me yesterday."

He grins. "Oh she was cursing your unconscious self out too. Kept muttering about how she missed one phone call and now we're here. I think she was proud of you though."

My chest warms.

He clears his throat. "I know I originally said I didn't want to be involved in your investigation. I didn't want to be enabling destructive behavior, or whatever." He takes a shaky breath. "I never want to see you like that again. So next time, call me. I'll come with you to any mountain top. Plus, my car has four-wheel drive so it won't slip off the road as easily."

"Won't your aunt get mad?" I tease.

"I don't care about that. I want to be your detective partner. Co-detective? Assistant detective? What *are* they called?"

Is this real? I almost died. He saved my life, and instead of giving me a lecture like everyone else, he wants in for more?

"I don't think there will be a next time. But, if there is, underling has a nice ring to it."

He bursts out laughing. "Deal." He holds out his hand and we shake.

"What do you remember, from that night?" he asks.

I rub my temple. "Everything with Mason," I start. I

don't want to go into all the details of that, not right now. "I heard you yelling at me to wake up. Some flashes of inside the ambulance. The IV felt like fire going through my veins."

"It was warmed to help you heat up faster," Quinn says.

"Interesting. Umm, then I remember lots of yelling when we got to the hospital, and that's about it."

He nods. "Anything else?"

"What did I forget?" I ask.

His eyes search my face, looking for something.

What am I forgetting? What does he want me to remember?

There's a loud knock on the door.

Quinn instantly sits up straight. The door swings open, and my dad walks in, followed by Jamie. Jamie's holding a bouquet of roses in a red vase. My dad stops walking and Jamie runs into him. My dad swivels his head dramatically between Jamie and Quinn.

"I found this guy coming up to visit and thought I'd introduce myself," Dad says, gesturing to Jamie. "We didn't get to officially meet outside the hospital."

When Jamie declared that he liked making out with me. My face is on fire now.

Quinn stands up, running a hand through his hair. He takes a step away from my bed.

"I'm glad you're doing okay," he says to me.

"Thank you. For everything," I say. How can you properly thank someone who saved your life?

He gives me a quick smile, shakes my dad's hand, and then Jamie's.

"Nice to meet you," he says to Jamie. Then he squeezes out of my hospital room, disappearing into the hall.

Jamie stands there awkwardly, then steps forward, extending the roses to me. "These are for you," he says.

"Thanks, they're beautiful." I take them from Jamie and try to sniff them. I get the faintest sniff of pollen, mixed with the copper smell of all the dried blood in my nose from the break.

"Should I leave you two to talk?" Dad asks from the doorway.

There's another knock, and my nurse walks in with a thick stack of paperwork. "Discharge time," she sing-songs, her black bob bouncing.

"I'll talk to you later," Jamie says. "I'm glad you're safe."

"Thanks for helping them find me," I say, holding the roses gratefully. I wouldn't have known how important he was too if Anika, and Quinn, hadn't told me. My head starts spinning, thinking about both of them.

The nurse frowns at me. "What are you feeling?"

Jamie slips out of the room, closing the door behind him.

"My head is bothering me again."

She gives a sympathetic sigh. "Makes sense. You're still recovering from a concussion. Dad, do you want to start putting things in the car?"

My dad nods, shouldering a duffel bag and grabbing one of the many bouquets of flowers.

The nurse disconnects all of the monitors on me, and removes the IV port on my arm. The worst part is getting all the tape off.

"Remember, now isn't the time to be making any big decisions," she says nonchalantly.

I turn and stare at her. "What do you mean?"

"Anything involving legally binding decisions, or contracts. Or which of those boys to pick," she says with a wink.

"What are you talking about? Did they say anything?"

She stops moving, looking at me. "I'm sorry. I shouldn't have said that."

"No, explain. Please?" I beg.

She looks back and forth in the room, checking to see if anyone else is there. "I may have heard that one of them declared his feelings in the ambulance bay," she starts.

I already knew that.

"The other one was distraught enough from finding you that they let him ride in the ambulance to make sure he was okay. And apparently..."

"Go on," I urge.

"You told him you wished he'd kissed you." Her voice gets tinier and tinier with each word.

I sit there with my mouth wide open. *That's* what Quinn was asking about. He wanted to know if I remembered saying that to him. That confession was dangling between us the whole time he was here, and I had no idea. And then Jamie, the guy who yelled about kissing me, walked in? I'm glad the monitors are off so no one has to hear how that news rocks me.

I'm going to milk this concussion induced amnesia as long as I can. Forever if I have to. If anyone asks about anything uncomfortable, it will conveniently be forgotten.

"You didn't hear that from me," she adds. She shakes her head back and forth. "Promise me you'll take it easy; you need rest. Don't worry about the two of them right now. Or ever if you don't want to."

She stands there, waiting for my reply.

"I promise."

"Good," she smiles. Dad walks back in, and she's all business, going over all the different signs I might be dying to watch for over the next few days. *Oh joy.*

Community Gathers After Killer Pleads Guilty

Isa Mondragon, Editor-in-Chief
    February 20th, 2023

Local man Mason Wilkins pled guilty to the murder of Jacob Peters, and attempted murder of Ellie Garcia. His sentencing is scheduled for April 6th.

Wilkins, Peters, and fellow classmate Devon Burton built an app together for a business competition in 2022. Peters took that prototype and created Unter, a ridesharing app. The majority of the cars on Unter were stolen vehicles, contributing to an uptick in car thefts in the area. Details about Peters accomplices in procuring those stolen vehicles are still forthcoming.

According to statements from police, Wilkins learned about the existence of the app only weeks ago, and confronted Peters about his share of the profits. When Peters refused to share, Wilkins returned with a weapon to intimidate Peters. Wilkins and Peters got into an argument, and Wilkins shot Peters.

The weapon belonged to their third app partner, Devon Burton. Wilkins knew where the Burton family stored their weapons, along with their garage code. Wilkins stole the weapon and it was used in both the murder of Peters, and attempted murder of Ellie Garcia.

After a conversation with Garcia, Wilkins was worried she would learn of his killing Peters. On February 15th he led Garcia up to the reservoir during a blizzard, and rammed her vehicle off the road. He then started a fire, and chased her into the woods.

Garcia heroically fought Wilkins off and restrained him until law enforcement were able to locate them. Garcia was involved in catching the River Killers last October.

Wilkins' grandmother has been sick with leukemia the past year, and Mason has been her caregiver. "He wanted the money because of me. Mason is a sweet boy who only wanted to take care of his grandmother. He gave up his dreams of going to MIT to help me. What he did is unspeakable, and I pray every day for both of those boys' souls," Doreen Wilkins said.

There will be a candlelit vigil for Jacob Peters Friday on the high school football field at 5PM. The community is invited to share their memories of Jake by sending them to jakepetersvigil@ gmail.com to be used in a slideshow.

THIRTY-THREE

Friday February 24th 5:10PM

Topher pulls his truck onto the side of the road
across from the school. There's a line of cars in the center
lane, trying to get into the overfilled parking lot. Officers in
green vests are trying to direct cars to the back lots, but it's a
mess of honking and yelling. A great way to pay respects to
someone's memory: fighting for parking.

A swarm of news vans are parked on the sidewalk in
front of the building. The sight of them makes me shrink
down in my seat. I know they can't see me all the way over
here, but still.

Hundreds of tea lights pop on one-by-one. The lights
flicker in and out, mimicking candles.

"Who decided that we need to hold up dollar store
lights en masse whenever people die?" Anika asks.

"It's a metaphor for life," Sophie says from the backseat.
"I think it's beautiful."

"What's the metaphor? That we're all fragile flames, waiting for the right wind to blow us out?" Anika replies.

"When you look at the size of our universe, we're all insignificant. Yet, we can still light up the dark," Topher says.

All of us turn to stare at Topher. He looks back, his eyebrows raised, like he didn't just spit out poetry.

"When did you get so deep?" Anika asks.

"That's beautiful," Sophie sighs.

"I still think there's a dollar store conspiracy involved," Anika grumbles.

Sophie whacks her in the arm.

We all sit in silence, watching the waves of light ebb and flow. Seeing all those lights pressing against the dark expanse of the night sky makes my throat burn. I'm so lucky to still be here; seeing this.

"Is this enough?" Topher asks, turning to me.

I needed to come here, to pay my respects in some way to Jake. I didn't want a repeat of the last vigil where I was swarmed by the crowd and the press, so this seemed like a good compromise. I'm not the one who killed Jake. But Mason had no idea about the app until I asked him about it. He might have gone on with no idea, and never confronted Jake. Anika and Topher keep reminding me that Jake was in trouble with the Serpents and they would have come after him eventually.

I'll never know what might have happened. Jake's death was about money and greed. He was hurting so many in this town to make money for his app, and when he refused to share any of it, he paid with his life. Is sitting here staring at those lights enough for the small part I played?

"Let's do a Schrute style funeral. You know, where they all state a blatant fact about the person," Sophie suggests.

Anika rolls down her window, despite the cold. "Jake, you had blonde hair," she yells into the air.

"You were tall, but not too tall," Topher says, copying her.

"You had green eyes, and then brown eyes depending on your shirt," Sophie says.

I wrack my brain for a fact to state about him while rolling down my window. "You were a complicated person," I finally say.

All together we roll the windows back up. It's clichéd, but I do actually feel lighter. Topher pulls back onto the road. I stare at the reflection of the tealights in the side mirror until they're no longer visible.

Topher takes the truck too fast over a speed bump, and I fly up from my seat and crash back down, despite my seatbelt. My heart starts racing, and my collarbone and ribs remind me of the beatings they're still healing from.

"Slow down," I snap.

"If you don't like my driving, you shouldn't have driven your car over a cliff," Topher says. Anika laughs in the back seat, then cries out as Sophie whacks her again.

"Shut up," I mumble.

It's been a sore subject around the house. There's no way my car could be rescued, and the insurance payout for it was pitiful. If I want my own car anytime soon, I'm going to have to get a second job. I can't even ride my bike anywhere because my left arm is still in a sling for one more week. So, I'm dependent once again on Topher. Or walking. Thankfully I'm back on his good side.

Topher pulls up right in front of the frozen yogurt shop. With everyone at the candlelight vigil, Main Street is practically empty.

"Give me five minutes alone before you come in," I say.

I carefully undo my seatbelt, then walk to the shop. The bell rings when I open the door, but there's no one behind the counter. I walk around noisily, but Jamie still doesn't appear. He was supposed to be working tonight. I grab a cup and head toward the strawberry banana. It's one of the most popular flavors, and often running low this time of night. When I pull on the handle, the machine jerks and whines, searching for the last bits of yogurt.

"You're doing a pretty lousy job of keeping this place stocked," I call out.

"Excuse me?" My boss Angie walks out from the back room.

"I'm so sorry! I thought you were Jamie."

She looks me up and down, and winces when her eyes land on my face. The bruises and cuts are healing, many of them nasty shades of yellow and green. I'm so used to seeing it at this point I forget how shocking it is until others react exactly like Angie.

"He's on his break. What are you doing here?" She looks pointedly at my sling.

"I had an intense craving for yogurt," I say.

She raises an eyebrow. "Well, if I was you, I'd make sure to fill your craving on your own time, and not where I have to watch it on the cameras." She looks up pointedly to the security camera in the corner, pointed at the cash register. Which also has the wall Jamie and I were kissing against in its view.

My face heats. "Won't happen again."

"I'm glad to hear it. It's good to see you," Angie says. "Take care of yourself, we need you back here ASAP."

The bell rings and Topher, Anika, and Sophie walk in. I glance at the clock. They only waited three minutes. I knew they wouldn't give me much time alone to talk to Jamie.

Anika is still salty that I didn't tell her about the first kiss the day it happened. When she keeps reiterating that the two of us make no sense, I feel justified in that decision.

Angie settles behind the cash register as we all get our yogurt and pay. We have the pick of tables, and settle at the one in the back corner of the room.

The bell over the door rings again, and Sandra walks in. Topher gets up and walks over to chat with her by the yogurt machines.

"Did he ever tell you who he went on a date with on Valentine's Day?" I ask.

Anika shakes her head.

"Do you think they..." I trail off, nodding to Sandra and him.

Anika and Sophie look over at the two of them. Topher is grinning, and Sandra is laughing. "I hope not," Anika says.

"How can you say that?" Sophie asks.

"They're going to different schools in a few months. He's been moping about his grades the past few weeks, I don't want to see what he's like going through heartbreak."

"Wow," Sophie says, rolling her eyes. "Sandra deserves someone good. If there's something there, I'm happy for them."

"You're a good human," Anika says, nuzzling into Sophie's shoulder.

The bell jingles again. I turn and see Kacey, Isa, and Quinn. Isa and Kacey wave to me. Did they somehow know I'd be here? I get up from my chair and walk over to them.

"Are you stalking me?" I ask.

"Nope. We really wanted yogurt. And figured if we happened to run into you here, we could say hi," Kacey says.

"You've been ignoring my calls," Isa adds with a wink.

I glare at her. "You've been writing about me anyway."

"It's not my fault you've completely wrapped yourself up in all the best stories about this town. What kind of journalist would I be if I left out all mentions of the girl who was almost killed bringing Mason to justice?" Isa asks.

I cross my arms and glare at her.

"Hey, I stuck strictly to the facts that were already public knowledge," Isa says.

I roll my eyes. "I guess that's true."

"You know where I am when you're ready for your tell-all. I'm glad you're okay." She grabs my hand and gives it a squeeze. Then she rolls off to the yogurt cups.

My eyes land on Quinn. Why does he have to look so good in a black hoodie and jeans, while my face is a horror show?

"You're looking a bit better," he says, holding his arm up for a half hug.

So we're the hugging type of friends now? I wrap my good arm around him for a brief moment, ignoring the way my body reacts to him.

"Thanks, I'm trying out a new highlighter," I say, gesturing to my cheeks.

"I think you still look like shit," Kacey says, scrunching up her nose.

"Trust me, it's a lot better than it was," I laugh.

"There's a reason I didn't go into medicine," Kacey says. "Try not to go out and get yourself almost killed again, okay? I need Quinn's rent money." Kacey gives me a tiny hug, then joins Isa at the yogurt machines.

Quinn and I stand there staring at each other. He rocks back and forth on his heels, his hands in his pockets. He knows I wanted him to kiss me. But I can pretend that I don't know that he knows.

"So," I finally say.

"So," he replies.

We both smile at each other, and those familiar butterflies make their appearance. The bell on the door jingles, and of course, Jamie walks in then. He freezes in the doorway, the winter air blowing through the store. He stares at me, then Quinn, then back to me. He looks down at the ground, and then makes his way behind the counter, walking right between us.

I'm tugged in two directions. I want to follow after Jamie and say all the things I've rehearsed the past few days. But I want to stay here with Quinn too. So, I do nothing.

"Have you listened to the podcast yet?" Quinn asks.

"Which one?"

"The one about you," Quinn says. "And me," he adds.

I freeze. "What are you talking about?"

Quinn pulls out his phone and shows me the screen. It says SLEUPHORIA on the cover of a notebook covered with stickers. I glance at the episodes. There are three out so far. The first episode is *Sleuphoria: An introduction.* The second one is *Who is Ellie Garcia?* The newest is titled, *Who is Quinn Raineros?*

"What is Sleuphoria, and what does it have to do with me?" I ask.

"We're thinking they combined sleuth with Euphoria. Since your high school is surprisingly crime ridden," Quinn explains. "There's a TikTok, Instagram, and Threadlit. This thing is going to blow up. I knew we should have started our own podcast. Then we could have cashed in on the merch money."

My head is spinning. It's been weird enough having Isa

mention me in her articles. Now there's a podcast episode out there about me? With more coming?

"You don't look so good; do you want to sit?" Quinn asks. I nod and follow him back to the table. "How's your head?" he asks.

"It's fine." The headaches still come, and I get motion sickness easily, but each day there's a little more improvement. I should be able to go back to school for the first-time next week.

My phone buzzes in my pocket and I immediately check it. It's a text from Evan.

EVAN: Mom and Dad are getting nervous. They'll be there soon.

I huff. I know I should be grateful that they let me out at all after the stunt I pulled last week. I hate knowing all the worry and stress I'm putting them through. But their hovering is suffocating. Going to college is sounding more appealing if this is what I have to look forward to.

ELLIE: Thanks for the heads up.
EVAN: DMI

I flip my phone around to show my friends. "What acronym is this?"

Everyone looks at it. Foreheads wrinkle and heads tilt.

"Don't mention it?" Topher finally suggests.

Everyone lets out a collective, "Ohhhhh."

I sigh. "Don't go to prison. When you come out, you still think acronyms are a thing and make up your own."

Everyone laughs. I catch a glimpse of Jamie staring my

direction from behind the counter. When our eyes meet, he immediately looks away. Then he disappears into the back of the store. I get up from my seat and sneak behind the counter. I find Jamie in the back room, digging through the boxes of powdered mix. The muscles in his arm flex as he stands up with a bag in hand. He jumps when he sees me, dropping it on the ground.

"You're lucky that didn't break," I say, pathetically.

He shrugs. "What are you doing?"

"I wanted to see you," I say.

He raises an eyebrow. "Really?"

"Yes, really."

"Here I am," he gestures.

"What's wrong?" I ask.

He blows out a slow breath. "It's weird to see you here with all your friends."

"Why?"

"Because you were run off a cliff a few days ago. I figured you were still recovering, but it looks like you're feeling just fine."

I take a step back. "This is the first time I've gotten out of bed in days, and if I don't take more drugs in the next twenty minutes, my head is going to start killing me again. Even with that, I chose to come here because I knew you'd be working and I wanted to talk to you. But if you're too busy being a jealous jerk, then I'll go."

Jamie runs his hands over his face. "Why does every-thing come out so wrong whenever I talk to you?"

"Sounds like a you problem."

He removes his hands and takes a step closer to me. "I've been worried about you. I don't like the way we ended our last conversation and I've been dying to talk to you, but

I didn't want to dump all of that on you while you were recovering."

"You were worried about me?" I ask.

He looks at the floor. "Of course I was. You could have died."

I take a step closer to him. There are only a few feet between us now. "I didn't, and that's partially thanks to you. So, thank you."

He keeps looking at the floor, and says a quiet, "you're welcome."

It's silent between the two of us. Everything I'd practiced saying is gone.

He finally looks up from the floor. "How are you?"

"Good. Much better from when I last saw you."

He gives a small smile. "I'm glad. It's been quiet here, and at Pathfinders. It's not the same without you antagonizing me."

I grin. "Don't worry. I'm thinking of new ways to bother you in the meantime."

He raises a brow. "Like what?"

"You'll have to wait and see."

His face changes instantly. "I know this probably isn't the time, and if you don't want to talk about this now, I understand. I'm not sure if you were awake, but I said some things in the ambulance bay at the hospital..."

"I heard them," I admit.

His eyes widen. "And?"

I roll my shoulders back and take a deep breath. "We're about to graduate high school, go who knows where. I don't want to get into a relationship and break up in a few months."

He flinches. But I'm not done.

"I've missed antagonizing you, too. And, I really like

kissing you. So maybe, we don't put a label on things and see what happens."

He crosses his arms. "Are you asking me to be in a situationship?"

That *is* what I just described. "Pretty sure that qualifies as a label."

He snorts. "What about that other guy?" He nods to the front of the shop.

I pause. "What about him?"

"Are you using me to make him jealous? Or as a consolation prize?" he asks. "I've seen the way you two look at each other."

I need to be honest. "You're not a consolation prize. You're loyal, determined, kind, occasionally funny, and I like being around you. I had a crush on Quinn last year, but I'm not the same person as I was then. He's a good friend, and that's it.

"I used to have my entire life planned. How to graduate college a year early so I could apply for the police force the second I was old enough, Bachelor's degree in hand. Then I'd work my way up the ranks and be a detective by twenty-six.

"Now, I haven't finished a single college application. I need to get on that, or decide if I'm taking a gap year. If I'm taking a gap year, I need to get a different job because there's no way I'm working here full time. Maybe I'll do the Europe backpacking thing; I don't know. I'm getting over a concussion and starting to feel like myself again, and I'm actually excited to see who that might be."

There's the speech I rehearsed. I knew it was in there somewhere.

Jamie stands with his arms crossed staring back at me,

his face unreadable. Finally he nods. "Let me think about it. I'll let you know."

That wasn't what I expected him to say. I'd expected passionate kissing against the wall, or for him to start screaming at me. "Sounds great." Not knowing his answer is in line with the rest of my life of unknowns. And that's okay.

We both stare at each other for another long moment. "I'll see you at work next week," I finally say.

He nods. "Be ready to fight."

"You're going down," I tease.

He scoffs. "With that sling? No way."

He follows me out of the backroom, heading to the cash register. I catch Quinn's eye as I'm coming out from behind the counter. He immediately looks away, talking to Kacey animatedly. My skin feels warm where he was looking at me.

I meant what I said to Jamie. I'm not the same person I was in October. My traitorous body might still react every time I'm near Quinn, but I'm sure it will get better with time. He's my friend, and if this town keeps up with its shenanigans, my underling detective. That's enough.

Something moving in the front window catches my eye. It's my parents, looking inside. Evan wasn't lying when he said they'd be here soon. They see me looking at them, and give little waves. Then, they start walking down Main Street.

They are not fans of my new 'I don't know what I want and that's okay' attitude. Mom blames it on the concussion. Dad thinks it's because I spent too much time at Pathfinders. Evan's been surprisingly supportive, sending texts, and occasionally talking my parents down on the phone. He told me to give them time, that they'll come around.

They better not follow me to my shift at work next week.

I settle in at the table with my friends. I'm so lucky to be here with them. Things could have gone very differently at the bottom of that cliff. Each of them has helped me find a tiny piece of myself I thought I'd lost, and gently placed it back. Anika and Topher, for holding me, standing by me, pushing me, laughing with me, crying with me. Kacey, for helping me remember what lights me up. Isa for showing me new ways to change the world. Quinn for listening as I found my voice again.

Maybe I'll discover new things with Jamie. If not, I'm glad I took a risk. I can always move across the world if it gets too weird.

Anika tells a joke, and everyone starts laughing. I join in, my ribs twinging with the movement. It's funny. I felt broken over the past few months. Like I would never be able to enjoy the things I used to. Yet here I am, with actual broken bones, and I feel the most alive I have in a while. I haven't had one panic attack since waking up in the hospital. It might be temporary, but something changed at the bottom of that cliff. I showed myself what I'm capable of. Even when I'm in a situation I have never planned or prepared for, I made it out. And I can do it again.

I'm Ellie Garcia. I don't have a clue what's coming next, but I know I can handle it.

ACKNOWLEDGMENTS

I legitimately thought I would never write these acknowledgements. I've wanted to be a writer as long as I can remember. There's a strange phenomenon that happens when you've had a dream for so long, and you finally reach it. I finally had my finished book in my hands. And... my life was still the same. I still had to change diapers, schedule doctors appointments, and deal with hard things. But now I had book promotion to figure out, social media algorithms to decode, while also getting daily stats on how well I was doing.

Then you add in the dreaded second-book-syndrome. Second books are notoriously hard to write. When you write your first book, it's in a bubble. You are creating just for you. But when you're working on your second book, you're starting to get feedback on your writing, and writing with an audience can be daunting.

All of that, plus some other big life things, were the makings of the perfect depressive spiral. I was so mad about it. I'd FINALLY accomplished my dream. People were being so supportive. What was wrong with me?

I couldn't create in that space, so I took a break. And then beat myself up about that too.

Why am I sharing this? Because a few months into this, I saw another author share that the year after their debut came out, they too got extremely depressed. So many other authors shared their experiences in the comments, and I felt so seen. It wasn't just me. In fact, this was normal.

I gave up on the idea that I had to publish my second book a year after my first one. One of the reasons I chose indie publishing in the first place is because I knew that the stage of my life I was at, I needed as much flexibility as possible. So, I gave myself that flexibility. I took a promotion break, made non-writing goals, did a ton of EMDR for old traumas, my kids got older and more independent, and slowly, page by page, I started piecing together this book. And then... I read ACOTAR.

ACOTAR and TOG changed my life. They reminded me why I fell in love with reading in the first place. They were an escape. I felt seen in the characters mental health journeys. They gave me courage to take bigger leaps. I finally found friends and community. It completely refilled my creative well. I was writing all day, every day, and I did three rewrites of this book in four months. I finally figured out the biggest plot holes, and had a book that fit the vision I'd had of this story, but couldn't quite reach.

I always knew Ellie was going to go on her own mental health journey when I first started this book three years ago. I didn't know I was going to have to go on my own. Again. I'm very passionate about showing and depicting mental health struggles in books, because I know how lonely and isolating it feels when you're in the thick of it. I know how helpful it has been to see that I'm not the only one feeling things. I remember having my first panic attacks as an eleven-year- old, and no one knowing what was happening to me. When I started having them more frequently in high school, thankfully my mom knew what was happening and was able to give me a name for it. I hope that sharing my own experiences, and seeing Ellie go through hers, can help someone know they aren't alone. It will get better. It may be a winding path with hidden falls. But it will.

Now, to the people I couldn't have done this without. First off, there are people who have been there for a long, long time, that were left off the acknowledgements of my first book, and I am deeply sorry.

Hayley, thank you for deciding to talk to my emo little self back in seminary. We were such babies, but it's been a pleasure growing up with you, sharing emotionally devastating books with you, and going through similar journeys. You are such an inspiration, and you always make me laugh with your Twilight memes. Thank you for reading my first attempts at novels, and being a cheerleader always.

Joice, I believe in serendipity because I had the best roommate in you. Thank you for all the laughs, shopping trips, makeovers, teaching me how to dance, and accepting my weird self. Thank you for always inviting me to Diwali and telling what Indian foods white people should start with. But most of all, thank you for cheering me on in my dreams. You never judged me when I wanted to stay in and write a scene for a novel that would never see the light of day. It's been such an inspiration watching you never give up on your own dreams, and how you've made so many new places your home. The world is lucky to have you in it.

Amanda, Katie, and Lucero... You three are some of the most inspiring woman I have had the pleasure of meeting. We met in a hellhole, but it was all worth it to meet you. Thank you for accepting me for where I was as a little baby twenty-something, and for all the laughs and ridiculous conversations. I'm sorry you had to suffer through my Hamilton obsession. I've learned so much from you all, and it's a privilege to know you. Thank you for being the kind of people where when you say you're going to stay in touch after you've parted ways, you actually do. Whenever I hear Moana, I think of you three. Which is a lot.

Jenna, I'm so glad I accidentally emailed you a link to a book event. Thank you for sharing my book with others. I've gotten to have experiences I never would have thanks to you!

And to you, Julie, Brittany, and Nancy—thank you for loving on and supporting our family. I will literally never forget how much you all changed my kiddo's and our lives.

Nancy, thank you for inviting me to visit your bookclub. It was such an amazing experience, and you have some pretty cool friends. At the meeting everyone was joking about how I should include the discussion about Xcel billing in my next book, and I had a scene with it in here that I had to cut... but there's always the next book!

Stevie, thank you once again for being my critique partner, and reading through the early, early drafts of this book, even when you were extremely busy. Your feedback helped tremendously, and helped this book not be an absolute depressive mess.

Bridget, thank you for all the support, checking in on me, and giving your insight into some of the technical parts of this story. I love that you're always down to seriously discuss whatever, whenever. You are a rare gem of a human and I'm lucky to have known you for most of my life.

Mallory and Collin, I am so, so sorry that your car ended up being the inspiration for this book. Thank you for your friendship and all your wild stories. You are wonderful people and we're lucky to have walked with you through the weirdness that was a pandemic.

Amy, thank you for the gorgeous headshot (and perfect family photos, let's be real.) I love seeing the world through your lens, and am glad to call you a friend. Thanks for always listening to my rants about the patriarchy.

Helen, thank you for sticking with me through all the crazy ups and downs since we've met. Thanks for sharing so many book adventures with me, and for letting me vent about plot problems. You've been such a light spot, and I feel so seen with you.

Tayler with Bailey and Bloom, thank you for your outline help! It helped so much in the beginning stages. You went above and beyond reading my first book just to help with this one, and I hope to keep working with you in the future.

Cameron, thank you for creating the coolest cover ever. Again. The first thing everyone mentions is how cool it is, and it brings so many new readers in. I love chatting with you about art and having no idea how my ramblings get processed in your brain and you spit out the cool stuff you do. Thanks for working with me again, and for all the years of friendship.

Rachel... thank you, thank you, thank you. You have been a cheerleader in all of my creative endeavors, and I can't express how much it has meant. This book would not exist without you, period. You talked me through some moments where I really wanted to give up. Thank you for being my beta reader, and for loving Ellie and the gang so much. There aren't many who are as authentic, creative, caring, and thoughtful as you and I'm glad to know you.

Thank you to all the readers and friends from past and present who showed up to signings, shared about my book, told your friends about it, and took the time to read my words. It all means so much, and I'm so lucky to have you all.

To the wonderful authors and writers of Bookstagram... thank you for befriending me, helping me work through technical difficulties (screw you Amazon), and walking this journey with me. You're the only people who understand how wonderful, stressful, and complicated it is to take a pen to paper and share those words with the world. I admire you all so much, and hope to keep playing with our imaginary friends together.

To my Gomez family... thank you for taking me in and loving me. You all have been so supportive of me and my creative endeavors, and it means so much.

Tanner, thank you for always listening as I untangle my plot threads, and for the coolest cards. You're the best brother ever.

Brinley, thanks for loving on my boys and for telling me what you want more of in book two. I hope to not let you down with these actually finished stories. You're the best sister.

Mom and Dad... thank you, thank you, thank you for always supporting me in my writing. A lot of people aren't lucky to have such supportive parents. Sorry for all the times I just ramble on and on about my stories, trying to piece them together. Thank you for making sure I stayed sane this summer, and had writing time. I never would have finished this without you.

Aaron and Julian, I love you boys so much. It's a privilege to get to know all of the versions of you, and watch you grow and experience everything life has to offer. Being your mom has been more than I could have ever imagined. Thanks for letting me borrow your Hot Wheels to figure out the physics of all the car scenes. May you chase after your own dreams, and the only cars you steal be from each other.

Sammy, my best friend. Thank you for all of the date nights where you let me talk out plots in the car. For always making sure I get writing time. For never judging me for walking around with dozens of imaginary friends I need to talk to. For loving all the different versions of me over the years, and being willing to work and change together. For never missing the mark when sending reels. I keep telling you I'm so happy with our life, and I'm going to say it again,

IN WRITING. (Take that random superstition that saying something good is happening will make the universe take it away.) I look at what we've built together, and the people we've become, and I am beyond grateful you are my partner in this weird world.

ABOUT THE AUTHOR

Kylee Awiech graduated from the University of Colorado Denver with a degree in English. She was the drummer in a girl-band, and participated in programs with the coroner's office and police department in high school. She previously worked in a library. She lives in Colorado with her husband and two boys. When she's not writing she can be found playing with her family or cross-stitching. She doesn't google medical symptoms anymore because #therapy.

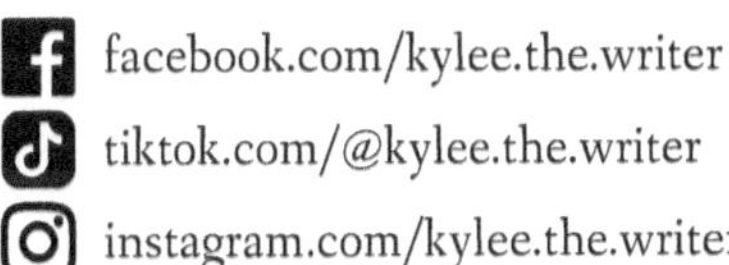
facebook.com/kylee.the.writer
tiktok.com/@kylee.the.writer
instagram.com/kylee.the.writer

www.ingramcontent.com/pod-product-compliance
Lightning Source LLC
Chambersburg PA
CBHW030146310726
48970CB00005B/1616